Your Irresistible Love
(The Bennett Family, Book 1)

LAYLA HAGEN

Dear Reader,

If you want to receive news about my upcoming books and sales, you can sign up for my newsletter HERE: http://laylahagen.com/mailing-list-sign-up/

Chapter One

Sebastian

"This was a great idea," Logan says as I sign the papers for our parents' present. Their thirty-sixth wedding anniversary is coming up in one month.

"It'll make them happy," I agree, nodding at my brother. Handing the papers to my assistant, I rise from the chair, pacing my office to stretch my legs. From the seventh floor of the building, I have a great view of San Francisco. One of the perks of being the CEO of my own company is that I get the best office. The second one is that no one dares to contradict me. It gets boring once in a while, but my family is always around to shake things up and remind me they don't care much about my title.

"So, how many times did Mom ask you if you're bringing a date?" Logan asks, leaning back in the chair in front of my desk.

"Nine." My face breaks into a grin. "You?"

He gives a long whistle, crossing his fingers on top of his head. "Only four times. I should consider myself lucky."

"She's not giving up, is she?" Shaking my head, I glance at the family photo resting on my desk. Dad looks at Mom with the same loving expression I remember seeing my entire life. Since she's been happily married to my father for so long, and they raised nine kids together, my mother believes all of us must follow in their footsteps. So far, building a business empire from almost nothing has proven easier than finding what my parents have.

"No, Mom isn't giving up. And I'm afraid Pippa's becoming Mom's right hand. She actually calls us San Francisco's most eligible bachelors."

I snort, jamming my hands in my pockets. If my sister Pippa were the only one calling us that, I wouldn't have a problem. As it is, every damn magazine running an article on Bennett Enterprises mentions most eligible bachelors at some point. That has the unfortunate effect of drawing women to us like moths to a flame. The wrong kind of women— mostly gold diggers and social climbers. I can't remember the last time I've met a real woman.

"Pippa set me up with a hottie last week," Logan continues. "Hottie turned out to be a bimbo. That dinner was so boring I wanted to poke my eyes out."

My brother's tone is even, but his eyes harden when he mentions our sister. Pippa is the only Bennett sibling who was brave enough to marry, and she's now divorcing. I want to punch that bastard. By the look of Logan, that makes two of us. I suspect her matchmaking attempts for Logan and me are her way of coping.

"Back to Mom and Dad's present, are you telling them about it now, or do you want to wait until the party?"

"Let's wait." Wiggling my eyebrows, I add, "You know, for dramatic effect."

Thirteen years ago, I asked my parents to sell the ranch where we grew up and hand me the money. I needed capital to start this business. They agreed on the spot. We were piss-poor, and the ranch was everything they had, but they trusted me blindly. It paid off. Bennett Enterprises became one of the world's major players in high-end jewelry. I've taken care of my parents, but I know that giving them back the ranch my father built with his bare hands will be the best damn thing I could ever gift them. The minute I found out it was up for sale, I made an offer on it. Can't wait to let the rest of my siblings know.

"Sebastian," my assistant interrupts us, "Ava Lindt has arrived. Should I bring her in here?"

"Yes, bring her in. Let's meet our new marketing consultant."

As my assistant leaves the office, Logan says, "I bet Mom will nag you at least two more times about bringing a date."

"No bet," I reply. "I know she will."

Chapter Two

Ava

I enter the office with my chin high, shoving a strand of my blonde hair away from my face. My little navy suit fits this place perfectly. The two men inside greet me with smiles.

Well, damn.

I've seen photos online of the Bennett brothers, but I was convinced their looks were at least partly due to some photoshopping. I was wrong; they're just two very fine specimens of the male variety.

One of them walks up to me and extends his hand. "Ava, I'm Logan."

"Nice to meet you. I'm happy to be here."

I shake his hand firmly, knowing the first impression counts. Logan is about six feet tall and has dark hair and striking blue eyes. "And this is my brother and our CEO, Sebastian."

As Sebastian walks closer, he fills the entire room with his presence. He's a few inches taller than Logan, and his eyes are as dark as his hair. Otherwise, the brothers share the same fine features: sculpted cheekbones, strong shoulders. Still, something about Sebastian makes it impossible to look away from him.

"Welcome to Bennett Enterprises, Ava," Sebastian says.

God, even his voice is sexy. He holds out his hand. I shake it without thinking. His touch is like a magnet, pulling me in, sending my pulse into overdrive. I swallow hard as he keeps my hand a fraction too long. Finally, he lets go. To my embarrassment, I discover my palm is sweaty. As discreetly as I can, I wipe it on my skirt.

Well, as far as first impressions go, Sebastian sure knows how to make himself memorable. Before I stepped inside this office, I was already fascinated by his story: the billionaire who rose from nothing, who donates a large chunk of the company's profit to charities and shuns the spotlight. A rarity by all accounts.

Now, I'm fascinated by him.

He gestures for Logan and me to sit in the chairs in front of the desk, and he drops in the seat behind it.

"You come highly recommended." Sebastian nods at me. "I expect the next marketing campaign to be a success."

"It will," I assure him. His lips curl up in a half smile, as if he's enjoying a private joke. I squirm under his gaze. It travels from my face further down. His gaze dwarfs and undresses me at the same time. Squaring my shoulders, I make myself taller. "Where will my office be?"

"Next to mine." Sebastian points with his thumb to the left. "It's a room we use for small meetings. However, for the four months you'll be here, it'll be your office."

"I'll be on your other side," Logan says. "It's best if you're close to us. Sebastian and I take an active interest in the advertising campaigns."

"We practically did all the marketing in the early days," Sebastian adds.

"Very well, I'll keep you both informed."

"I will attend the first meetings you will have with our marketing team to make sure everything goes smoothly," Sebastian offers.

"Great," I say appreciatively. CEOs usually don't bother with me, instead sending me to deal directly with their teams. I usually spend a few months on each project, and there were instances I never met the CEOs.

"Did you fly here directly out of Sydney?" Logan asks, referring to my last project location.

I shake my head. "New York. The consultancy's headquarters is there, and I always fly into the office between projects."

"Why don't I give you a tour of the company?" Logan suggests, looking at his wristwatch. "That way I can tell you more about us. We can go down to the creative department where all the magic happens. If we're quick, we can grab lunch afterward. I should still make it in time for my afternoon meeting. Unless you have other plans? I know your official start date is tomorrow. It was great of you to come today."

I relish the compliment. It's little things like these, on top of my usual work, which make clients remember me. "I only have plans later."

I'm about to add that a company tour is a wonderful idea, when Sebastian interjects, "I'll take her."

Logan shoots him a confused look. "Why?"

"I want to be nice to our consultant. Is there a problem?"

"You don't do nice." Logan's voice is stern, but his lips form a smile. "I'm the nice brother, everyone knows that."

"Fuck off, Logan," Sebastian says good-naturedly. I barely withhold a grin.

"See," Logan tells me, as if to prove a point, "that's his idea of being nice."

"I'll take my chances," I reply, charmed by the playful rivalry between the two brothers. I expected them to be arrogant and cold, and they've proven me wrong. Their fun side is a pleasant surprise. I've read about the Bennett family. There are nine siblings, and most of them are involved in Bennett Enterprises. As an only child, I can't even grasp the idea of such a big family—though I've always wished to have one. I imagine you never get lonely.

Logan clutches his heart theatrically. "You choose my brother over me? I am profoundly hurt."

"I don't want to make you late for your meeting." I try to be diplomatic. Truth is, I long to be alone with Sebastian, against my better judgment.

"I'll see both of you later," Logan says, taking off.

The second he leaves the room, the air thickens with tension. Sebastian gazes at me intensely with thinly disguised curiosity. Being the object of his attention sets me on fire. The burning spreads through my body, filling me up, but I hold his gaze.

Abruptly, he stands up. "Let's go. Do you want to do the tour first or grab lunch?"

"I'm not hungry yet. Let's do the tour first. I'm looking forward to it."

He nods, gesturing me to join him. He shows me my office briefly, and then we walk in silence down the corridor. When we step inside an empty elevator, he puts a hand at the small of my back. It electrifies me, sharpening my senses, zapping to life all my nerve endings. Damn it, Ava, get a grip.

Chapter Three

Ava

Alone with him in the elevator, I keep my eyes firmly on the ground. His masculine scent is intoxicating. We stop briefly on every floor, and Sebastian explains which departments work where. Every division is here, except production—it's in the smaller building adjacent to this one.

"How come you keep the production here too?" I ask. "Most companies outsource that activity, or move it to a cheaper location, not San Francisco."

Leaning in to me, he says, "We don't have large production runs, so the factory itself is small—more like a workshop. Keeping it here is motivating for the employees. Whenever they are frustrated with everyday tasks, all they need is a trip next door. They can see it's not all numbers. It's beauty."

His enthusiasm surprises me. CEOs are usually all about numbers and profits, the core and essence of the company long forgotten. Then again, Sebastian created the company. He is a passionate founder.

Something tells me he is a passionate man in

everything he does.

I steel myself, mentally cursing. I can't lust after Sebastian. I have a no-fraternization clause in my contract. My boss would fire me in a minute if I crossed the line from professional to something more. I can't afford that. I'm saving for a down payment for my own apartment in New York, which costs an arm and a leg. Owning my own place has been a dream since forever. While I was growing up, Mom always worried about rent and being evicted. When she was alive, the idea of having a place we could call ours seemed like a safe haven. I wish my mom could be around the day I finally have the keys to my very own apartment.

Anyway, a man like Sebastian—with his unbelievable looks and impressive wealth—is not in my league. Not at all.

Our last stop is the first floor. The elevator comes to a halt, and the doors open to reveal a chaos that contrasts starkly with the order above. For one, it's an open office. Then, everyone wears casual clothing, running around as if their life depends on it. Sketches, energy drinks, and empty pizza boxes clutter the desks.

"This is the creative department," Sebastian announces as we step out of the elevator. He raises his voice so it's audible over the background noise of voices, printers, and general madness. "I call it our playground."

"Brother," an attractive blonde calls from across

the room. She hurries our way, stopping in front of us. She wears a figure-hugging green dress and nude stilettos, which I eye with appreciation.

"You must be Ava," she says. I answer with a nod. "I'm Pippa."

"The creative genius behind everything," Sebastian supplies.

"Aww, my sweet brother, singing my praises."

Sebastian puts an affectionate arm around his sister. She fakes pushing him away for a split second, then returns the half hug. Warmth and a little jealously fill me. It must feel wonderful to have such a tight-knit family.

"I wish I could stay longer with you two, but I need to get about a million things done. Ava, let me know if Sebastian doesn't treat you right. I'll kick his ass."

"He's been very nice so far," I say. Sebastian chuckles at my emphasis on nice. "He's even taking me to lunch."

"Well, you two have fun." She takes off, heading back to her desk.

As my eyes follow her gorgeous stilettos, I realize the room has quieted down. Most people are behind their desks now, throwing furtive glances at Sebastian. Thanks to this newly created order, I notice the jewelry holders scattered on the desks throughout the room. They hold different things from raw gemstones to finished necklaces, bracelets, or earrings.

"This is so interesting," I say, as we pass through

the desks. "Can I see the production workshop, too?"

"We can do that another day if we want to get lunch."

"Okay."

I come to a stop in front of an empty desk, pointing to the necklace on the holder. "This ruby is beautiful." Sebastian merely gives me a tight, uncomfortable nod, but I lean over the desk, closer to the gemstone, and continue. "I've worked with luxury goods companies before. However, gemstones and diamonds are magic. There is something so pristine about them, so pure."

I catch Sebastian staring at me. His gaze is filled with disbelief, of all things. "They don't look like this when they're dug up. They must be polished first."

Straightening up, I shrug. "Everything needs work and polishing to shine."

"We agree on that." He steps right behind me, his proximity making it impossible to gather my faculties. In these blissful seconds, all I'm able to do is feel—soak up all the things he exudes: power, masculinity, and something else I can't pinpoint. Maybe it's his commanding presence, but I feel safe around him.

"Rubies are my favorite," I continue. "When I was little, I was convinced fire was in them."

"You're not alone. There are ancient legends and stories in which people believed there was fire in rubies."

"There is a bit of fire in everything and everyone," I say.

Sebastian lets out a sharp breath. Feeling the hot air at my nape weakens my knees, so I turn around. Big mistake. His gaze smolders. Biting my lower lip, I force myself to break eye contact. As we head back inside the elevator, I ask, "Why is everyone down here so stressed out?"

"We have a small collection presentation in two weeks for our international buyers."

Frowning, I inquire, "Don't they receive catalogs?"

"They do, but inviting them over for a private presentation makes them feel special. Also, we have more negotiating power if we bring them to our territory."

"Smart," I admit.

"It's good you'll be here for the presentation. It's nowhere near as elaborate as our big runway shows, but it'll give you an idea."

"That's great." My job is to set up a more aggressive marketing campaign for the next season, which will culminate with one of the Bennett runway shows. They're so famous they often attract more press than fashion mogul shows.

"You'll love the show." We only travel for a few seconds in the elevator; and when the doors open, we step out in an underground garage. "Rubies are the focus."

"Will you be there?" I make sure to keep my distance as I walk alongside him.

"I haven't attended shows in years. Neither the big ones nor the ones for buyers. Reporters are always milling around. They're like hawks when they see me. I'm not much of a front man."

That is true. Business magazines regularly showcase Bennett Enterprises as a poster child for the most successful American companies. I did my research before I came here, reading everything that's been written about them. Sebastian leaves interviews and editorials to his siblings. Nevertheless, that doesn't keep magazines from mentioning him.

"I avoid the spotlight. Thankfully, most of my brothers like it. Blake and Daniel especially enjoy it. They're the party brothers," he says with a smile and a wink. We come to a halt in front of a black Mercedes, and he opens the door for me. Such a gentleman.

"So if Logan is the nice brother, Blake and Daniel are the party brothers, which brother are you?"

The sexy one, a voice in my mind says. That's not fair to the other brothers. From what I've seen in magazines, they're all yummy, but I doubt they'd have the same effect on me.

"You'll have to find out."

"I've never backed away from a challenge." I hold my chin high.

Sebastian pins me with his gaze, his eyes snapping fire. "Neither have I."

Oh, my God. Sebastian Bennett is a flirt and I love it. I'm teetering on the brink of dangerous territory.

Chapter Four

Sebastian

"Where are you taking me?" she asks ten minutes later, while we're speeding through San Francisco.

"To one of my favorite restaurants."

"I hope it's not an expensive one."

I blink. I've never heard these words from a woman before. Generally, the more expensive the location, the better. But Ava Lindt is full of surprises. The first one was down in Creative today. I watched her carefully while she was inspecting the rubies. Women usually look with greed at the gemstones. However, the expression on her face was one of pure interest and awe.

"The verdict is still out there as to what kind of brother I am. I must do my best to impress you."

"I see." She laughs softly, and I find it a relaxing sound. It pleases me that I'm the reason for it. It also makes me imagine what other sounds I could get out of her.

"Is there anything you don't eat?" I keep my fingers crossed, hoping she won't be one of those women who eat almost nothing and call themselves full after half a salad.

"Nope. I'll have anything. As long as it's tasty, I'm in."

I nod appreciatively. Ava Lindt is proving to be more real than any woman I've met in years.

"Is it far away?" Ava crosses her legs, making her skirt lift, revealing a bit more of her thigh. I force my eyes on the road, fantasizing about what she hides under her strict little suit. I must be out of my mind. I just met her.

"You don't trust me?"

"Well, I did just meet you. Isn't there a saying about not getting in cars with strangers?"

"You do know I'm the CEO, right? You act as if that doesn't matter in the slightest."

"And you like it." Her eyes widen, her mouth forming a small, delicious O.

"I do," I admit. "Most people are afraid to even breathe in my presence."

"I'm not afraid of you." Her dismissive tone riles me.

"Perhaps you should be," I retaliate, because I've thought about devouring that delicious skin of hers since she set foot in my office. With her hair on one side and her neck bared to me, I wanted to kiss her right there and feel her shudder in my arms.

I grip the steering wheel tighter. I will not get involved with an employee. Well, technically she's a consultant, not my employee. *Damn semantics, Bennett... The whole thing is out of the question.*

We arrive at the restaurant ten minutes later. I let the valet take my car. This is one of the best restaurants in San Francisco. Of course, I might be biased since one of my sisters owns it, but reviewers agree with me. It's high on one of San Francisco's hills with a magnificent view over the city.

"Mr. Bennett, welcome," the headwaiter says. "We have a corner table available on the terrace. You'll get the best view."

"Oh, this is beautiful," Ava exclaims as she sits down, looking beyond the terrace.

I order the house specialty for both of us. Ava squints at me.

"I could have ordered for myself," she says after the waiter leaves, jutting her chin forward and rolling her tiny shoulders. God, she's delicious all worked up like this.

"I know the restaurant better. You'll like it."

"You're bossy." She crosses her arms over her chest. Even though she has a petite frame, she has curves in all the right places.

I lean slightly across the table. "You have no idea."

A few seconds later, my sister Alice appears at our table. "Sebastian, you should've told me you were coming."

"It was a spontaneous decision. Alice, this is Ava, our marketing consultant. Ava, Alice is my sister and she owns this restaurant." Out of my three sisters, Alice resembles Mom the most. She has the same small figure and light brown hair.

"It's very beautiful," Ava says.

Alice looks speculatively at us. I hold her gaze, but don't return her inquisitive smile. I make a mental note to keep my eyes off Ava during lunch, or the Bennett rumor mill will start.

"I'd love to eat with both of you, but I'm in the middle of a meeting with a potential partner. I came to say hi."

Ava and I make small talk after she leaves, until the waiter brings our drinks. After sipping from her soda, she says, "I want to know more about the company and about you."

"Do you always grill CEOs?"

She grins. "No. CEOs are usually people hired from outside. You are the founder, the essence of this company. By knowing you, I will understand the company's values better. The foundation of a successful advertising campaign is authenticity. I've read all there was to read about the company online. Nevertheless, I know the press has its way of twisting stories, depending on the angle they're going for. I want to know the facts directly from the source." She speaks with so much passion, the sudden urge to lean across the table and kiss her hits me like a ton of bricks.

"So I'm a source?" I smile. "No one's dared to call me that before. Not to my face, anyway."

The waiter interrupts us, serving our food.

"Oh, is this Dungeness crab?" Ava laughs throatily.

"Yes, it is."

"San Francisco is famous for it."

"I know; that's why I ordered it. Thought you'd want to try it."

With a wink, she digs in.

"Anyway, back to you being a source. You are the company. And you're not half as bad as I feared you'd be. So. . ."

I'm used to curiosity from women, though of another type. Within five seconds of meeting a woman, I can tell what she wants from me: either to get a leg up in society, or my credit card.

Watching Ava watch me, I detect honest curiosity on her face. I smile, putting my fork down. She makes sense, but I'd be lying if I said the campaign is the only reason I'm considering giving in to her request. Something in her round eyes beckons me to open up to her. And that is dangerous. Openness leads to vulnerability.

"What do you want to know?" I ask.

"How did you start out?"

I lean back in my chair, studying her. "My parents had a ranch when I was a kid. They'd been struggling financially forever. Raising nine kids is no piece of cake. All of us were working hard at the ranch, even the small ones. At fourteen, I realized we'd never get out of poverty if we continued that way. It was the only life my parents knew; I don't blame them for anything. They are wonderful people and they both worked their fingers to the bone, but it wasn't enough."

"You didn't go to college."

"No. I had to work. At sixteen, I left the ranch to try my luck in other jobs. At some point, I got involved in commerce. Nothing expensive at first, but later I moved to precious stones. At twenty-one, I'd made some good money, but it wasn't enough for what I wanted."

"And that was?"

"To set up my own high-end jewelry company. I sat down with my parents and asked them to sell the only thing they owned—the ranch—and give me the money. Within five days, they put it up for sale. Everyone was behind me."

"I like your family already." Her eyes are glassy all of a sudden, but then she blinks, lifting the corner of her lips in a smile. The moment of vulnerability is enough to wake something in me: a need to protect her and keep her from feeling vulnerable again.

"They trusted me completely. I'll never be able to repay them."

"You're doing that already. You take good care of them now."

"I try to. After selling the ranch, they moved in with my father's brother and his family. They had a neighboring ranch. It was a tough time, but within six months, I made enough profits to help them. Anyway, Logan helped me build this company. He's as much of a founder as I am. He doesn't get nearly enough credit. The press always presents me as the sole creator."

"That's true. I suppose it makes for a better story.

One man who succeeded against all odds and all that."

"Yeah. Anyway, as the company grew and the profits came in, I set up my parents so they never had to worry about money again. My siblings all went to college—Logan included. I brought in my other brothers and sisters to help. The company is vast, and most of them found their place in it."

"So out of all of you, who works in the company?"

"Pippa and Logan, obviously. I'm the oldest, then come Logan and Pippa. You've met Alice. She decided to do something else. The first set of twins is next, Christopher and Max. Max is in London, and Christopher in Hong Kong, building our presence in those markets. The next set of twins—Blake and Daniel—are undecided yet, and the family baby, Summer, is a painter."

"Wow. Your family sounds fantastic. Blake and Daniel are the party brothers, correct?"

I grimace—shouldn't have mentioned that to her. People always pick on Blake and Daniel. A few women I've dated even went far enough to suggest I should completely cut them off. But they are family, and family comes first. Always.

"Yeah. Blake and Daniel will come around," I say evasively, with no desire to hear another person talk about how I should crack a whip and put some sense into them.

"Well, everyone is different. As long as they don't hurt anyone, I don't see why they shouldn't do whatever they like."

I appreciate her nonjudgmental tone. "Many people view this as a corporation. I see it as a family business. A big one, it's true. But there you have it; I'm not the core of the company. My whole family is."

There it is again, that vulnerable look in her eyes. I want nothing more than to wipe it away with a kiss and a hug, but I stay put.

"So basically, you built up this company to make sure your family is well taken care of. You are the most interesting man I've met." The sincerity in her words catches me off guard. Oh, I've heard this sentence from women before. It usually comes after I give them an expensive gift, not after I talk about my family. "I can't wait for the show in two weeks." Her eyes light up with excitement.

"Maybe I'll go too this time." Seeing her curiosity, I want to go, if only to watch her experience everything. "Got enough material for your marketing campaign?"

"This isn't just about the campaign. You're fascinating. I could hear you talk all day."

"Careful there, don't feed my ego. I've been told it's oversize already."

"I'm sure that's true, but you might be one of the few men who deserve that ego."

"Actually, Logan's the one with the big ego. He likes to tell everyone he's the nice brother. Don't believe him."

She tilts her head to one side. "Tell me more."

"Enough about me. Tell me about yourself."

"Pffft, my story isn't nearly as interesting as yours."

I lean forward. "I think you're interesting."

In fact, I think she's very interesting. I chuckle, remembering Logan saying he got so bored at his last date he wanted to poke his eyes out. Blake refers to such dates as so boring I couldn't even get it up.

Well, judging by the stirring in my boxers, that's not the case here. Of course, the nipples almost showing through her shirt also contribute to that. I had a glimpse of them when she unbuttoned her suit jacket. Imagining how puckered they must be drives me crazy. Her reaction to me tells me exactly the kind of effect I have on her. A lovely blush spreads on her neck. Smiling, I lean back to give her some space. "Do you have siblings?"

"No, I was an only child. My mom died when I was in college."

"Sorry to hear that. How about your dad?"

"Never met him. He took off before I was born."

My jaw ticks. I detest men like him. Switching to a safe topic, I say, "Tell me about New York."

"I've lived there since I was born, but I don't see too much of it lately. I'm always somewhere else with clients. Singapore, Sydney, San Francisco." She pauses, frowning. "I wonder if they sign me up to clients based on the letter the city starts with."

"Do you like traveling? I find it exhausting."

"I love it. It's a lot of work, but I manage to squeeze in plenty of sightseeing. Can't wait to explore. Believe it or not, I've never been to California."

"I can show you around." My words surprise both of us. I haven't had time for such things in years. More accurately, I didn't make time, but her enthusiasm is catchy. I like how carefree she makes me feel. I haven't felt this way since I was working at my parents' ranch, before I took it upon myself to take care of my family.

A grin flickers on her face. "I might take you up on that."

"I'll make sure you do."

As we leave the restaurant, I notice her flexing her neck. "You look tense."

"I wrapped up the last project in Sydney five days ago. My boss didn't let me take a few days off. I was assigned directly to this project."

"I promise not to go too hard on you in the first days."

Her pupils dilate, and I swallow hard. Well, you know you're on a slippery road when you start making involuntary innuendos. The valet brings the car and as I open the door, the words slip out. "Are you seeing someone?"

"You're technically not allowed to ask me that."

"Of course, I can. I'm the most interesting man you know. Don't I get a hall pass at invading your private space?"

A red hue stains her cheeks as she whispers, "No, I'm not seeing anyone."

I drive her to the complex where she told me her serviced apartment is, and invite myself upstairs. I can't believe my eyes when she opens the door to her room.

"When did you arrive?" I ask.

"This morning."

"This place looks like you've lived here for months." There are photographs and little keepsakes from her numerous trips.

"You like it?" She smiles proudly.

"It looks almost like a home." It's warm, bright, and colorful, like her.

"Well, I spend so much time traveling and living in hotels or serviced apartments that I try to make it seem like home everywhere. It feels less lonely."

"You don't have to be lonely. There's me and a bazillion other Bennetts to keep you company. My family is very friendly," I add, before I can stop myself. I should go, but something makes me want to stay. "Aren't you going to invite me for a drink?"

"It's early afternoon, and I don't have any drinks. Besides, I already have plans for today. I have to leave in about half an hour."

"You're kicking me out?" I ask in disbelief. I like this woman more with each passing moment.

"I am. I officially start working for you tomorrow, so the rest of the day is mine. I'm exploring the city." She presses her luscious lips together in a tight line.

"I like a woman who is confident enough to spend time by herself, but wandering through San Francisco on your own is not the best idea. You don't know the city."

"Sebastian! Thank you for your concern, but I live in New York, and I have traveled to some very shady cities. I know how to take care of myself."

I back off, trying to rein in all the feelings she stirs in me: protectiveness, desire, and something more.

"Besides, don't you have work to do? I heard you're a workaholic."

This sobers me up. Yes, I am; but she made me forget that for a few hours. Stepping in front of her, I brush the hinge of her jaw with my fingertips. I take endless pleasure in the way her pupils dilate and her tiny body quivers at my touch. "Enjoy your day. See you tomorrow morning."

Chapter Five

Sebastian

"I can't believe you took her to Alice's place. How was lunch?"

I look up from my papers to find Pippa in the doorway. Alarm bells ring immediately at her characteristic smile. When we were kids, that grin usually meant I broke a window—don't tell Mom. As of late, that grin means I'm trying to set you up with someone.

It was a bad omen then, and it is now.

"The food was good." Despite my neutral tone, Pippa's smile morphs into a grin.

As I said, bad omen.

I hold up the report I'm reading to show her I have no time. Instead of taking the cue, Pippa proceeds into my office, sitting in the chair opposite me and resting her elbows on my desk.

"Oh, but it's all in the company, not in the food, right. So, how was the company?"

"Ava's smart," I reply curtly, still surveying the

report in my hands.

"And beautiful and sexy. You want to add anything to that list?"

With a groan, I give up and push the papers away. It's not as though they'll stop Pippa when she's on a mission anyway.

"What's your point?"

Her brows lower and she answers in the most innocent tone possible, "No point. Just trying to get a feel for the situation."

"There is no situation, Pippa."

Her grin returns, all traces of innocence—real or feigned—gone. "Yet, Alice told me you and Ava were giving each other hot looks."

"I don't get involved with employees."

"Ha!" Pippa points a triumphant finger at me, as if I admitted to a mortal sin. "So you have thought about Ava like that."

"Pippa, I'm a man. She's a smart, beautiful woman, and sexy as fuck. Of course, I thought about it. But—"

"You'd be perfect for each other." Pippa rubs her palms together in excitement.

"Damn it." I drop my head in my hands, sighing. I've opened Pandora's box.

"Hear me out."

"By all means, go on," I say in defeat. I can make boardrooms go quiet by only looking at those in attendance. Shutting up my sister? Any of my sisters, for that matter, and sometimes even brothers, if they feel like meddling? Impossible. Of course, there's something to be said about the fact that we've all seen each other playing in mud and had each other's backs, but still. Years have passed since then. I'm thirty-three. One would think they'd find me at least half as intimidating as our employees do.

"The two of you are very much alike."

I lounge back in my leather chair, frowning at her. "Meaning?"

"You both have a shield of steel"— Pippa grimaces—"you show everyone, and. . . ah, what is the phrase, 'a heart of gold' inside?" She cringes. "I always thought that expression sucks. I mean, steel and gold are both as hard as it gets. Why is a heart of gold considered a good thing? I mean, who decided that should be a thing as opposed to say. . . a heart of cupcakes? That sounds much better, doesn't it?"

I'd point out that gold is a soft and malleable metal, but Pippa knows this. I have a hunch I'm missing her point. I lost her somewhere between gold and cupcakes, so I don't answer.

"What I mean," she insists, oblivious to my predicament, "is I think you have lots in common."

I scoff. "And you noticed that in the fifteen minutes we were downstairs?"

"You know I can read people."

Yeah, except that asshole you married. I swallow my words though because I know Pippa is still hurting, no matter what she says. The truth is she does have an extraordinary talent for reading people—most of the time. She got that from Mom. It's a dangerous talent, especially when both of them decide to use it against me.

"Okay, let's wrap up this conversation." Pippa pushes herself to her feet, smoothing her skirt.

I shoot her a suspicious look. "You're not one to give up until you get what you want."

Putting a hand on her hip, she leans slightly forward. "But I already got what I wanted."

"And that was?"

"To make you admit you're not indifferent to Ava's fabulousness. Now you'll be thinking about her all day."

"No, I won't. I hate to break it to you, but I'm the CEO of this company. I have more important things to do than that."

She waves her hand, as if saying, That's nothing. "You won't be able to concentrate."

"You're crazy," I mutter, rising from my desk to walk Pippa to the door.

"Of course, I am. But I channel my crazy into creativity, making beautiful jewels that will bring happiness to high-maintenance women and clueless men worldwide."

We stand midway between the desk and the door, but Pippa doesn't budge any further, just looks at me expectantly.

"You're not going to leave until I tell you I love you despite your craziness, right?" I ask.

"Well, the men in our family are the only ones who do love me. A girl has to make the most of what she has." Pippa says this with a smile, like it's a big joke, but I know it's not. I know my sister. She masks everything with a smile and a joke. Much like Ava, I realize, remembering that fleeting moment of vulnerability she let slip today.

"Did Terence contact you again?"

Pippa flinches, hunching her shoulders. In a matter of seconds, my sister seems to have shrunk a few inches.

"He tried. How do you know?" she whispers.

"Wild guess. What did he want?"

"I didn't pick up," she answers a little too quickly.

I raise my eyebrows.

"I haven't spoken to him." She smiles, pulling herself straight again, setting her jaw. "I'm throwing away all the things he didn't bother to take with him when he left. I swear I keep finding his shit everywhere." I read between the lines. Terence moved out a month ago. If she still hasn't thrown away all of his things, it means she's still holding on to them.

"You know I'm here if you need to talk, right?" I ask gently.

"Brother, I just talked your ear off."

"You know what I mean."

"It's not worth talking about him. It's a waste of breath and words."

Pippa married Terence three years ago. I never liked him much. Something about him seemed off. I made him sign a prenup stating that if he and Pippa separated before their tenth anniversary, he wouldn't get jack shit. He played his cards right—for one whole year. In their second year of marriage, things took a turn for the worse. They fought continuously and spent more time apart than together. One night, his mask fell completely. He and Pippa were fighting, and he told her he couldn't wait for ten years to pass. Then he'd divorce her and get his share of the money. He crushed my sister's heart. Now they're in the process of getting divorced. That asshole won't get one cent from my sister, but no matter what, I can't undo the hurt he caused.

"He shouldn't be calling you."

"I don't want you to get in a fight with him," she warns.

"I'm not making any promises."

Logan already gave the moron the beating of his life. None of this will make Pippa feel better though.

"Logan told me about the present for Mom and Dad's anniversary. They'll be very happy."

I smile at Pippa. Yes, my parents will be very happy indeed. They gave it up for me. It's only fair that I give it back to them. They had my back when I needed it the most and risked everything for me. That's one of the reasons my parents, along with every single sibling of mine, own shares in Bennett enterprises, no matter if they are actually involved with the company or not. I remember what it was like to have nothing and the permanent insecurity that brought. My family won't have to endure that again. Ever.

Tilting Pippa's chin up, I kiss her forehead. "I love you, crazy pants. Now go create beautiful things I can sell."

She smiles before heading out the door. "I will. Now go tear Ava's panties—err, I meant shield of steel—down."

Shaking my head, I sit behind my desk, picking up the report again. As Pippa predicted, I have a hard time concentrating on the report, wondering instead if Ava wears lace or silk.

Chapter Six

Ava

I barely sleep during my first night in San Francisco. It's not unusual; it takes some time to adjust to new beds. Tonight, my bed isn't at fault for my lack of sleep.

Sebastian Bennett is.

There is something about this man. He can make my knees go weak and my heart somersault at the same time. It's not just his good looks that have me thinking about him, though he's delicious. He's different from what I expected, and from other powerful men I've met. He shows respect to everyone, even waiters and valets. I almost melted when he spoke about his family today.

I twist in my bed, burying my head in the pillow. I can't obsess over him; I need to drill this into my head. It would help if he'd acted indifferent, but his thinly disguised flirting made me simmer. An ache forms between my legs as I remember his stirring presence.

Unable to sleep, I text my best friend, Nadine.

Ava: Arrived at the new job today, wanted to let you know I'm okay.

Nadine: Is Sebastian Bennett as good-looking as in pictures?

Ava: Don't get me started. He's too hot for his own good.

Nadine: Too bad about your work clause. But nothing's sweeter than the forbidden fruit, right?

Ava: You know I won't do anything.

Smiling, I shake my head. I fall asleep with Sebastian on my mind. Dreaming is not forbidden, after all.

***

I arrive early at the office the next morning. Except for the security guard downstairs, I don't bump into anyone. Perfect. I like starting my days before anyone else. I can get work done without interruptions. As I sink in my chair, I notice a small envelope on my desk, with my name on it.

Frowning, I open it and find a gift certificate for a spa and a handwritten card.

You deserve to relax. Enjoy your time at the spa.
Sebastian

Warmth billows inside me. Slowly, unexplainable emotions overcome me. No man I've dated has done something so thoughtful for me, and here comes this man I've known for one day, offering me something

I need very badly. I'm sure he's busy, yet he took time to buy this and even write to me. I have no proof, but I'm certain this is his handwriting.

Sighing, I push the card and the voucher back in the envelope. I can't possibly accept it, though I could use a few hours of pampering. I walk to his office, intending to leave the envelope on his desk, but find Sebastian inside, bent over some papers. Like yesterday, he takes my breath away when he looks up at me.

"You're here early."

"I like to start my day early, when there's no one around," I say. "That way, I don't get interrupted."

"Clever. That's why I like to come in early, too." He sizes me up, his eyes resting on my hips and then my chest. The intensity in his gaze sets me ablaze. Wow. Okay, this must stop. It's going to be a long four months if I daydream about jumping him every time I see him.

"What can I do for you?" he inquires. Why, thanks for asking, Mr. Bennett. How about showing me all the things you can do with your tongue and fingers and. . . "Ava?"

I bite the inside of my cheek, holding up the envelope. "I found this on my desk. It's very thoughtful, but I can't accept it."

"Why?" His eyebrows shoot up. "You said you didn't have time to relax after your last project."

"Yes, but. . ." All the reasons I had in mind become a muddled chaos as he fixes me with his eyes, piercing me. Goose bumps cover my skin as I try to pull myself together. No chance. The man sets me alight with only his eyes. I shudder, imagining what he could do with his hands, or lips. Damn it. This needs to stop.

"Take pity on me and accept the gift to relieve me of my guilt," he says.

"What are you guilty about?"

"I terrorized your boss to send someone as early as possible or I would give the job to another consultancy."

"You terrorized my boss?" A giggle tumbles from my lips.

"I did." He crosses his arms over his chest, his delicious lips curling upward. "Am I wrong in thinking you find that a little amusing?"

"I find it very amusing. He usually does all the terrorizing. The thought that someone has done the same to him is very satisfying."

"There's a naughty girl hidden down there underneath your business suits, isn't there?" he asks. Is my mind playing tricks on me, or did his voice become throatier? I wet my lips, averting my gaze.

"Take the card, Sebastian. Give it to someone else."

"I'm not expecting you to fall all over me because of a spa visit." His bluntness sends tendrils of heat low in my body.

"You're cocky."

"You like it." When I don't say anything, he continues. "Look, I want you to have a good time. Let me do this for you."

"You're doing this. . . why?"

He smiles mischievously. "You were practically glowing at the restaurant yesterday. I loved that look on your face, and I'd love even more to be the reason you smile."

I am speechless, and swooning. How can he do that to me? Why do I want even more? Sebastian closes the distance between us, pointing to the envelope.

"Take the gift card."

"Sebastian."

"Ava."

"I can't—"

"You will. End of discussion." His tone is so final, so full of authority, that I actually take a step back. He advances toward me, as if determined to dominate me. "I want you to relax." He bends his head to my cheek, whispering in my ear, "Think about me while you're there."

Chapter Seven

Ava

The rest of the day passes in a haze. I sit through multiple meetings with the marketing department. Sebastian joins me in a few. I try to keep my distance from him and fail. The man is relentless. He always sits next to me, touching my hand or my leg—by accident, of course. He's smart enough to make it look that way.

The meetings go well. During the first one, I discover his team is pleased with my presence here, which is refreshing. Marketing departments are usually hostile toward me, considering the outside agency an intrusion. This one seems open and eager to collaborate. Good. This means I can concentrate on my job. By the third meeting, I realize it's not that they are pleased with me; they just don't like the new marketing manager, Martha, much. She was hired a week ago.

"Why did you hire the marketing manager from outside instead of promoting someone from within the department?" I ask Sebastian after that meeting is over. "Your team doesn't look very happy."

"I know, but bringing in new blood can be good. That's why we decided to work with your consultancy as well. She's on probation for four months anyway. If it doesn't work out, she'll go."

At six o'clock, I'm utterly exhausted, sitting in my office and going through my notes from today's meetings. My neck is even stiffer than yesterday. I eye the voucher still lying on my desk, tugging at my lips with my teeth. On a whim, I call the spa. A woman greets me.

"Hello. I have a gift card and I'd like to use it as soon as possible."

"Why don't you come by tonight, and we'll see where we can book you in?"

"This sounds wonderful," I tell her honestly. I was expecting to wait at least a week. "Can you give me the address?"

As I scribble down her instructions, I realize it's on the same street as my apartment. Did Sebastian take the time to look up a spa nearby? I can't believe he gave this so much thought, but it can't be a coincidence.

"See you in an hour," I tell her.

Since it rained the entire afternoon, clouds populate the graying silk tarp of sky. I step outside the building, drained of energy. Inhaling deeply, I find the air doesn't bring the burst of freshness I was hoping for. Heaviness languishes in the air from the earlier rain. Arrows of light descend through the clouds, but it looks like the sky won't clear today.

***

I make myself a promise as I walk into the spa. I will relax and enjoy this without any remorse for having accepted Sebastian's gift.

"Hi," I tell the receptionist. "We spoke on the phone earlier."

She smiles politely, taking the gift card I hand her. "Yes, we did. What would you like to do while you're here, Ms. . .?"

"Lindt. I have a really stiff neck. Something to relax my muscles would be great."

"May I suggest a massage?"

"Sounds like just what I need."

"I'll send you to Andrew. He's the best." She frowns at her computer screen, clicking around a few times. "He's free in one hour. What would you like to do in that time? I can fit in a mani-pedi or a facial. Or I can book both and move Andrew an hour later. Your gift card certainly covers the expenses for all those."

"It does?" How much did Sebastian spend on me? There's no amount on the card.

"Yes. Shall I book everything?"

I tap my fingers on the counter, pondering my answer for a few seconds. "Okay."

I avoid thinking about Sebastian in the mani-pedi and the facial, but my will dissolves when I walk inside the massage room. I am naked except for a tiny thong beneath the towel I wrapped tightly around me. Andrew asks me to drop my towel and lie on my stomach on the massage table. He turns his back while I do as he says, and then he covers my butt with the towel. Well, I don't feel less naked. He pours warm oil on my skin and begins to knead my flesh between his expert hands, and I forget all about shame.

"The neck area keeps giving me problems," I tell him.

"I'll concentrate on that."

As I feel Andrew's fingers on me, my mind flies to Sebastian's strong hands. They'd make my entire body burn. His memory alone lights every nerve. His vivid, dark eyes haunt me, and soon I fantasize he's with me in my hotel room, doing what Andrew does, only moving his hands much lower. I'd let that man do anything to me, and that's a scary thought. Breathing hard against the towel, I curse aloud, making Andrew jump.

"Sorry, Andrew. I remembered I forgot something at the office," I lie.

I cannot fantasize about Sebastian Bennett. At any rate, I don't know much about him. He could be the ultimate playboy. He certainly has the looks for it. I learned early on not to trust men. Dad left Mom before I was even born, leaving her to fend for us both.

A dull ache hovers in my chest. It's been nine years since she died, and I still miss her every day.

While I grew up, it seemed so often that it was the two of us against the world. She never—to my knowledge at least—dated again. It's not that she instilled in me to mistrust men, it's that the men I've dated gave me reason not to trust them. I've always longed to have a large family, but my two long-term relationships ended because the guys cheated on me, and blamed me and my job for it. Finding a decent man and counting on him seems like an impossibility, akin to comfortable high heels or sexy period panties. At thirty-one, I threw in the towel and only count on myself.

Sebastian seems to be every woman's dream. He's kind, thoughtful, and intense. Just remembering his piercing stare sends tendrils of heat low in my body. I need to get laid. Badly. It's been an embarrassing number of months since I last had sex, and I know Sebastian's proximity will be much easier to bear if I don't have so much sexual tension bottled up inside me. It'd also be easier if the attraction was one-sided, but I saw how he looks at me. I take a deep breath. Four months. I have to resist for four months; then I'll be gone.

I leave the massage room, take a wrong turn, and end up in an unfamiliar corridor.

"Excuse me," I ask a cleaning lady who passes by. "Where is reception? I got lost."

The woman, petite and in her forties, opens her mouth, but instead of answering, coughs. Furrowing my brow, I study her appearance. Her nose and eyes are puffy—signs of a cold or an allergy. Either way, she's sick. She gives me directions in a low voice.

"Thank you. Are you okay? You're very sick. You should take the day off."

She shakes her head, her eyes widening. "Can't afford it. I have two little kids back home. I'm much better now, though. I thought I'd collapse a few hours ago when I was waitressing. At least here it's quiet."

Gulping, I say, "Take care of yourself. What's your name?"

"Nora."

"Have a good day, Nora." My voice is shaky, and the hair at the back of my neck stands on end as I make my way to the reception. Nora's determination to give her kids the best and moonlight between jobs hits home too hard.

"Was everything all right?" the receptionist asks.

"Yes, but I want to ask you for a favor. You have a cleaning lady, Nora, who's sick. Tell her to go home, and that you'll pay her anyway."

"Miss, the bosses won't—"

"I'm paying for it. Here." I put more bills on the counter than her wage must be, but I don't care. In fact, I add more bills, struck by an idea. "Also, I want to buy her a gift card for a treatment of her choice here at the spa. Please tell her it's on the house, though."

"Why are you doing this, miss?"

I smile, remembering what my mother used to tell

me. "Sometimes an act of kindness is enough to keep one going."

***

"Let's wrap this up. Good work, everyone," I say three days later, smiling broadly. There is a sense of accomplishment as the marketing department and I leave the meeting room. I head to my office, glancing inside Sebastian's as I pass. My stomach constricts slightly. He's inside. I've kept my distance for the past few days, but knowing he works on the other side of the wall makes concentrating a chore. I've had the same dream the past two nights. I'm in the massage room again, only Andrew isn't there. Instead, a man with dark eyes and full lips curled into a smile welcomes me, wearing nothing but a towel.

Around lunchtime, someone knocks at my door. I look up from my computer screen to find Sebastian standing in the doorway.

"Lunch?" he asks.

"I have a lot to do." It's not exactly a lie. "I'll grab something quick later."

"I see." He walks inside my office, pushes aside some folders I'd spread out, and sits on the desk. "How is the team treating you? I thought it'd be best if I didn't join you in all meetings, so you had a chance to work with them without the boss breathing down their necks."

"I appreciate it. They are very cooperative with

me. I think they'll warm up to the marketing manager too, eventually."

"I'll keep an eye on that. Martha has excellent credentials. It'd be a pity if things between her and the team didn't work out."

"I agree. She's very competent."

Sebastian taps his fingers on the desk, a crease forming on his forehead.

"I went to the spa," I find myself blurting out. His crease instantly disappears, a smile inching its way across his features.

"Did you enjoy it?" he asks softly. His gaze is anything but soft. He looks at me like a man determined to read my most hidden thoughts, discover my deepest desires.

"Oh yes. You were very generous. Thank you. You were right. I needed a few hours of relaxation badly."

"What did you do?"

"Many things, but the massage was the best part. The guy, Andrew, had the most amazing hands."

Sebastian's eyes narrow. "I know how to give a good massage. I know which points to press to relieve. . .tension." The last word rolls off his tongue with so much sensuality that I nearly lose control and kiss him on the spot.

I find it within me to roll my chair a little further from him, and decide to confront him. "Are you flirting with me?"

"Yes, I am."

I back away from the intensity of his gaze. I was

expecting him to at least skirt around the subject. But something tells me Sebastian isn't that kind of man. He's the kind that gets what he wants, no matter how.

"Sebastian," I say weakly. "Don't. I have a no-fraternizing clause in my contract. I'd get fired in a blink for getting involved with you."

He pauses for a few seconds. "I didn't know that."

"Now you do."

"What if you didn't have that clause?" He shifts closer to me. I remain silent, and he tilts my chin up to him. "Answer," he demands. What would it be like to be wanted by a man like him? To be loved by a man who holds so much intensity in his gaze alone?

"I never got involved with clients, not even when I had no such clause," I stammer. "It's a matter of principle. Work is work."

"I never get involved with people I work with either."

I breathe a sigh of relief. "You're a smart man. I'm a smart woman. Let's not do something stupid together."

"Stupid never sounded more appealing. I want to get to know you, Ava," he murmurs. I open my mouth, but he holds up his hand. "Hear me out. You're fun, sweet, and refreshing."

My breath catches. Licking my lips, I smile. "Is this because I'm not acting all impressed that you're the CEO and everything?"

"Maybe." His eyes light up. "I'm looking forward to impressing you."

"You are very direct."

Leaning lower, he whispers, "And determined."

Words fail me. His lips are so close, and I love every word coming out of them.

"Lunch, anyone?" Logan's voice resounds from the doorway. I jump so violently in my seat I almost knock over the glass of water in front of me. Sebastian catches it, looking as nonchalant as ever.

"Logan. Impeccable timing, as usual." Sebastian doesn't take his eyes off me. "Yes, let's you and I go have some lunch. Ava here doesn't have time for us."

I gulp as the two men leave. Four months. I'll never survive them.

Chapter Eight

Ava

"Ava, wait for me," Sebastian calls from behind me the following Monday. I push the button to keep the elevator doors open and give Sebastian a small smile as he enters. Instinctively, I take a step back before his scent can overwhelm me. This man sneaks pheromones in his cologne, I swear. I gulp, looking straight at the doors.

When we reach our floor and the doors open, Sebastian holds out his arm, "Ladies first."

Several mishaps occur as I step out of the elevator. First, my heel gets caught in the tiny space between the elevator floor and the actual floor. I lose my balance and fall on all fours. The cherry on the top? My skirt flies up to my waist. I desperately reposition my skirt, then turn to look at Sebastian. I've given him a full view of my granny-period panties. I know this because his eyes widen—and not in a good way, but in a what-decade-are-you-lost-in way. I groan, and this seems to snap him back to his gentlemanly ways, because he steps out of the elevator and helps me up.

"So, is this a trick to get you in my arms?" he murmurs, his hands on my arms. I shake him off, mouthing a quick thank you and scurrying to my office. Behind the safety of the closed door, I slump in my seat and swear. The day Sebastian Bennett sees my ass, I'm wearing granny panties.

Just my luck.

Now I feel obligated to show him that particular asset in a more appealing light too. Jesus, Ava. Where did that thought come from? He definitely doesn't need to see your ass again. Maybe the sight has put him off me. As depressing as that thought is, it's for the best.

I distract myself from the mishap with e-mails and phone calls, and it works. Until after lunch, that is, when I can't postpone a trip to Sebastian's office any longer. I need to discuss some things with him before bringing my ideas to the table for the next campaign.

***

Determined to ignore the morning incident, I walk into his office and sit on the chair in front of his desk. The problem is, the second our gazes meet, I notice the twinkle in his eyes, accompanied by a bona fide smirk. I can practically see my god-awful panties reflected in his pupils. Opening my mouth, I intend to say, Thank you for taking your time to discuss this. Other words come out instead. "I don't usually wear granny panties."

Sebastian bursts out laughing, plunking his forearms on the wood desk. "What do you wear?"

"Normal stuff. Modern stuff."

How did I get myself in this conversation? My mouth is definitely not connected to my brain today. Or maybe my brain stopped working altogether, letting hormones take over.

I pull myself straighter and try again. This time, the right words come out. "I want to talk to you about the campaign."

To his credit, Sebastian stops laughing, though the twinkle still dances in his eyes. Damn him. We spend about an hour discussing my agenda.

"We can wrap up this conversation. I'll draft up the next steps and meet with the team."

He gives me a nod. "You're very efficient. I like it."

I smile, wanting to get out quickly now that the meeting is over. I'm sure my brain will come up with a few more ways to embarrass me if I stay here too long.

"Ava," Sebastian calls when I'm at the door.

"Yes?"

"If you think I can't imagine exactly what is underneath your granny panties, you're wrong. I still want to know what kind of modern stuff you usually wear. And I will find out."

Chapter Nine

Sebastian

My words have precisely the effect I want on her. A delicious blush spreads on her neck, visible even from here. I smile long after she leaves, remembering her outburst when she entered the office. I discover something new about her every day. During our first lunch, I had a sneak peek of the vulnerable layers hiding behind her laughter. Today, I learned she also could be a complete goofball, which is adorable and hilarious, since she works so hard to keep up her image of consummate businesswoman. I like that she doesn't have a stick up her ass. I cannot help but relax in her presence. She's playful, without playing mind games. Most of all, I am the one pursuing her. I'm so tired of women pursuing me, their eyes on my wallet and social position.

My phone rings. Dad is calling. I pick up immediately. "Hi, Dad."

"Hello, son. Am I interrupting you?"

"Not at all. I have time for a little chat."

"Well, it won't be long. Your mother wants to

know if you're bringing anyone to our anniversary."

I grimace. "You're kidding, right? How did Mom and Pippa get you into this matchmaking thing?"

"You know what they say, happy wife, happy life."

Smiling, I refrain from commenting. My father never does anything he doesn't want to. He can't be coerced or convinced. If he does something, it's because he thinks it's the right thing to do. I've learned many things from my father. He instilled in us from a very young age the importance of family and hard work. No matter how tired he was from work, he never complained, and he always made time to listen to us. Above all, he always took care of Mom and spoiled her. However, he never got into her matchmaking games before.

"I'm coming alone. I was expecting Mom to keep nagging. Since when did you go over to the dark side?"

"Since I think it's high time my son got married."

Right. Time to make up an excuse. "My assistant sent me an important report. I'll call you later, okay?"

I smile, and I swear I can hear Dad's smile on the other end. "I'm sure you will."

When I hang up, my smile widens. Maybe because Ava is so complex, or maybe because her presence is so refreshing—it's addictive, but I want to know more about her.

I should be more careful; I've been burned enough times. Women have a way of hiding their true intentions very well. Ava isn't like that, though. She can't be.

I want to know what she fears, what makes her cry, and what makes her laugh. After today's incident, I want to know what kind of lingerie she wears, only to remove it, and find out what makes her come apart in bed.

***

Logan and I attend the meeting with the marketing department in the afternoon, and Ava presents her proposals. Everyone is impressed, including Logan, who usually plays devil's advocate.

"I have to admit," Logan tells her afterward when it's just the three of us left in the meeting room, "I was skeptical when we brought you in."

The three of us sit at the long table, Logan and me on one side, Ava on the opposite.

Ava narrows her eyes. "And why is that?"

"Consultants usually rip you off. I imagined marketing consultants to be even worse."

"Wow. You do know how to compliment people, don't you?" She says that with a smile and a headshake.

"There goes your nice brother facade," I tell him. "You can never keep it up for long. Told you to find another angle."

"It does work in negotiations," Logan counters.

"That's true."

Ava has her hair down today, and sweeps it on one side, baring her neck. It takes all my self-control not to imagine kissing her there. Or anywhere else.

"Tell me more about that," she says, looking at me. She has a curiosity about everything that reminds me of the way I was years ago, when I first started out. "Let me guess, Logan is the good cop, and you're the bad one?"

I nod, still eyeing her neck.

"Plays well, right?" Logan says. "He always keeps out of the limelight, so people already assume he's an ogre. Don't tell anyone he isn't, or we'll have to find another negotiation strategy."

"Your secret is safe with me." Ava laughs, and Logan joins in. That's how I know I'm not the only one who feels at ease around her. For my brother's sake, I hope he isn't fantasizing about her neck or underwear too. A vein pulses in my neck at the thought, and I turn to watch him. He leans back in his chair, lacing his fingers on top of his head. I've seen my brother when he's after a woman, and this isn't how he acts.

"I want more secrets," she says.

"Okay, enough secrets," I interject when he opens his mouth. "Logan, you'll be late to your dinner appointment."

"Right, yeah. I'll get going."

"I love this banter between the two of you," Ava says after he leaves. "You were right; this doesn't feel like a corporation at all. Thank God neither of you is a brooding ogre."

"You haven't tried to talk budgets with him. He's not the good cop at all when it comes to that."

"Is the rest of your family like the two of you?

Pippa and Alice seemed funny."

"You'll meet all of them at some point. I'll let you make up your mind. How was your weekend? Did you do any sightseeing?"

"Not much. I was tired and didn't feel like drawing up itineraries and running around town."

"I can take you this weekend."

Ava drops her eyes, rubbing the side of her neck. "Maybe not such a good idea."

"You were open to it during lunch last week."

"Yeah, but now I'm not."

"Why not?"

"You know why."

She says this in a final tone, and we both get up from our chairs. At the door, I grasp her arm and whisper in her ear, "You do realize I won't give up, right?"

Chapter Ten

Ava

The week goes by fast, and before I know it, it's Friday. I'm about to leave the office when Nadine texts me.

Nadine: How's hot stuff today?

Ava: Stop calling him that. I grin as I type. You know I have to do the proper thing and keep this professional.

Unsurprisingly, she answers right away.

Nadine: I googled Sebastian—again. Did you take a good look at him? The only thing you HAVE to DO is HIM.

Ava: Enough with the caps lock. Go back to whatever it is you're doing. I shake my head.

Nadine: My appointment is forty minutes late. It's so boring I want to poke my eyes out.

Ava: Well, I must work.

If I think this will deter Nadine, boy, am I wrong.

Nadine: No you don't. You're thinking about him, you little perv. So, no other gift cards?

Sebastian texts me in the meantime, asking me if there's anything I'd like to discuss with him or

Logan. I answer quickly that everything went smoothly this week before returning to Nadine's text.

Ava: Nope. And no other display of unsexy underwear.

Shame grips me as I remember the incident, but I smile at Nadine's reply.

Nadine: Thank God. One display was enough. Come on, show the guy the sexy stuff you've got.

Ava: Nadine, go get laid and stop bugging me.

Nadine: I haven't found anyone worthy, so I'm basically living through you. God, women who haven't gotten laid in months should come with a warning sign, shouldn't we?

I laugh out loud.

Ava: Yep, we should.

Sebastian texts again, asking if I have weekend plans. I'm still waiting for Nadine to answer, but she doesn't write anything back, so I assume her appointment arrived. I toss my smartphone in my bag, unsure what to tell Sebastian. Then I fish it back out, and type to Nadine, **I know Sebastian's hot, but I have to keep my distance. There's my work clause, and other things, like my crappy experiences with men, the fact that I'm not a one-night-stand kind of girl, and that I'm here for a few months only.**

I press Send. She'll read it whenever she has time, though if I'm honest, I wrote it more for myself. To my surprise, the phone buzzes right away.

I can work with that.

Frowning, I'm about to ask her what she means, when I realize I haven't sent the text to Nadine. I sent it to Sebastian.

Ground, swallow me now, please. Well, the list of embarrassing things I do around Sebastian has gotten longer and it's only my second week here. Tugging at my lower lip with my teeth, I assess the damage, preparing a reply.

This wasn't meant for you—DELETE.

I don't think you—DELETE.

Damn. What do I write back? Drawing in a lungful of air, I close my eyes, trying to clear my head. Unfortunately, all my mind comes up with is an image of Sebastian, looking ridiculously hot in his suit. I start wondering what he looks like naked.

Ava: I'm not a business project, Sebastian.

He doesn't reply right away. My stomach twists as I wait, holding my breath.

Sebastian: No, you're a smart, sexy woman I can't stop thinking about.

To address your concerns:

1. I'm not like the men you've met.

2. I'm not the "one-night-stand type" either.

3. I can't make time stop yet, but I can give it a try.

See? All things we can work with.

I smile. I can't help it as warmth spreads along my nerve endings. This man knows how to charm. Despite everything, I want to let myself be whisked away, even if only by his words. I'm about to type back when Sebastian strolls into my office, sporting a grin the size of Texas.

"So," I say.

"So," he replies.

Pulling my eyebrows together, I say with a businesslike tone, "I'm confused by point one in your message. Please expand. How are you not like the men I've met?"

Sebastian crosses the room to me.

"Well, for one, I'm much better looking." To his credit, he looks me straight in the eyes as he says this. Also to his credit, he definitely is much sexier.

With all the confidence I can muster, I reply, "You don't know that."

"I'm fairly certain."

Grinning, I huff out a breath, straightening in my chair. "My God, you do have a giant ego."

"You said I deserved it." Sebastian leans into me, as if to make a point.

Of course, having him so close whips my breath away. Still, somehow I manage to reply, "A mistake I shall not repeat."

Seeming to realize his effect on me—and very satisfied by it, judging by his conceited smile—he pulls back. "You didn't say anything about the other points."

"Nothing but words." I wave my hand dismissively, even though my center throbs. They were good words, but I'm not about to own up to that.

"I'll prove it to you." His low, raspy voice does nothing to dull the ache between my thighs. "I told you I like a good challenge."

Chapter Eleven

Ava

Thankfully, Sebastian leaves my office after our encounter. I'm restless the entire evening and sleep evades me at night. I toss in my bed for hours, checking the time on my phone now and again. At about one o'clock in the morning, I receive a text. The sender is Sebastian. My heart flutters as I draw the phone closer to me.

Sebastian: Are you asleep?

I shouldn't respond. I really shouldn't. The temptation is too big though.

Ava: No. I can't fall asleep.

He answers fast.

Sebastian: Neither can I. I can't take my mind off you.

I bite my lip, trying hard to ignore the heat igniting inside me.

Another text arrives.

Sebastian: Why can't you sleep?

For a second, I debate not writing back, but I give in to temptation again.

Ava: Same reason as you.

Sebastian: You can't stop thinking about yourself?

Smiling, I shake my head. He's really gonna make me write it. Oh well, here goes nothing.

Ava: I can't stop thinking about you.

My breath catches when I read his next reply.

Sebastian: I want to see you tomorrow.

I try to backpedal, because seeing him outside the office is a really, really bad idea.

Ava: I already have plans. I'm sightseeing in San Francisco.

Sebastian: Great. I'll pick you up at nine tomorrow.

I type back quickly.

Ava: There's no need. I can go by myself.

His reply comes in three seconds.

Sebastian: See you at nine.

I stare at the screen for a long time, but don't write back. There's no point contradicting him. He'll do exactly what he wants anyway. The problem is I want him to do that. I toss in my bed, sweating. Jesus, I don't remember being so painfully aware of the ache between my legs in a long time. The feeling grows unbearable, and I briefly wonder if it's possible to die from it. I can already imagine newspaper headlines. Death by sexual frustration, or something equally ridiculous.

***

I wake up at seven o'clock sharp, even though I

set my alarm for eight. Bolting to a sitting position in my bed, I acknowledge the reason behind my early rise: adrenaline. The knowledge that I'll spend the day with Sebastian makes me grin and spikes my blood with something dangerous and addictive.

I can't wipe the stupid smile off my face the entire time I'm getting ready. I shower first, using my best-smelling shampoo, and then use the razor to get rid of unwanted hair from my body. I'm aware that I'm putting more effort into looking perfect than I have in a long while. It's for tonight, I tell myself. The presentation for the buyers is tonight, so I'm preparing myself for the occasion. Great excuse. Except, why would I shave my pubis for the show?

At nine o'clock, I hear three knocks at my door. Drawing in a deep breath, I open it and thank heaven for having spent the past hours beautifying myself. Sebastian looks perfect. He wears jeans and a black cotton shirt. It's simple, but it hugs his torso and biceps in a mouthwatering way. His gaze rakes over my body, resting on my breasts and lower on my hips.

Holding up two brown paper bags, he leans against the doorframe, saying, "I bought breakfast. We can eat it on the way to our first stop."

"Okay." I go toward the desk and grab my purse, then pause, turning to him. "I have one rule for today."

"Only one?"

"Yes."

"Okay. Let's hear it."

"No flirting," I say seriously.

He strokes his chin, as if he were expecting this. "That's no fun."

"Then I'm not going anywhere." I drop my purse on the table.

"You drive a hard bargain, don't you?"

"Yeah." I cross my arms over my chest, looking at him expectantly.

"Let's go, Ava."

"Promise."

"I don't make promises I can't keep." He strides inside the room, slings my purse over my shoulder, and hooks an arm around my waist. "But I can promise you'll have fun today."

Sebastian proves to be a perfect tour guide. I showed him my itinerary when we got in his car, and he nodded, scribbling two more stops on it. Five hours into the tour, and he hasn't thrown one flirty line my way. Oh, he's thrown plenty of insinuating stares, and I've returned every single one of them, because apparently I can't stick to my own rules around him.

We grab a sandwich for lunch and crash on a bench in the Golden Gate Park.

"Why do you know so much about the city?" I ask, munching on my sandwich. There must be an apricot tree nearby, because the smell of apricots invades my senses. It's so thick, I feel like I can bite into it and it would taste like Mom's homemade apricot pie.

"I live here."

"Yeah, well, I've lived in New York my whole life, and I don't know that much about it. Kind of embarrassing."

Sebastian doesn't answer right away. "One of my first jobs in San Francisco was as a tour guide. I still remember a lot of that stuff."

"Wow. So, what other jobs did you have?"

"Hmm, let's see. I was a driver, a waiter." As he recites a number of other jobs, I take in his body language. He holds his head high. He's proud of every single job he's had. Heck, he has every right to be proud; he's a self-made man. I'm proud of him too.

"That's why you treat everyone with respect," I conclude.

"I honestly don't think there is an easy job. I got a lucky break, but others don't. This doesn't mean their work is less valuable or easier."

I look at him in awe. If only more people thought like him.

"Ready for the next round?" he asks.

"Let's stay for a few more minutes. My feet are killing me."

Without any warning, he lifts my legs, pulling my feet into his lap. I lose my balance and prop myself on my elbows on the bench. How did I end up on my back after only half a day with him?

"What are you doing?" I ask, as he gets rid of my flats. "Oh, foot massage."

"Relax."

That's exactly what I do, letting him work his magic hands on my tired feet in silence. Holy guacamole, this man is perfect. And off limits, unless I want to lose my job, which I can't afford.

"You're spoiling me," I say.

"It makes you smile. I like your smile."

"Sebastian. . ."

"Stop saying my name like that." His voice has turned low and breathy.

"How am I saying it?"

"Like you're begging me to stay away from you and kiss you at the same time."

I have no answer, so I look away from him. Even as I try to focus on the beautiful nature surrounding us, I feel my body succumbing to sinful sensations.

After a few minutes, Sebastian asks, "Do you know that this is the first Saturday I haven't worked in years?"

I feel my eyes widen. "Why change that now?"

He shrugs, as if the answer couldn't possibly matter. He stops the massage, instead trailing his fingers over my bare ankles, turning my skin to goose flesh. He fixes me with his eyes, burning my control away.

"I like spending time with you."

"I said no flirting."

"That's not flirting. It's the truth. You have an enthusiasm that lights you up permanently. I feel carefree around you."

"Are you seeing someone?" I blurt, attempting to

take my feet out of his lap, but he grips them firmly.

"You're breaking your own no-flirting rule." A satisfied grin stretches across his features.

"It's not flirting," I counter. "It's a question."

"I wouldn't be here with you if I was seeing someone. I'm not a fan of cheating."

"Why aren't you dating anyone?" I ask, not really buying it. He is Sebastian freaking Bennett, the CEO of the most beloved jewelry company in America.

"I'd date you, but you're putting up a good fight."

"Stop it, Sebastian. You'll get me fired."

He pulls me so abruptly to him my ass almost lands in his lap. I stop short of that, planting my palms firmly on the bench, trying hard not to acknowledge that the only things separating his crotch from the backs of my knees are his jeans and underwear. Unless he's wearing no boxers. Maybe I should check. Where did that thought come from? I have no business checking if he's going commando or not.

"How about I get your boss fired?" he says.

"You can't do that," I murmur.

"You have no idea."

I push myself out of his lap, putting some much-needed distance between us. "Seriously, why are you single? I've seen how women look at you. They'd fall in your bed in a second."

"Yes, and then they find out who I am."

"What do you mean?" I ask, genuinely confused.

He twists the watch on his wrist, rolling his shoulders. "When you have as much money as I do, women start seeing your bank account instead of you."

"I'm sure that's not true. You're hot—kind of hard to overlook that."

"Why, thank you." The wry grin that melts my insides returns.

"I'm sure women don't do you just for your money."

"Do me? Why would you do me, Ava?"

"Hypothetically speaking?"

"Of course," he says solemnly.

"Because you're fun, kind, and caring." Realizing this must sound like I want to have your babies to a man, I try to downplay it. "But mostly because you're hot." I lick my lips. "I bet you can do some very hot things in bed." My face reddens. I never meant to say the last sentence out loud; but apparently, my mouth didn't get the memo from my brain.

"I can tell you exactly what I'd do to you," he says, making me shiver. "Hypothetically, of course."

"No, thanks." My voice is undependable, while he looks perfectly composed. Obviously, he's better at this game than I am.

"I can assure you, the reality would be much more delicious than you can imagine."

I sigh at how much like a promise his words sound. This man won't tire until he has me, and I'm not sure I mind anymore, risks be damned.

Clearing my throat, I push myself a few inches from him and say, "See, plenty of reasons for women to want you. They can't all be after your bank account."

"If they aren't in the beginning, they learn quickly. I've been burned plenty of times."

"Maybe you've gotten burned because you're too hot. Are you sure you're not paranoid?"

"I wish I was. I envy my parents. They had nothing when they were young, but they found each other, fell in love, and stayed that way. Wish things were that simple now, too."

I open my mouth to reply, then clamp my lips shut. I'm not sure what to tell him. Sure, I gave up on believing in happily-ever-after too, but that's because the men I've been with couldn't keep it in their pants.

Looking to switch the topic, I say, "Look, they're selling popcorn."

Before Sebastian has time to reply, I jump in my flats and run to the popcorn stand. By the time the popcorn guy hands me a bucketful, Sebastian is by my side, opening his wallet.

"I've got this covered," I say. "You already bought my sandwich."

"You won't pay for anything while you're with me." Holding a ten-dollar bill between his fingers, he stretches his arm to the vendor. I block his hand.

"Sebastian, this is not a date."

"Nope, it's me being a gentleman," he says. My insides squirm, even as I try to hold my ground.

"I'm not letting you pay."

He looks at me with narrowed eyes. "I'm not asking for permission."

I throw my hands up in despair. "Are you going to go caveman on me every time I don't agree with you?"

Sebastian drops the money on the counter, telling the vendor to keep the change, and drapes an arm around my waist, pushing me away from the cart.

"I'd like to go caveman on you somewhere else. I picture us in a bed, you under me. You'd love it."

"I thought we said no flirting," I say weakly.

"You said that. I never play by anyone's rules except my own," he whispers in my ear.

Thankfully, he says nothing else as we fall into step, heading toward the next stop on my itinerary. I become aware of the throbbing in my feet almost immediately.

"Let's do the rest of the itinerary another day. I won't even be able to stand tonight at the show if I don't rest my feet. Can you get me back to the apartment?"

"Sure," he answers. We walk toward the exit of the park.

"Your turn," Sebastian says after a while. We're nearing the parking lot where we left the car. "Why aren't you seeing anyone?"

I deflate at his choice of topic. "Kind of hard with my job. I travel too much and I can't make long-distance relationships work. My last two exes cheated on me. I'm not keen on repeating the experience, so no more long-distance for me."

"I'm sorry."

"Yeah, well, I must be doing something wrong," I

say as we reach his car.

"Don't you blame yourself."

"Fool me once, shame on me." I smile sadly. "Fool me twice. . ."

"Listen to me." He tilts my chin up, pushing me against the closed door. "The world is full of assholes. Just because you've encountered a few doesn't mean you don't deserve someone better."

"Thank you," I whisper. "I needed to hear that."

"You deserve someone who makes you happy and fulfilled. Someone who worships you." He watches me with such honesty I have no choice but to believe him.

"Why do you say all the right things?" I murmur. "It makes resisting you very hard."

"So stop resisting me," he says as he opens the car door for me.

Once inside, he says, "Let's go up the Twin Peaks. I know it wasn't on your list, but the view is great from there." Looking at my shoes, I sigh, but nod.

We drive up the North Peak, and once we get out of the car, Sebastian hands me a windbreaker. It's so long it'll even cover my ass. "Trust me, you'll want to put this on. It's much windier here than in the city." We both put a jacket on, and I follow him to the viewing place. The sun hovers above us, and a sea of mist stretches in front, floating above the city, while a green blanket stretches over the hills in the distance.

It's amazing.

Despite the jacket, I shiver. So when Sebastian slings his arms around my middle, moving his chest against my back, I don't pull away. I nestle in his arms as if it's the most natural thing, and he rests his chin in the crook of my neck, his hot breath caressing my skin. I find myself wishing we could stay like this for hours, but all too soon, it's time to go. Smiling, Sebastian takes my hand, leading me to the car.

***

We drive to my apartment in silence. When we reach it, Sebastian stops the car and gets out. Even though I could easily let myself out, I stay put, choosing to watch him open the door for me. I enjoy being treated like a lady.

I'm about to tell him I'll see him on Monday, when a gust of wind rustles my dress. Sebastian's eyes widen.

"You're wearing lace underwear and expect me not to flirt?"

"You're not supposed to see it," I say, horrified.

"Who is supposed to see it?" he says with a growl.

I snap my gaze back to him. "What?"

"You said I'm not supposed to see it." He places his hands on the hood of the car, trapping me between his mouthwatering biceps. "Who is, then? Who are you wearing lace for?" He's jealous, and it's unbelievably sexy.

"Myself," I say boldly. "Isn't a girl allowed to do that?"

"Mmm, you're not a girl. You're a woman. A

fucking gorgeous one."

"No, I'm not," I say dismissively.

His brow furrows. "What?"

"Well, I'm okay, I guess. Pretty."

"You are gorgeous. Just agree with me once, woman." Leaning into me, he adds, "If you don't, I'll kiss you senseless."

"Okay." I'm almost out of breath. "I agree with you."

"See you tonight at the show."

"You're coming?" I ask.

"Yeah. What will you wear?"

"I bought a crazy fancy dress. I love it."

He steps back, freeing me. As I step by him toward the building entrance, he says into my ear, "Wear lace underneath the dress tonight. It turns me on."

Chapter Twelve

Ava

Crazy fancy is the term for the show, and I've been to some fancy events in my life. The location is one of the most famous restaurants in San Francisco, with a beautiful garden surrounding it. Organized mayhem reigns inside. The back of the restaurant has been transformed into a runway with large screens on either side of it. There are no rows of chairs, like in a traditional fashion show. Instead, there are round tables scattered in the room. Most tables are for four, but there are some larger ones as well. Still, the place maintains a warm and welcoming feel by having candles on each table.

Looking at the people milling around the room, I grow prouder of my attire with every passing minute. I'm wearing a dark blue sequined designer dress I bought on sale in a boutique downtown that was surprisingly well stocked. They had some mouthwatering dresses from the latest collections, but I only tried on the items they had on sale. I'm saving the bulk of my salary for the down payment on an apartment.

I inspect everything about my surroundings. Part of my job will be to help put together the next collection show. I am pondering what I can do different while maintaining the essence of the show. Of course, Gemma, the event coordinator, can give me all the details about this, but experiencing it firsthand always beats looking at lists and video recordings. I take my time observing the decor, the way people react to it, and to each other, as well as the things—or people—the press is most interested in. The main collection shows always have excellent coverage. All the major fashion magazines, business magazines, and even the occasional lifestyle magazine cover them. I wasn't expecting so much press for a buyer show, too.

Most of the reporters are still waiting for the show to begin, but several are cornering the guests. Among the cornered ones, I see Logan and Pippa. She doesn't seem to mind the spotlight, even though her smile doesn't reach her eyes. Logan looks downright annoyed as the reporter throws question after question at him. A few feet away, I recognize the party brothers from the pictures I saw from the last show. God, this family has some extraordinary genes.

Logan joins me a few minutes later. "Ava, you look great."

"Thank you. Is the press done with you?"

"Ah, if they had it their way, they'd never be done." Shaking his head, he puts his hands in his pockets. "I don't know why I'm always surprised that they can't talk to our PR people and leave me and my family alone."

"Speaking of family," I say as nonchalantly as possible, "where is Sebastian?"

Logan raises his eyebrows. "He's not coming. At least, he hasn't told me he is."

My shoulders slump, and I try my best not to look too disappointed, but I'm not fooling Logan.

"Did he tell you something else?" he asks.

I give a noncommittal shrug and excuse myself, mumbling that I need to find my table. Why am I so disappointed? It's as though he promised he'd be here.

I was so eager to see him, though. I'm wearing lace underwear, like he asked me to. I mentally slap myself. I'm wearing the lace for me. I look for anyone else I might recognize, to take my mind off Sebastian. I spot the marketing department sitting at one of the larger tables, and wave at them. Martha sits with them. They are finally starting to warm up to her.

I'm heading to them when I feel my phone vibrate in my tiny purse.

I take it out, and my stomach jolts as I read the text message.

There is a room to the left of the bar. Get inside.

It's from Sebastian.

I drop the phone carefully in my bag, looking over my shoulder as if I'm preparing for a clandestine mission. Giddy with anticipation, I stride toward the bar, eyeing the door Sebastian meant. It's flanked by a massive bodyguard, but he gives me a once-over as

I approach and opens the door for me.

"Get inside. Quick," the man booms. Taking a deep breath, I glance over my shoulder one last time, then step inside the room. It's small but elegant, with a tiny table with a selection of the food available outside for the guests. A champagne bottle rests on it, along with two glasses. A giant window on the wall overlooks the restaurant, but I realize at once, it's a one-way glass. It looked like a mirror from the other side.

Sebastian sits on a small couch. He rises slowly when he sees me. You'd think that seeing him in a suit every day would have prepared me for this, but it hasn't. He wears an elegant navy suit, and wears it well. His hair still has that fuck-me look from this morning, and his entire appearance screams of masculinity and testosterone.

"You look perfect," Sebastian says.

"You don't look too shabby yourself." I only realize I'm still standing by the door when he closes the distance between us and locks the door. His hand touches my waist for a brief second, and it's enough to turn my knees to rubber.

"Why did you lock it? You have a bodyguard outside."

"I wouldn't want him to step inside at a bad moment."

He welcomes me in the room, pointing to the couch.

"This is where I stay until the show is over," he explains as I sit. "After that, the press will be asked to leave so the guests can enjoy the after-party."

"So you're incognito during the show."

"I am. I told you before I don't like journalists. Whenever they see me, they start questioning me about my private life instead of focusing on the company. It's up to you if you want to be incognito with me."

"Why does that sound dirty?" I giggle, which I don't do often. What does this man do to me?

"I can make anything sound dirty," he breathes in my ear, and I know this is a slippery slope.

"Is that so?" My flirty tone surprises us both.

"I'll prove it to you."

He eyes my lips for two incredibly sensual seconds, but instead of kissing me, he brings the bottle of champagne.

"You should be sitting with your brothers at one of the tables near the runway." I strain my eyes, looking through the glass. I can see the runway, and I will see the models, but only a hawk could see the jewelry they'll be wearing. "You won't see anything from here."

He waves his hand impatiently. "You can't see a damn thing anyway. The whole show is that, a show. The jewels are small. Everyone looks at the screens. Will you stay?" I startle when he pops the bottle open and pours champagne in the two glasses. Nodding, I take the glass he hands me.

"I need to eat something first," I say nervously. "Before I drink, I mean. I haven't eaten since I last saw you; and if I drink right away, I might lose my head."

"We don't want that, do we?" Sebastian muses, gesturing to the table as if saying help yourself.

I put my glass down and grab a plate, filling it with a little bit of everything. After the first few bites, I realize I won't be able to eat much anyway. Not with Sebastian so close, and so impossibly sexy. When it becomes clear I can't take one more bite, I abandon the plate on the table, take my glass again, and join Sebastian on the couch.

The second I sit, he leans in, wiping the corner of my lips with his thumb.

"You have a bit of cream," he murmurs. I smile shyly and take a large gulp of champagne, cleaning my mouth as discreetly as I can before putting the glass down again.

Sebastian doesn't take his eyes off me, and it becomes increasingly harder to breathe. I've been the object of his attention before, but now, in this small room with no one to see us, and tons of expectations, it's too much.

"You look very beautiful tonight." His tone is raspier than before. It does things to me. Delicious things. "But then again, you always look beautiful. Even in your little suits."

No, no, no. Why does he say all the right things? *OhGodOhGod.* He nibbles at my ear. The second his lips touch my skin, something dangerous lights inside me. Desire. It spreads like wildfire, and when he tilts my head to his lips, I don't stop him.

Our mouths meet in a fierce crash. I moan against

him as his tongue meets mine. He responds in kind, pressing me closer to him. No man has kissed me like this, with consuming desire and desperate need. I don't know how I end up lying on the couch on my back, under him, but I don't care. He's on top of me, propping himself on one arm in order not to crush me.

His lips feel so good on mine. I don't want him to stop. I savor his exquisite mouth with fervor as his free hand travels my body. Before long, it finds its way under my dress, caressing my thigh, traveling further up until. . .

He groans, pulling his lips away, placing the hand on my waist. "You're wearing lace."

"You told me to," I say between moans as his lips descend to my neck.

"Obedient girl; I like it. So you're wearing it for me?"

"For both of us," I murmur.

He cups my chin, looking me straight in the eyes. They're hooded with desire, and knowing I have such a powerful effect on this man turns me on to no end. I become putty under him as he kisses me again, allowing myself to feel. And by God, this man knows how to bring out every single sensation without doing anything except kiss me. His hands remain on my waist.

We're still lying on the couch, Sebastian on top of me, when my body succumbs to the consuming need and I push my hips into his, soaking my thong as I realize he's hard. He bites my lips gently, intensifying the kiss, luring whimper after whimper out of me. I fall into the bliss that this kiss is, fisting his hair, drawing him even closer to me. The deeper I let myself fall, the safer I feel in his arms. The more I taste of him, the more I want. Gradually, the slick warmth between my legs turns to unbearable heat. I become insatiable.

Pulling apart, we both laugh.

"Your lips are swollen," he says. "You look sexy."

"Oh no." I touch my lips. Shit. They feel swollen. "Everyone will know."

"Relax. No one will pay as much attention to your lips as me. If they do, I'll rip their heads off."

"Stop being such a caveman, Sebastian."

"I can't."

"I want you to know I haven't done anything like this before. I'm not a floozy."

He laughs softly. "Floozy?"

"I'm serious."

"Me, too. I know you're not that kind of woman." He moves a strand of hair behind my ear, pushing himself off me, sitting on the edge of the couch. I follow suit. The second I'm sitting, I realize the show has begun. Reality hits me hard.

"Sebastian," I whisper, even though it's just the two of us here. "We can't do this; you know that."

"Because of your clause?" He scrutinizes me, and I detect something besides desire in his green eyes. Worry.

"Yes."

"Only because of that?"

I blink, fearing he might be able to see through my facade, the fears that my past relationship failures instilled in me. "Let's not complicate this, all right?"

"The thing is, Ava, this is already a complicated matter. I can't get you out of my head since you walked into my office. I like to hear you laugh and see your eyes light up. I like watching you do mundane things like typing on your laptop, giving a presentation, or eating. What do you suggest I do?"

He renders me speechless, and all I can do is stare at him. His eyes look so sincere. Not that I am an expert on the matter. God knows, I've misjudged men and their intentions for thirty-one years. But Sebastian is sincere.

"I can't risk my job," I say eventually, because that's the truth.

Breath huffs out of him as he shifts closer to me and locks a strand of my hair around his fingers. "Is there no way around it?"

"Let me think for a few days." The fact that I'm even entertaining this thought is dangerous. Yes, my boss is in New York and I'm alone in San Francisco, but this doesn't mean he can't find out.

"Okay." His voice is full of hope. I almost kiss him again, but catch myself in time. "I want you to have something."

"What?"

He searches his pocket, retrieving something that makes my heart skip. My ruby necklace. Well, not my ruby. I don't own it, but it's the one that stole my heart during our company tour on my first day here.

"Let me put it around your neck."

"Sebastian—"

"I want you to have it."

I jump to my feet, cold suddenly gripping me. I replay our conversation from the walk this morning, specifically the part where he said women are only interested in his bank account.

"Do you think you have to buy my affection? This is why women take advantage of you."

In a fraction of a second, his face grows cold, his whole body stiffening. I can tell I've struck a chord. A deep one.

I shake my head. "I won't accept it. Nothing against you, but I don't want expensive gifts from men, much less a ruby. The day I accept one, it'll be on my ring finger and the man giving it to me will ask me to marry him."

He blinks, his expression unreadable. "You're somethin'."

"We should watch the show," I say in a calm voice.

"Yeah, we should."

We sit on the couch again, keeping a small distance between us. Sebastian keeps the ruby necklace in his hand the entire time we watch the show, playing with it between his fingers. Once or twice, I feel his gaze on me, but we both remain silent.

The thoughts roaring in my mind are dangerous.

Kissing Sebastian was like being reborn. His lips were fulfilling, his touch freeing. His groans addicting. He makes me want to throw all caution to the wind. I'm not one to be reckless, but he demands it. I'm on the brink of obliging. What would it be to let this man sweep me away? Would he blow through my defenses the same way he kisses? Unrestrainedly and unapologetically?

I think he would.

Chapter Thirteen

Sebastian

Admission is the first step in overcoming an addiction, right?

I am addicted to Ava Lindt. There, I admitted it. I have a hunch that in my case, admission won't help me overcome it. In fact, I don't want to be cured. I want her, and I will have her. One kiss wasn't nearly enough. Ava Lindt is unlike any woman I've met, and she's fucking perfect.

Alarm bells ring somewhere in the recesses of my mind. I should control myself and not jump straight into this, considering my past relationships. I should be careful; I want to be reckless instead. I need it.

"Sebastian, I'm talking to you," Logan says.

"Huh?"

"You either have developed adult-onset ADD, or you're thinking about a woman."

"Logan, don't get on my bad side today—"

"It's Ava, isn't it?" When I don't answer, he pumps his fist in the air. The gesture wouldn't look half as ridiculous if we were on a soccer field, instead of in my office wearing suits. "Did you do her?"

"If you speak of her like that again. . ." I give him a meaningful look.

He flaps his hand dismissively, rising from his chair. "I can recite at least ten dirtier ways of saying that. If I call up Blake or Daniel, we can get that number to twenty."

"Stop thinking in numbers all the time. And no, we didn't. I'm working on it."

Pacing in front of my desk, he says, "If you finally found a woman who isn't working on bagging you, she's a keeper."

"Interesting yardstick you're using." My clipped tone does nothing to tone down his enthusiasm. I decide to keep to myself that she all but told me I was out of my mind when I gave her a ruby and expected her to accept it. He'll tell me to marry her. I swore off that years ago, after one too many disappointments with women. Ava's here for four months, and she said she doesn't want to do long-distance relationships. We can enjoy each other while she's here, no other expectations.

"I can't wait to tell Pippa."

I eye my brother. "What are you? The family's messenger? Don't tell her anything, or I won't hear the end of it. Why don't we actually talk about the next meeting?"

"That's what I was here for before you fell into your weird trance." He drops in his seat again, and we go through the retail stores' numbers. Some of the stores are underperforming, such as Tylon's and

Derenbilt.

"We have to cut Tylon's loose. It's bleeding money and they keep making empty promises."

"I agree. Derenbilt is also disappointing. We'll give them until the end of this quarter to deliver results, or stop our collaboration."

Logan nods. We talk about the upcoming meeting a while longer, and then he says, "Pippa's refusing to let me go with her to the divorce hearing."

"I know; she doesn't want me there either." When she told me that she and Terence have the first hearing coming up, I insisted on going with her, but she wouldn't hear of it.

"I don't want her to see him on her own again. What are we going to do about it? "

"Nothing. She's a grown woman. We have to respect her decisions."

"I hate it when you're being sensible." Logan snorts, looking away. "It makes me look like even more of a hothead. I want to make sure our sister is all right and that asshole gets what he deserves." He balls his hands into fists.

"So do I. Which is why he'll go bankrupt faster than he can sign the divorce papers. I had some interesting calls from people he wants to work with. Apparently, he listed Bennett Enterprises as a client."

Logan snaps his head to me, his eyes bulging. "I knew he was an asshole. I never realized he was a blithering idiot too. He actually had the guts to list us? We set that business up for him so he wouldn't feel inferior. Can't believe we worried about his ego," he finishes through gritted teeth.

"We were worrying about Pippa, and his ego was hurting her." When Terence started showing his true colors, Pippa thought it was because he was feeling inferior. I knew it was because he was an asshole, but I wanted to see my sister happy. Some men don't take it lightly if their women earn more than they do. Especially if said wives are worth billions. So Logan and I literally set up a business for him, ran it, and he called himself CEO. Since he's incompetent, I suspect he'll go bankrupt soon with or without my involvement, but I prefer to have a hand in it so I can get my vengeance on the bastard.

Chapter Fourteen

Ava

I stay in my office the next three days, keeping contact with others to a bare minimum. I'm not trying to avoid anyone—not even Sebastian—but I'm buried in work. Right now, I have to attend a meeting of the board. Logan and Sebastian invited me, saying it'll be great for me to get an overview of the company. I very much appreciate it, since clients usually don't bother, leaving me to my own devices.

Sebastian is ruthless in the boardroom. He is fair and listens to everyone's opinion, but he's ruthless nonetheless. He commands everyone's respect, and when he decides something, no one but Logan dares to contest it.

During the break, I chat with Pippa.

"Your brother is quite the iron-fisted boss."

"Someone has to be," Pippa comments.

"Sure. And he does it well. Usually, when bosses attempt to be strict, they come off as assholes. Sebastian comes off as someone who knows what he's doing," I finish with confidence.

Pippa scans me, pursing her lips and winking at me. I freeze and then take a gulp of burning-hot coffee, keeping my eyes on the floor. So I can't even compliment him without someone realizing I've got the hots for him.

Her phone buzzes, and she gives me an apologetic glance. "I need to take this call."

I nod, finishing my coffee by myself, then send Nadine a message.

Ava: Sebastian is killing everyone in the boardroom, and I find it hot. How can it be? I hate when Dirk does it.

Her reply comes quickly and I smile reading it.

Nadine: That's because Dirk's a dick (hence his nickname). Sebastian, my dear, is a bona-fide alpha. It is irresistible, and trembling knees are totally appropriate. After a few seconds, she sends a new message. **Can you film him and send me the video?**

Heat surges in my cheeks.

Ava: Umm, you PERV. No.

Nadine: Jeez, I didn't ask for a video of the two of you doing it. He'll be fully clothed (or if he holds meetings in the boardroom naked, tell me and I'll come work for him, even if I have to sweep floors).

I type back as quickly as I can.

Ava: Sorry to disappoint, he's fully clothed. You're still not getting a video. I know you; you have X-Ray vision.

Nadine: *Snort* Remember our rule. If you do him, always use a condom. You have no idea who else he might be doing.

I don't reply. After the break is over, we all take our seats in the meeting room, except for Sebastian, who paces near the window, lost in thought. He discards the suit jacket, remaining only in his shirt. As I admire his broad shoulders and toned body, I wish I had X-ray vision too.

***

After the meeting is over at eleven o'clock, I disappear into my office. It's almost lunch when I receive an e-mail from Sebastian. The subject: Presentation Missing.

I frown. I'm not supposed to have the presentation ready until tomorrow. Even so, we agreed that I wouldn't send him the presentation beforehand. I want to gauge everyone's first reaction as I walk the marketing team through it tomorrow. I click the e-mail open. It contains one single line.

I can't stop thinking about the kiss.

I bite my lip, staring at the screen. Part of me thought he wanted to forget the entire thing. Usually men run for the hills at the word marriage, even if it doesn't concern them. But Sebastian didn't kiss and run. I should've known he wouldn't back away from a challenge. After all, he told me so himself.

I type back, **It was a good kiss.**

The ping announcing a new e-mail sounds a second later. **Good? You're hurting my pride.**

Grinning, I wait for one whole minute before writing him back. **It was great.**

His reply comes in instantly. **Great enough to repeat it?**

Adrenaline fuels me. I'd forgotten how sizzling flirting feels. It's dangerous territory.

This time it takes two whole minutes for his reply to land in my inbox. It feels like an hour. Maybe I'm the dangerous brother.

I lean back in my chair, contemplating the mess we're in. Here he is, still wanting me. Don't be stupid, Ava. You can't throw all you've worked for away for a fling. My heart constricts, because I know this wouldn't be a fling. Sebastian Bennett is too kind, too smart, and too perfect. Shaking my head, I go back to working on the presentation, losing myself in my work before long.

At one o'clock Sebastian bursts into my office, looking furious.

"I'm the CEO, you can't ignore my e-mails." He makes the assistant passing outside my door jump.

"Oh, did you send me more e-mails?" I check my in-box quickly, and discover that he did send me another e-mail, in which he asked me if we could grab lunch together. "I don't have time—"

"I won't hear any excuses."

"Sebastian, I really want to get this presentation done."

"I'm the CEO; you have to listen to me. This is nonnegotiable. Come on, grab your things."

"You're bossy," I say. In an attempt to stand up to

him, I fold my arms over my chest; but I can't deny it, I cower a tad under his unwavering gaze.

"And you like it." His fake frown melts into a grin.

"Maybe," I admit, starting to rise from the chair. I do it with exquisite slowness, torturing him. "Are you the bossy brother?"

"You're about to find out. Let's go."

"This needs to be quick, Sebastian. I mean it."

"Duly noted."

Picking up my bag, I ask him, "Where are we going today?"

***

Sebastian brings me to a beach for our lunch break. After finishing our tacos, we walk along the shore.

"This is nice." I admire the light waves caressing the shore.

"I knew you'd like it."

"I love the ocean. Lucky me that I've been sent mostly to coastal locations in the last year." I peer out to the sea, watching the water reflect the sunlight.

"I didn't want to offend you with the ruby that night," Sebastian says. "I honestly wanted to have it because you were so taken with it when you saw it. I wasn't expecting anything in return."

"I figured that out. You shouldn't hand out rubies like that, Sebastian. People might take advantage of you."

He smiles sadly. "Most do."

"Then stop doing it. You don't need to shower a woman with gifts to get her to date you. Or if you have to, she's not worth it."

"I want you. I can make these the best four damned months of our lives, Ava. In bed and outside it." Inching closer to me, he cups my right cheek in one hand. My face flames at his caress, and I suck in a breath when the fingers of his other hand trace my collarbone. The heat in his eyes mirrors the promise in his voice, prompting a frisson of need low in my abdomen. There goes my breath again. "But you said you need time, so I'll give it to you."

"Thank you."

I observe longingly the people jogging on the shore. I really should start running again. It's a routine I've formed in the past year, go to bed early, wake up early, and go for an hour-long run before work. All I've done since arriving is eat and drool at the thought of this impossibly sexy man.

"How often do you come here?" I ask him.

"You want the truth?"

"Yep."

"The last time I went to the beach was when my youngest sister graduated high school. They threw a beach party; she got drunk and called me to take her home. That was a few years ago."

"Why come now?"

He comes to a stop, watching me closely. "You make me miss things I didn't even know I missed."

"Like what?"

"Jogging on the beach."

I gasp. "How do you know I was thinking about that?"

"I can read your mind," he says cockily. From the way his eyes linger on my lips, my drooling and daydreaming did not go unnoticed. To make matters worse, I catch myself biting at my lip. That's the effect this man has on me.

"I'm in big trouble."

"You are, and because I want to add more trouble to that, I'll tell you what I was thinking about." His eyebrows arch slightly as he focuses his green eyes on me.

"I'm listening." My voice comes out a breathy mess.

"You and me, panting and sweating. . ." He says nothing more, instead leaning his muscular torso down to me. Two can play at this game. I'm going to make him say it.

"What would we be doing that brings us to that state?"

He wiggles his eyebrows. "Jogging together."

The surprise of his words brings on a hysterical round of laughter.

"Why, you were thinking about something else?" Sebastian's laughing too.

"I thought you said you could read my mind." I force myself to breathe deeply to calm down.

"You have a very dirty mind. I know the perfect beach for jogging." His stance is laid-back, but his tone is challenging.

I take the bait. "Fine, let's go on Saturday."

A look of immense satisfaction crosses his feature as he says, "It's a date."

Chapter Fifteen
Ava

On Saturday, I arrive at the beach a full hour earlier than my scheduled jogging session with Sebastian. He tried to insist on picking me up, but I won the argument. Well, won isn't the right word, because there's no winning against him when he puts his mind to something. We compromised. I agreed to let him drive me back to the apartment after the run.

The truth is that I wanted to have a whole hour to myself. The last three weeks were so full of Sebastian. If I'm not seeing him at the office, I'm thinking about him. He consumes my thoughts every waking moment. Every sleeping moment too, I might add.

After I'm done stretching, I break into a light run on the sand. How did I get out of shape so fast? I stop often, clutching my left side, panting. When I can't move anymore, I grasp mentally for any motivational crap about sports and health and all that jazz. I am sidetracked by the sight of the mouthwatering donuts the couple lying on the sand a few feet away from me is eating. I sigh, forcing my legs to carry me forward. I know better than to break into a run again, so I advance with quick steps. I'm meeting Sebastian at the other end of the beach, and there are still a bazillion miles until I get there.

Except for the couple with the donuts, the beach is deserted, so I don't have anything to distract me from the miles I still have to walk.

"Morning, beautiful."

A jolt shakes me, and I turn around. A short, balding man in his late forties—or possibly fifties—stands behind me. He wears jogging attire, but by the sleazy look he gives me, I can tell he's not here for jogging.

"Err, do I know you?" I don't bother to sound interested.

"You do now." He says the words with all the confidence in the world, as though it's the best pick-up line. "I'm Ray, what's your name?"

"None of your business." I turn around, intending to put as much distance between us. He catches up with me.

"You're right. I was trying to be polite. I live in one of those blocks." He points vaguely to some skyscrapers in the distance. "We could go there for a quick fuck."

My jaw drops. Is he serious? I've never heard such

a lame-ass pick-up line, and I live in New York.

I force my voice to sound calm, even though I'd like nothing better than to smash this idiot's nose. "No thanks, I'm going to pass."

"Oh, come on. Don't play hard to get. You came here looking for it. Do you want to get paid, is that it?"

This actually makes me stop. "What?" I bark at him.

"Flaunting your tits like that on the beach."

"I came for a run." Clenching my fists, I glare at him. I'm wearing tight jogging pants and a bra.

"Sure you did."

"I'm not going anywhere with you." I stomp my foot, placing my hands on my hips.

"You need some convincing."

"No. Please leave."

"She said no," someone booms from behind me. Relief washes over me at the sound of the familiar voice. Sebastian. Knowing that Sebastian's here makes me feel safe. "Leave or you won't ever be able to walk again when I'm done with you."

Ray's about two heads shorter than Sebastian; he's no match for him. He must realize this too, because his smirk fades as he eyes Sebastian. "Get out of our sight before I call the cops," Sebastian says.

Sebastian doesn't take his eyes off Ray until he's at a considerable distance from us. He turns to me, laying his hands on my shoulders, pulling me closer to him. I blink away tears.

"Are you okay?" Worry laces his voice.

"Yeah, just mad."

"He's an asshole, forget him."

"I'm mad at myself. I could've dressed differently."

"Ava Lindt, listen to me. You have the right to dress any way you want. Even if you walked around naked, it wouldn't give him the right to treat you like that."

When I don't react, he pulls me into a hug. I lose myself in his strong arms, inhaling his scent. His shower gel must contain mint, because the subtle smell invades my nostrils. It calms me further. I was ready to take Ray on my own. I took some judo classes while I had an assignment in Japan, so I know basic defense techniques. But, God, does it feel good to have someone stand up and protect me. After I wiggle out of his embrace, his eyes probe me.

"I'm okay. Thanks for rescuing me."

"Do you want to call this off? We can run another day."

"Let's have a donut," I say unexpectedly.

"What?" A small grin blooms on his features.

"That's the fastest way to forget about that asshole."

"Whatever you command." He bows mockingly.

"Oh, so you're not going to be all bossy with me today?"

"Only after you've had your donut. I know better than to upset a woman before she's had her portion of carbs."

"Your sisters have taught you well."

There is no line at the shop, so we each grab a donut. Sebastian pays, of course.

"Is there any point in arguing over paying you back?" I ask as I slump on the sand.

"Nope."

"I thought so."

Sebastian takes a bite of his donut, remaining on his feet. That's fine with me. In fact, better than fine, because I have a perfect view of his holy hotness. He wears a sleeveless shirt and black shorts stretched over his muscles. I trace the contours of his biceps with my eyes, and barely restrain myself from reaching out to touch him. Then there is his ass, of course. Pure perfection. Then there is his. . .

Nope. I will not think about that. I will not. But of course, it's like saying do not think about a pink elephant. Then a pink elephant is all you see. Judging by the way his erection felt the night we kissed, pink elephant would be right to describe his shaft.

"Why did you come early?" Sebastian asks.

What? I didn't come at all. Haven't yet mastered the art of orgasming just by looking at a hot man? Oh. . . he didn't mean it that way.

"I wanted to warm up and get into the rhythm a bit. I truly suck, so please go gentle. I'm in terrible shape."

After we finish eating the donuts, Sebastian insists on stretching, which gives me more opportunities for gratuitous staring. I promise myself I won't keep this up while we're running.

I needn't have bothered.

The moment we start running, I'm convinced the muscles in my thighs will explode from the effort. Sebastian is fast and tireless. I can tell he'd like to go even faster, but he respects my speed—or lack of.

"Let's take a break," I pant after what seems like an eternity.

"We only just started."

"I can't—"

"Save your breath and get going."

I shut my mouth, breathing through my nose as I command my legs not to give up. After about a mile, a cramp takes hold of my right thigh. I come to a halt with a shriek and grip my thigh, hoping to relieve the ache. All I manage to do is make the cramp extend to my ankle too.

"Fuck," I groan, collapsing on the sand. In a heartbeat, Sebastian kneels next to me, putting his hands to work on my thigh and ankle. He kneads my flesh expertly. Before long, the cramp subsides, but he doesn't stop touching me.

"You really are in terrible shape."

"I told you to go gentle," I groan. "Jesus, it hurts everywhere."

"Ava, I don't do gentle."

His words send a jolt of heat right to my core, his double entendre turning me on instantly. I push myself up on my elbows.

"How often do you run?" I ask. "Be honest."

"I go to the gym every morning. Running an hour is part of my routine."

I snort. "I knew it. Why didn't you mention that when I told you I haven't been running in over a month?"

Sebastian smirks, shrugging.

"Well, at least I get the satisfaction that you're also sweaty."

"Oh, I can think of a much more satisfying way to get sweaty," he says. Then he does that thing with his eyes again that turns me to mush. His gaze smolders, as if nothing exists except the two of us.

"Does it involve any clothes?" I mumble.

"No, it doesn't."

His gaze descends to my chest then lower on my disheveled body. Since he's not bothering to be discreet, I allow myself to inspect every delicious detail about him. Sweat dots his upper lip, and I imagine what kissing him would taste like. A little like salt, a lot like a man. Oh, God. How am I supposed to resist him when he's so irresistible?

I let my elbows slide forward, flattening my back to the sand, and close my eyes.

"Do you still want to run?"

My only response is raising my eyebrows. After a few seconds, I add, "My legs hurt. Actually, my whole body hurts. My legs are downright killing me."

I feel his hands on my ankles, applying pressure on the points that hurt most.

I let out a moan. "This is so good."

"Stop making those sounds, or I won't be responsible for my actions."

I freeze, then attempt to retract my legs, but he

doesn't let go. "Let me do this for you."

"Why are you so amazing?" I ask.

"Because you deserve it."

I melt on the spot, swallowing any words, and simply enjoy him.

"What are you doing this afternoon?" he asks after a while.

"I haven't decided yet. What are you doing?"

"My parents are celebrating their wedding anniversary."

"Oh, right," I say, remembering what Pippa told him on my first day here. "Thirty-six years. Will it be a huge party?"

"No." He chuckles. "My parents don't like that. It'll be intimate, family only. Well, our family is huge, so I'm sure it won't be intimate by most people's standards, but it'll be fun."

"When do you have to be there?"

"In about two hours."

"Let's get going, so you can shower and everything."

He gives me a long look. "You really hate jogging, don't you?"

"Yes, and I'm not even sorry."

The drive to my apartment is pure torture. Ignoring the sexual tension on the beach was hard. In the car, it's downright impossible. We are too close, too sweaty, and too turned on. At least, I know I am. I cross my legs, hoping to squelch the ache in my groin. No such luck. To make matters worse, we remain stuck in traffic for half an hour because of an accident.

"Shit! I'm running late," Sebastian exclaims, punching the side of the steering wheel.

"You can shower at my place, and then you can go directly to your parents' house. Oh wait, you don't have anything to change into, right? "

"Actually, I do. I have the suitcase for Washington with me. I'm flying tonight, after the anniversary."

Oh, yeah. He's flying to Washington for a business trip. I almost forgot.

"Why aren't you flying tomorrow?"

"I have meetings scheduled tomorrow too."

"It's a Sunday, workaholic."

He shrugs, smiling. We arrive at my place a while later. Sebastian showers first, and then it's my turn. I immediately spray myself with cold water, but it doesn't relieve the pressure in my core at all. Only one thing will.

After fixing the showerhead up, I close my eyes and take a deep breath. Parting my legs, I slide my hand down to my shaved pubis. I moan when my fingers reach the tender flesh. It's been so long. I circle my clit, biting my lip to choke any noises. The thought that Sebastian is in the next room turns me on even more. I increase the speed of my strokes, imagining he's the one touching me. I am sure he can do wonders with his hands. Without realizing, his name slips out. As pressure builds inside me, I can't withhold my sounds of pleasure anymore.

"Fuck, you're sexy."

A shiver runs through me—hot and cold at the same time. I blink my eyes open, moving my hands behind my back. Sebastian stands in front of the bathtub, completely naked. My greedy eyes want to take in every inch of his sculpted body, but a particular spot requires my immediate attention. Sebastian Bennett has a hard-on, and he is stroking himself in my bathroom, less than a foot away from me.

"Sebastian, what. . .?"

"You left the door open." His voice is low and raspy, and his eyelids hooded. "And you called my name. I took it as an invitation."

Holding my breath, I nod, consequences be damned. Sebastian climbs in with me. When his mouth covers mine, the same avalanche of feelings that gripped me during our first kiss storms through me again. I can't make out one sensation from the other, but what I do know is that he's filling up a void inside me that I wasn't aware of until now.

Need and desperation lace our kiss as he cups my head with both hands, pushing me against the wall. The cold tiles shock me, prompting my hips to buck forward, pressing my lower body against his erection. A new wave of sensation hits me at the same time he groans into my mouth. He unhitches his lips from mine, trailing kisses down my chest, nuzzling one of my nipples and pinching the other one. I fist his hair with one hand, grazing the skin on his shoulder with the other one. The tension inside me grows and grows as Sebastian slowly makes his way down. Very slowly. He stops at my navel, placing his hands on my hips.

When he lowers his mouth further, I brace myself to feel his lips on my folds, but he places them on my inner thigh instead. The soft touch of his kisses spurs a million sensations. I can't take it anymore.

"Stop teasing me," I whisper, kneading his hair between my fingers.

"Greedy girl."

"Yes, very. I need you. Now."

"Demanding. I've wanted this moment for too long not to enjoy you."

He continues with his ministrations, turning me crazy, until my body seems to be made of fire, sensation, and need. When he finally kisses my clit, suckling at it expertly, I turn to mush, barely standing. I grip the rail of the shower with one hand, the other one still buried in his hair. His lips feel amazing on my slick flesh, his tongue pressing on the bundle of nerves in the center, setting fire to each and every one of them. The warmth carries through my extremities, infusing my entire body with wanton need. Suddenly, I can't get enough. As if sensing this, the lash of his tongue becomes faster, harder. My breath comes in pants, and my legs are trembling so badly that I'm certain they will fail me. A bolt of heat knocks through me, and I see stars. Sebastian slicks one finger inside, stroking my inner flesh in a come-here motion that splinters me. I come hard, buckling forward from the shock and the million sensations exploding inside me, euphoria and satisfaction filling me. Only when I hear him groan a few seconds later do I realize he was pleasuring himself at the same time he was pleasuring me.

***

Back inside the room, we dress, and Sebastian wraps his arms around me from behind, planting small kisses on my earlobe.

"I'm sorry I can't stay longer."

"Mmm, you have remarkable self-restraint."

Flipping me around, he tilts my chin up. "I have about ten minutes left before I have to leave. When I make love to you, Ava, I will take my time with you." Leaning in to me, he adds, "I will make you scream beneath me."

I shudder in his arms, heat pooling between my legs again. He leans back, scrutinizing me with an unreadable expression.

"Do you want to come with me to my parents'?"

"We only got to third base and you already want to introduce me to your parents? You're a keeper." I elbow him in the ribs playfully, even as a fuzzy feeling takes hold of my insides. "I'd love to, but I don't want to intrude on family time."

"Nonsense. They'll be happy to meet you. You'll like them."

"If they're anything like you and Logan, I'm sure I will."

"Come with me." When I don't answer, he cups my cheeks with his hands, tilting my head up. "I want to spend the day with you, but I can't miss their anniversary. I'll be gone for a week; I want to get my fill of you."

Now that he reminded me, the desire to spend the day with him hits me hard and unapologetically.

"Won't they think it's weird if I come? I'm practically a stranger."

"They're very nosy, so they'll probably realize we're up to something. Especially since I haven't taken a woman to meet them in years."

"You haven't?"

Shaking his head, he caresses my lips with his thumb.

"Will you miss me?" he asks. "This week?"

"Yes," I say truthfully. God, this man hasn't even made love to me, but I already feel like I won't stand his absence. "Can't you send Logan in your place?"

"No. But you could join me."

"You know I can't."

"Maybe that's better, so I'll actually concentrate."

"You can't concentrate with me around?" I tease, rejoicing in the knowledge that I'm not the only one with that problem.

"No." He drags his fingers down my cheeks and over my lips. "As of late, I spend my days imagining I'm taking you on my desk, or on yours. I don't have a preference, really."

"Sebastian." I lick my lower lip, my mind joining his fantasy. "I'll go with you today, but I need at least half an hour to prepare."

"You look great like this."

"I'm wearing shorts. There's no way your parents can see me like this."

"Fine, I'll wait for you in the car. I have some calls to make."

After Sebastian leaves, I stare at my closet for a good few minutes. I need an outfit that says I'm happy to be here, and no, I haven't slept with your son.

Yet.

In the end, I go for a light yellow chiffon dress and flats. There, let them figure out what it means. I still have ten minutes left. Perfect. That gives me enough time for a trip to the shop on the ground floor of the building. I eyed a beautiful vase there a few days ago. Since I have no need for it, I didn't buy it. I don't know the Bennett house, but I have a feeling it'll fit there perfectly.

Ten minutes later, I walk out of the building clutching the huge box containing the present against my chest, a stupid grin on my face.

Chapter Sixteen

Ava

"What's this?" He holds open the door of the car for me, and I fidget into the seat, careful not to drop the box.

"Your parents' present."

He jerks his head back. "I gave you twenty minutes notice. When did you have time to find a present?"

"I have my tricks. I'm awesome like that."

"Yes, you are." He nods as he closes the door then gets inside the car. "You didn't have to buy them anything."

"Of course, I did. Thirty-six years. They deserve national recognition at the very least."

"I completely agree with that."

"I don't know any couple who's been together this long. Did they ever. . . you know. . . take breaks?"

"They had ups and downs along the years, like every couple I suppose. But I always remember them being loving and supportive to each other, and to us kids."

The moment he revs the engine to life, something stirs inside me. This feels so much like we're a couple.

"Are we all right, Ava?"

I swallow. How can he read me this well? "Yeah."

"What about your contract?"

"We'll have to be careful so Dirk doesn't find out." My insides clench at the thought of everything I'm risking. If I lose my job, I won't be able to afford saving for a deposit for my own apartment. I don't even want to think about the damage it would do to my career.

"So if this was an option, why did we wait until now?"

"Because you're so easy to fall in love with, Sebastian. I can't lose my head and throw all my hard work down the drain."

"I'm not asking you to give up anything for me, and I know you don't want a long-distance relationship. I'm not a big fan of them myself. Let me make these four months the best of your life."

"You're sweet," I say.

"If anything happens, I'll move damn mountains for you if it's necessary."

"I can take care of myself, Sebastian. Always have." I slide lower in my seat, watching him. He's not just sweet, but also perfect. Utterly perfect. I don't say that out loud though. Instead, I bombard him with questions.

"Tell me about your family. Who's going to be there? Is there anything I should be careful with?"

"I could write an entire book about this."

"Give me the CliffsNotes version."

He furrows his brow, as if this requires his utmost concentration. "Mom's very nosy. My entire family is, but Mom is very smart about it. She can get the deepest secrets out of you and you won't even know it."

"Sebastian Bennett, are you afraid of your own mother?"

Sebastian laughs softly, and there is a glow to him that makes me happy. He loves talking about his family.

"Of course not," he says seriously. "But I have a lot of experience. I've learned what to say or not to say around her. You, on the other hand, are easy prey."

"Pffft, I can handle her."

"You've been warned."

"Who else?"

"Well, my sisters take after my mother. You've met Pippa and Alice. I'm surprised Pippa hasn't cornered you at the office already. Summer is the eternal romantic." His smile broadens at the mention of his baby sister.

"Tell me about your brothers. They can't possibly be as good-looking as they are in photos, right? Though, you and Logan are. And Blake and Daniel too, I saw them at the party," I finish. Sebastian glares at me. I grin. "Are you jealous?"

"My brothers know better than to flirt with you."

"Why? What did you tell them?"

"Nothing, but in my family, it's often not necessary to say something out loud. They catch the drift quickly. The other twin set will also be there. They flew in yesterday."

We arrive at our destination half an hour later. I'm mesmerized, hardly believing that we're only seventy miles away from San Francisco. There is a thick forest beyond the double gates in front of us, an oasis of green tinted with brown.

"This place is huge, isn't it?"

"It is." He grins proudly.

The double gates open as soon as we approach, and we enter the woods. We drive on the paved road for a few minutes before the trees thin out and the edges of a clearing come into view.

In the distance, I spot a three-story house with a cream-colored facade and red tile roof. The sheer number of people milling in the garden in front of the house shocks me.

"How big is your family?"

"Dad has five brothers, Mom four. Everyone was busy making kids. We're a big and crazy clan. You have been warned," he says, before sliding out of the car. I follow suit, too excited to wait for him to open the door.

"Let's go say hi to my parents first."

I feel a tad ridiculous carrying the huge box in my hands, and I attract curious stares.

"Mom, Dad," Sebastian says when we arrive in front of an older couple. He has his mother's eyes, but his father's strong bone structure. "This is Ava. She's from New York and is working with us for a few months. She doesn't know anyone around here, so I thought I'd introduce her to our crazy family."

"Congratulations on your anniversary." I blush at Sebastian's introduction. "I bought you something." I put the present on a nearby table, with a pile of other presents.

"You shouldn't have bothered," Mrs. Bennett says warmly.

"It's my pleasure. I hope I won't intrude too much today."

"We're happy to meet you, dear." His mom pulls me into a hug. I'm surprised, but I welcome it, and hug her back as tightly. She smells so. . . motherly. Not just feminine, but motherly, as if the act of spreading love is deeply ingrained in her nature. I absorb all of that. I received a lot of hugs from my mom, and I've missed the warmth of a mother figure so much since her death.

We chitchat for a while, and then his parents excuse themselves to mingle with other guests.

"Are you going to introduce me to everyone?" I ask.

"That'll take the entire day. I'll introduce you to my siblings."

"It's wonderful that you're all here."

"Yes. Speak of the devil. . ." He points to two men in front us, each holding a glass of whiskey.

"Ava, these are Daniel and Blake."

"Fancy seeing you here," Blake says, as if we've

known each other forever.

"We've heard about you from Logan," Daniel adds.

"The party brothers," I say. "I saw you two at the launch party."

"Oh, why didn't you come talk to us?"

"You were busy talking to the press."

"Someone has to," Daniel says, unaffected. Blake raises his glass, as if drinking to Daniel's words.

"Then you disappeared," Pippa says, appearing next to us. "I saw you in the beginning, and at the end. Where were you during the show?"

I try to keep a straight face as she looks from Sebastian to me. The art of wordless communication was perfected in this family.

"I was around," I say vaguely.

"Ah, here is the other set of twins," Blake says, gesturing behind me. I whirl on my heels. Where Blake and Daniel look completely different, Christopher and Max are identical twins. It was obvious in the photos I saw, but I thought I'd be able to tell them apart if I faced them. As they come to a halt in front of me, I give up trying to spot differences. There aren't any. They both have jet-black hair, dark eyes, and well-built physiques.

Sebastian introduces me, and Blake says, "Ava, you've met the party brothers," he gestures at Daniel and himself, "now meet the serious brothers."

Christopher and Max crack identical grins at their nickname.

"God, I missed being home," Max says, while

Christopher nods.

"We weren't always so serious," Christopher explains.

"That's true, you pranked everyone." Pippa wiggles between Christopher and Max and elbows them both in the ribs.

"Played their identical twin card as often as they could," Sebastian tells me.

"We got away with it most of the time."

Pippa snorts. "Once, Christopher wanted to profess his love," she says, clutching her heart theatrically, "to a girl at school, and he asked Max for help. Max had to pass as Christopher a few times in the whole scheme."

"Wait, why did you need Max's help?" I ask Christopher.

"Logistics," Christopher says vaguely, not looking half as amused as his siblings.

"Anyway," Pippa continues, "everything went great until the girl kissed Max, thinking he's Christopher."

Ah, that explains why Christopher isn't smiling, whereas everyone else—Max included—looks on the verge of bursting with laughter. Taking a good look at the Bennetts in front of me, I observe that all the men share their father's build. They're tall and have broad, strong shoulders.

"That was the last time we pulled a prank like that." Max puts a firm hand on Christopher's shoulder, and the latter finally smiles too. Both of them leave and the focus is back on Sebastian and me. Pippa is drilling Sebastian with her gaze.

"Please tell me Logan is taking good care of you," Blake tells me, oblivious to the staring match between Pippa and Sebastian.

"Actually, I don't see much of Logan, but Sebastian's doing a great job."

The twins stare at us in disbelief.

"If you're in need of some real fun, you can always call me," Daniel offers.

"Or me," Blake says.

"Or both of us. Really."

"Ava is a smart woman," Sebastian says. "She'll know to avoid you. Both of you."

With that, Sebastian whisks me away.

"By the way, Summer is looking for you, Sebastian," Blake says from behind us. "She wants to give you hell for missing her exhibition last week. We were there, but the moment she realized her favorite brother wasn't going to show up. . ."

"I'll find her," Sebastian says over his shoulder.

"You are irresistible when you go all caveman," I whisper to him.

"You haven't seen anything yet."

He treats me to Mrs. Bennett's homemade lemonade.

"So are these all cousins?" I point to the nearest group.

"No. They're adopted Bennetts."

"What?" I chuckle.

"Friends of ours. From college or high school. They like to stick around, because we're a cool bunch."

I wonder if I can apply to become an adopted Bennett. I'd totally do it. After drinking a third glass of Mrs. Bennett's wonderful lemonade, I need to pee badly.

"Where are the restrooms?" I ask.

Sebastian gives me precise instructions before leaving to find Summer, and I hurry across the garden and inside the house.

The interior of the house is pleasantly cool. With my bladder threatening to explode, I don't pay much attention to anything until I get to the bathroom. After I exit, I take my time to look around. The house is decorated with dark furniture with a reddish tint, and paintings hang on almost every wall. It looks cozy and warm, exactly the way I always imagined a home should.

I'm inspecting one of the paintings—with kittens and a dress—when Mrs. Bennett appears at my side.

"Are you enjoying the party, dear?" she asks.

"Yes. There are so many of you, though."

"I miss those days, having the kids home. They visit often, but it's not the same. We've been blessed with great children."

"You are," I agree, hoping the jealousy isn't too thick in my voice.

"Family is the most important thing. Other things come and go, but family stays."

"I suppose so." Upon seeing her confused glance, I add, "I don't have any family left."

"You poor thing."

"I'm quite self-sufficient," I assure her.

She rolls her eyes. "I can understand why Sebastian took a liking to you. My son likes to think he's self-sufficient too."

I don't hide my surprise. "But he's got all of you."

"Ah, yes, but my son feels responsible for us. He's so adamant to look after everyone around him." She's right. I remember all the times he's done little, nice things for me. "He doesn't look after himself anymore. Even after all these years, after he gave us all of this, he still doesn't let himself relax and enjoy life. Though I hear this has started to change with your arrival."

Heat rises in my cheeks. "Well, I wouldn't say it's on my behalf."

"A little bird told me he took you on a tour of the city."

I grin. "He did."

"Any more tours planned?"

I open my mouth, then clamp it shut. Now I see what Sebastian meant about his mother's ability to make one talk. I decide to keep it vague. "There's nothing planned."

Mrs. Bennett looks at me suspiciously. "You're welcome in our home whenever you want. To tell you a secret, I always wished to have more daughters. Alas, I only got three. And six boys. They drove me mad."

"I can imagine."

"I can't wait for them to get married and give me grandkids. The house will be full again."

I laugh softly, following her dreamy gaze to one of the paintings.

"That's a beautiful painting."

"Summer did it. She has the soul of an artist. She expresses herself in various ways. Up until a few years ago, she was convinced acting was her calling. Now she paints. I'm so proud of her."

I smile, remembering my own mother. She too was always supportive of me. In fact, so supportive that she never told me she had cancer until it was too late. During my third year at college, she got sick. Her insurance didn't cover the costs of treatment, so she simply didn't get any. If I'd known, I would have quit my studies and worked hundred-hour weeks if necessary to pay for her treatment, which is exactly why she didn't tell me. The sickness ate at her, and she lost weight dramatically. She was in stage four when she couldn't hide it anymore. I tried everything to help her, but it was too little, too late.

She died before I began my senior year at NYU and I never got the chance to take care of her.

Mrs. Bennett and I return outside, and Blake and Daniel immediately approach me.

A while later, we're served cake. Mr. Bennett gives a toast, speaking beautiful words about his wife. Mrs. Bennett gets teary-eyed, and I'm not doing much better. She holds it together until Sebastian presents them with an envelope, announcing he bought the ranch they sold years ago. His parents hug him, thanking him over and over again. Though they don't want to move away from their children, they plan to turn the ranch into their second home. My heart squeezes as I watch Sebastian with his parents. There is so much tenderness in him. He loves his family so fiercely, it makes me wonder how it would feel if he ever came to love me.

***

Sebastian

Summer is playing hard to get. She was around when I gave my parents their gift, and then she disappeared again. Ah, my baby sister. The most spoiled of the lot of us. I smile, remembering the day she showed up in my office, lacking her usual good humor and glow. It took so long for her to tell me why she came to see me, I started to suspect she was pregnant or something. Nope. Turns out, she had discovered she wanted to be a painter, not an actress. She didn't tell Mom or Dad. She came to me first.

We come from a family used to the hard work of a ranch, and she felt guilty for her eternal quest for her true calling. I told her I doubted anyone in the family would show her anything except support. I want her to have all the opportunities in the world. Why settle?

My search for Summer is interrupted again, this time by my father.

"Son, you have the look of someone who knows he has some apologizing to do."

"Guilty. I completely forgot to show up at Summer's exhibition."

My father smiles. Though in his sixties, he's in top form. He refuses to go to the gym, but keeps in shape by doing most of the things around the house himself. That includes repairing the roof and other potentially dangerous activities, which drives me mad with worry. Unfortunately, I can't tell a man who spent most of his days shouldering the hard work at the ranch suddenly to stop doing what he's used to.

"Lovely girl you brought with you today," he comments. Ah, let the cornering begin. I'm surprised my mother hasn't attempted it yet, but the day is still young. "There is no greater gift for a man than a loving wife."

"Dad." I keep my voice respectful. "Let's not get into this today. I brought her here because I thought she'd like it." We walk in the shadow of an old oak.

"Don't you want to get married?"

I snort. "Pippa was married, and look how that turned out."

"Your mother and I are celebrating our thirty-sixth anniversary."

"I know, but times are changing."

My father gives me a look that says, You might be CEO, but you know nothing.

Well, the man earned his right to think whatever he wants. Logan approaches us, and after he and Dad have a short exchange about their dismal fishing results from last weekend, Dad leaves.

"You brought Ava today," Logan says.

I groan. "Obviously."

"You really like her, don't you?"

I debate denying it, but Logan is not stupid. "Yep."

"Did she give in?"

"Maybe."

"Are you only going to give one-word answers?"

"I won't discuss private matters with you," I say.

"Why not?"

"That's my business."

Logan surveys me, flashing a shit-eating grin. "You've got it bad for her, brother. I don't remember seeing you like this in a long time. You took last weekend off, you—"

"You don't look like you have a stick up your ass anymore," a female voice supplies from our right. Logan's grin widens. I groan again. Summer joins us. "Mom's been interrogating Ava, and I was around, of course, so I overheard them."

"Of course," I say.

"She's lovely," Summer says. "And she's got it just as bad for you."

"Summer, I was under the impression you were mad at me and ignoring me. I'd prefer it that way."

She flaps her hand impatiently. "Yeah, I was. But you brought a woman with you today, so you're totally forgiven."

"Why am I being cornered by my own family? I—"

"You can't boss us around in our free time," Logan says. "You cease to be CEO when you get out of the building."

"Which means we can try to beat some sense into you," Pippa says, appearing out of nowhere. They're taking this cornering thing to an entirely new level.

"This is getting out of hand. I'm going to have a drink and return later, when you're normal again."

As I stride away from the group, my eyes search the crowded garden for Ava. I find her near the entrance to the house. I remember her wide eyes as she said I'd be easy to fall in love with. Well, that makes two of us, because she's damn easy to love. She's not like other women I've dated, all fancy. She likes the life I grew up with, not the one my money can buy now. Women usually show thinly disguised disdain for my family. Some have outright told me that someone with my status should have a more sophisticated family. Ava's embracing them. Family is important to her, just like it is to me.

I start toward her, but before I blink twice, a guy starts chatting with her. A vein pulses in my neck. I get close enough to hear the conversation.

"Do you have time for dinner this week?" he asks.

What the fuck? I leave her alone for a bit and someone's already hitting on her? I'm about to interrupt their conversation and put him in his place, but her answer stops me cold in my tracks.

"Not a good idea. I've been in a relationship for a year."

She lied to me? Well, that seals it. I have many defects, but I'd never touch another man's woman. It's a matter of principle. The guy takes the cue, nodding curtly and blending in to a nearby group.

I step in front of her, raising an eyebrow. To my surprise, she grins.

"Have you been eavesdropping?" she asks.

"Why did you lie to me when I asked if you were seeing someone?"

"Relax, Sebastian." She rolls her eyes. That usually annoys me, but it looks cute on her. Damn it, I'm supposed to be mad at her right now. "I didn't lie to you. I told him that to get rid of him."

I eye her closely, not wanting to admit how much relief her confession brings me.

"Are you jealous?"

"Yes. Does that amuse you?"

"Very much. You have this expression between brooding and moody. It's very sexy."

I let out a low sound in my throat.

"That's even sexier," she whispers.

"Do you want to take a walk?" I say in her ear. "I need to take a break from my siblings. They're driving me mad already, and it's only afternoon."

She grins. "Sure. I love, love, love your family. They're so. . ." She holds her hands together. "I can't explain it, but I wish I had a family like yours."

"You're on the right track to become an adopted Bennett."

"How do you know?" she asks suspiciously.

"You've already been questioned by Mom and survived it. Summer was eavesdropping on your conversation, by the way."

"So is eavesdropping a family hobby?" she challenges. In response, I do something so completely out of character it surprises me more than her.

She yelps. "Did you just pinch my ass?"

"I'll do it again if I have to." What is this woman doing to me?

"I didn't know you were a pincher."

"There are a lot of things you don't know about me."

"Like what?" she challenges.

"I'll be happy to show you."

"So are we going to take that walk, or what?"

I offer her my arm, and she takes it with a smile.

"This place is heaven on earth," she comments as we make our way in the vast garden. I lead her to an alley lined by coast redwood trees, and watch her drink in the surroundings. "A tree house," she exclaims, coming to a halt.

"Summer used to paint here before she moved out of my parents' house."

The story behind the tree house goes back to when I bought the place for my parents. Summer was still young and wanted a tree house. I rounded up all of my brothers and we built it for her. I told them things would be different from then on, because I made good money and would take care of all of them. I also made them swear they wouldn't let money define who they were; that they wouldn't turn into self-absorbed assholes. Several expensive cars and homes around the world later, I can say they've kept their promise.

"Can we go inside?" Ava asks. Eyeing the fragile old ladder leading up to the house, I'm certain it's not the best idea, but when Ava adds, "I've always wanted a tree house," I nod.

The tree house isn't half as decrepit as I expected it to be. In fact, it's remarkably clean, which means someone's still using it. Ava inspects the old wood with curious eyes. She belongs in here, just as she belongs with my family.

The recognition fills me with both panic and warmth. Panic because I feel like I'm not only rushing into this, I'm diving headfirst; and warmth because nothing's ever felt more right.

Reaching for her waist, I pull her to me, tracing the contour of her mouth while pushing her against the wall. Opening her lips, I slip my tongue inside, tasting her sweetness. There's no restraint in her kiss as she presses her soft curves against me. My palm slides to her breast, cupping it over her bra. Needing to feel her soft skin in my hand, I make quick work of unclasping her bra and pushing her straps and her dress down, revealing her breasts. I break off the kiss, drinking in her bare skin, her puckered nipples calling to me. I press both breasts together with my hands, coaxing her peaks with my thumb and mouth.

"Sebastian."

My name sounds perfect in her mouth. I lure a moan out of her, and I suddenly become greedy for more sounds of pleasure. I could watch her slowly come apart all day long. When I get back from my trip, that's exactly what I plan to do. Right now, I will give her another taste of what I plan to do to her. Dropping my hand to her thigh, I cinch her dress up to her waist, groaning as I caress her over her thong. It's soaked through. Goose bumps appear over the delicate skin on her arms. I push the fabric aside, touching her slick flesh. She swallows hard, but that doesn't stop me. Her eyelids flutter closed, and I tighten my grip on her waist.

"Don't close your eyes," I say with a growl. Biting her lips, she looks up at me with wide eyes. When I touch her clit, she fists my shirt. When I pinch it between my fingers, her legs quiver, which gives me immense pleasure. I loved feeling her come apart today, now I want to see her. As I caress her tender spot, I watch her breath quicken, her pupils dilating. She clenches around me as I slide a finger inside. I want her like this, always. I don't know where the thought came from, but I know it's true. Nothing ever felt as right as being with her does. I want her smiling and laughing for me, and I want her panting underneath me. When her orgasm ravishes her, I hold her tight to me, steadying her and claiming her mouth.

Upon our return to the group, it appears that no one noticed our absence. One of my cousins whisks me away, while Mom gets Ava's attention.

The rest of the day passes by quickly, and before I know it, I'm dropping her off at her apartment. We're standing in the lobby, and neither of us wants to say goodbye yet.

"I had a great time today," Ava says. "Thank you for taking me with you. Your family is wonderful."

"I'm glad they didn't drive you too mad."

"Stop it, they are adorable. Are you heading straight to the airport?"

"Yeah."

"Okay."

I take her hand, as if I'm about to kiss it, then pull her to me, kissing her lips hard.

"See you in a week."

Chapter Seventeen

Ava

I thought concentrating with Sebastian nearby was hard, but concentrating without him proves to be impossible. On Monday, I have a dopey grin on my face the entire morning. I try to look as professional as possible during the weekly meeting with the marketing department, but I'm not sure I'm fooling everyone. When I return to my office, I make a promise to myself that I won't think about Sebastian for the remainder of the day. Then I discover a box of chocolates on my desk, and I squeal like a high school girl, of course. There is also a typed note on top of the box, with five words on it.

Enjoy your day.
Love,
Sebastian

Something I haven't felt since college blooms inside me. Butterflies. My smile gets dopier.

I set the box aside and start working, telling myself that I'll only allow myself to eat a chocolate if I go an entire hour without thinking about Sebastian. I break that rule within five minutes, opening the box and swallowing not one, but three of the tiny little bastards. They taste amazing. God, I need him back like, right away. He's barely gone and I miss him already.

Tuesday is better, and worse. It's better because I manage to control my smile and worse because I miss Sebastian even more. At eleven o'clock, I receive a huge bouquet of flowers. This time the card says,

I'd do anything to see your smile now.
Sebastian

Aaaaand behold the return of the out-of-control grin. Surprisingly, I do put in some solid hours of work afterward, skipping lunch. I end up staying at the office until seven, when Pippa bursts in.

"Pippa, this is a nice surprise."

"Wanna grab dinner?"

"Oh, yes. I'm starving."

She eyes the flowers on my desk, and then turns her attention to me, an expectant expression taking hold of her features. I pretend not to notice it.

We take a cab to a restaurant downtown that Pippa swears has the best pizza. The place is packed, so there must be some merit to it. We wait for half an hour before the waiter finds us a table.

"Bring us two margaritas," Pippa instructs him. She leans over to me. "They make some kick-ass margaritas."

"I thought they were known for the pizza?"

Pippa blushes. "That too. And hot waiters."

"Oh."

As I look around, I get what she means. Every single waiter could grace the cover of GQ.

"You were really oblivious to all the hotties running around here until I mentioned them?" She narrows her eyes triumphantly, as if she proved something to herself.

The margarita really is kick-ass. We order seconds, munching on our pizza.

"What's the deal with you and my brother?" Pippa asks.

"What do you mean?" I ask, a little too quickly.

"Oh, don't give me that I-have-no-idea-what-you're-talking-about look. You've been drooling over him since he showed you around."

"I have," I admit in defeat. "Why are you feeding me carbs? I can never lie when I eat carbs."

"I thought that was the margarita's job."

I grin.

"Spill. What happened between the two of you? Have you. . ." Pippa wiggles her eyebrows suggestively.

"No."

She gives me a doubtful look.

"Not yet."

"That's more like it. Why haven't you?"

"I. . . It's complicated because of my work clause."

"What do you mean?"

"I have a strict no-fraternizing policy in my work contract."

"Biggest bullshit I've ever heard."

"Well, believe it or not, it's an actual clause. We had some bad press a few years ago when one of our consultants got involved with a very well known, very married CEO. His wife was New York royalty, so she destroyed my colleague, and did some serious harm to the company name."

Pippa presses her lips into a thin line. "Okay, but you're on your own here. Your boss can't find out."

I paste a mischievous smile on my face. "That's what I'm banking on."

"Now we're talking," she says.

I'm uneasy, because Dirk is sneaky, but if I play my cards right, he won't find out.

"How about you? Are you dating anyone?"

"Nope. I'm divorcing my ass of a husband."

"Oh. I'm sorry."

She lowers her eyes to her plate. "Haven't gotten to the part where I want to date again. I'm going to grow cobwebs down there soon."

I snort into my pizza, and we both roar with laughter.

"You know what the antidote to that is?" I ask.

"Two more margaritas and a hot waiter to go?"

"I was going to suggest shopping, but your way will work better."

Pippa shrugs. "I'm not going to go home with a waiter. I don't really do one-night stands. But there's no harm in delighting my eyes."

"None at all," I say. Suddenly, I want to brighten up her mood. "We should schedule a girls' day out."

Pippa perks up. "How about Saturday?"

"Well, Sebastian returns Saturday."

"Ah, I see. Let's check our calendars to see when we both have a free weekend."

"Deal."

***

It's only back in my apartment that I start feeling the effects of the two margaritas. Or were there three?

I discard my clothes and collapse on my bed, but don't fall asleep. The smartphone on my nightstand beckons.

With uncertain fingers, I pull it to me and call Sebastian. He answers after three rings.

"Hi." For some reason, I'm feeling shy.

"Hi, back."

The sound of his voice sends tendrils of heat through my body. "I know you're busy, but I wanted to hear your voice."

"Mmm. . . so my plan is working."

"What plan?"

"Not calling you so you'd miss me."

"You little player," I giggle, my body aching for him. Oh, God, how will I survive until Saturday? "Thank you for the chocolate. And the flowers."

"I wish I was there to see your smile when you received them."

"Why are you spoiling me like this, Sebastian?"

"It's called courting."

I squirm in my bed, my toes curling up. I've never been courted before.

"I wish you could return sooner," I admit.

"Me too."

"So, what will I receive next?"

"Like I'd tell you. You'll love it." His voice drops an octave on that last note, and it's so damn sexy. "What did you do today?"

"I actually did some work in between daydreaming about you. Then Pippa took me to heaven."

He laughs softly. "What?"

"It's a place downtown with delicious margaritas, crusty pizza, and hot waiters."

"Pippa gave you margaritas in a place with hot waiters? I need to have a talk with my sister."

"Oh, she wanted to have some girl time."

"By taking you to the male equivalent of Hooters. So, how hot were these waiters?"

Now it's my turn to laugh. I pull the cover up to my chin, enjoying this immensely.

"Like I'd tell you," I tease. "Payback for not calling me yesterday."

"Did any of them hit on you?" His tone is still playful, but I detect a hint of uneasiness in it.

"Oh, yeah, one of them did. He took my number, said he'll take me to dinner this week."

"You gave him your number?"

My stomach clenches at the disappointment and hurt in his voice. It's time to end my little joke.

"I'm kidding, Sebastian. No one hit on me, and I

didn't give my number to anyone. I honestly didn't even notice the waiters until Pippa pointed them out. That's how wrapped up I am in you."

"Good," he says. "Because that's exactly how I feel. You are mine, Ava. Mine."

I fist the bedsheet, breathing hard. "Yours," I agree.

"I have to go now, but I promise I'll call tomorrow."

"Okay."

I spend the next day drafting more campaign proposals based on the latest feedback I got from the team. Massaging my temples, I try to come up with some more ideas. I'm pleased the team seems to accept Martha. Unfortunately, Martha isn't too happy in San Francisco. A little digging reveals she longs to return to Seattle, where she's from. I have lunch with the marketing team; and when I return to my office, I find a cup of coffee on my desk, and a note.

You're too tense today.
Love,
Sebastian
P.S. It's with almond milk.

I can't believe he remembers I like almond milk in my coffee. I gulp down some of the invigorating liquid, and as I play with the note between my fingers, a question springs to my mind.

How does he know I'm tense? He could have

guessed, but it's unlikely. Hmm. The presents always arrive when I'm not in the office. I narrow my eyes as I peek outside the door, watching the assistants in an entirely different light.

Sebastian has a little spy/helper.

***

"Are you putting everyone you know on this courting thing?" I ask Sebastian when we talk in the evening.

"What do you mean?"

"I know you have someone delivering your gifts in the office, and then I came home and the cleaning lady told me your mother dropped by today and left me some pudding."

"Ah, yes." He laughs into the phone. God, I like the sound. "She did mention you're too skinny."

"Skinny? Has she seen my butt?"

"Not as close as I have, but my mother has a good eye. If she deems you skinny, you'd better believe it."

"I called her and thanked her for it. It's delicious."

"That's my family. They like you."

"So you didn't put them up to this?"

"Trust me, you can't put my family up to something they don't want."

"Do they pity me? Because I don't know anyone outside of work here?"

"Ava, you're the least pitiable person I know."

"Oh yeah, I'm Ava, hear me roar." I try to let out a growl, but I sound very silly. "I've been jogging after work. To relieve some of that tension you know so much about."

"What? Alone?"

"Relax. The beach was full when I got there, so no one tried any funny business. Also, I wore a totally unflattering t-shirt."

"Everything looks flattering on you," he replies.

"Charmer." Secretly I swoon.

"Well, since you've been busting your ass with jogging, I'd better tell my mom to keep feeding you. Wouldn't want it to shrink."

"Can we stop talking about my ass?" I giggle into the phone, biting my lip.

"I happen to think it's a wonderful ass. Round and perky, begging for a little smack." I ignore the smack comment, even though it sends heat right to my core.

"When did you inspect it so well?"

"Oh, lots of opportunities. You know, your little suits aren't as safe as you think. They fuel the imagination."

"Your imagination," I correct him. "I doubt everyone looks at me with such ideas."

"I'd better be the only one."

"Caveman."

There is some commotion in his background, and someone's calling his name. I can't believe he still has meetings at this hour. "I've got to go," he says. "I miss you."

"I miss you too."

***

Thursday after work, I decide to treat myself and go to the spa. After another visit to Andrew, some of my tension has bled away, but Andrew can't give me what I really need. Only Sebastian can, and there are still forty-seven hours until his return.

Yep, I'm counting the hours.

Feeling mischievous, I decide to spoil myself with one more treatment at the spa.

"So how was your day?" I ask Sebastian that evening.

"Same as the others. I had a few New Yorkers in meetings. They are starting to get on my last nerve. Why do they have to sneer every word in that affected accent?"

At once, I get defensive. "Well, it's better than your neither-here-nor-there San Francisco accent."

"Are you kidding? It's much clearer."

"You really want to engage in a battle of accents, Sebastian? I've lived in New York forever, and had decent stints in Australia and even England. I can take you."

"I bet you can," he says. His voice is suddenly throaty, a sign he's not talking about accents anymore. As a matter of fact, neither am I.

"I was at the spa today." My voice is as throaty as his.

"Oh, the princess needed another massage?"

"Yeah, I have so much tension in my body." I stretch in my bed, guttural sounds escaping my throat.

"I have a cure for that. It's much more efficient, trust me."

"So much teasing." I barely keep my voice from faltering, but two can play at this game. "Do you want to know what else I did at the spa?"

"Yeah."

"I got a Brazilian wax," I whisper.

"Jesus, are you trying to kill me?" He lets out a low growl, which makes my skin tingle.

"Mmm…" I say in my best seductive voice. "The skin there feels so smooth."

"Ava, if you don't stop, I'll get on the first plane home."

I laugh. "Maybe that's my plan."

"What are you wearing?"

I shift against my pillows, my senses alert. We're slipping into dangerous territory. "A black nightgown."

"Describe it to me." His tone is commanding and oh, so alluring. It turns me on like nothing else.

"Guess," I whisper.

"Is it lace?"

"Yes."

"Oh, fuck, Ava. You are killing me here."

"Back at you."

"What other nightgowns do you have?"

"I have a red one with lace, and a white one." I stop, feeling self-conscious. I admit I love sexy nightgowns; but what's he going to think about me? That I moonlight as a high-end call girl?

"Go on," he invites.

"Come back to me quickly."

***

The next day at the office is brutal. I barely have time to eat lunch, and hop from meeting to meeting the entire day. Also, I don't receive any present from Sebastian. I suppose that means the courtship period is over. I can't help but feel sad about it. On the bright side, Sebastian will be home tomorrow.

Logan returns in the afternoon, sporting bloodshot eyes and dark rings under them. He was gone this week too.

"How was London?" I ask him when he passes by my office.

"Bloody jet lag."

"I see you picked up the slang," I say appreciatively.

"How was your week? I haven't had any time to read your e-mails, sorry."

"No problem. I want to have a short meeting Monday morning and bring you and Sebastian up to date. I'm working on the agenda right now, and I've checked Sebastian's business calendar and yours. You're free."

"You're amazing. Yes, of course we can meet Monday morning. Now I'll go home and sleep until then."

I smile, watching him leave. I roll up my

proverbial sleeves and throw myself into work. Having everything ready for Monday morning means I'll have to come to the office tomorrow too. That's okay. I love my job, and I got where I am by busting my ass and going that extra mile every single time. I sort of lied to Logan anyway, since I'm not only going to update him and Sebastian on what occurred last week. I already have some partners in mind that could help us bring the show to the next level. The ones they've worked with until now are good, but I've worked with better in the past. They're more professional, even though a bit pricier. I can make a good case to convince both of my bosses.

The show is still three months away, but these suppliers need to be booked early. In fact, they'll probably claim this is too short notice for them to take us on. I can work my charm on them if it comes to that.

I lose myself in my work, and only realize what time it is when my phone buzzes.

"Why aren't you home yet, you little workaholic?"

"Sebastian, this is creepy. Do you have someone watching me?"

"Of course not. Who does that?"

I lean back in my chair, holding the phone to my shoulder and flexing my wrists. They've grown stiff.

"How do you know I'm not at the apartment?"

"Mmmm, I can't say, but you'll see as soon as you get there."

I sit up straight, my heart doing a somersault. Is he

at my apartment? Maybe he decided to return earlier.

"I've got to go." He ends our conversation on that mysterious note.

I'm out of the office in a few minutes.

Once inside my building, I look for Sebastian in the small lobby, but he isn't there. Since this is a complex of serviced apartments, quite a few people have keys to my place. Oh, God, did he convince them to let him inside my room? My heart hammers against my rib cage as I step into the elevator and then continue down the corridor leading to my apartment.

With trembling hands, I unlock the door and push it open. The lights are out.

"Sebastian?"

No answer. Disappointment washes over me as I switch on the light. I notice the package on my bed. It's a rectangular box tied with a ribbon and a note.

Thought it'd be best if this wasn't delivered at the office.
Sebastian

So that's why I didn't get a gift today. Smiling, I sink on the bed and open the gift, careful not to damage the box, because it's so pretty. I cover my mouth with my hand. Inside the box is the most luxurious nightgown I've ever had the pleasure to see. Silk and lace.

I call him immediately.

"Sebastian."

"Aha, I know that accusing tone. It means you got home and saw your present."

"What did I tell you about expensive gifts?"

"You told me not to buy you rubies," he says coolly.

"No, I'm pretty sure I told you expensive gifts."

"Don't you like it?"

"Of course I do. It's perfect, but that's not the point."

"Consider it a gift for me."

"What?"

"I want to imagine you wearing it." A pause follows, then a whisper. "Touching yourself."

I dissolve in a puddle of need, and almost do as he says. I get a grip on myself. "Sebastian Bennett, I won't have phone sex with you. I want our first time to be the real deal."

He laughs softly, but when he speaks, his voice is husky. "Oh, Ava, it'll be so real you'll ache for days."

Chapter Eighteen

Ava

Sexual frustration threatens to suffocate me the next morning, but I don't give in to it. Also, I suspect that masturbation, far from satisfying me, would only increase my hunger for him. I contemplate trying out the age-old cure for horniness: a cold shower. Said and done.

I get in the bathroom, turn on the shower to its coldest, and step right under it.

SuchabadideaOMG.

I jump out so fast I lose my balance and fall flat on my ass. Groaning, I get up, massaging the base of my spine. Well, that's a way to start one's Saturday. Dressing up is quite literally a pain the ass. On the bright side, the pain replaced the horniness, so it wasn't all for nothing, though I'm not likely to repeat the experience.

I sling on a fluffy dress. There won't be anyone at the office today except the security guard, so I might as well take advantage. On the way to work, I pick up a bagel and a coffee, my mood lightening up.

When I arrive at the office, I check if there is anyone else on my floor. Nope. I'm all alone. Great.

I turn on the music on my computer. I work best listening to music, but I always use earplugs. Since I'm alone today, I forego them. I set the alarm on my smartphone for seven o'clock. I know I'll lose track of time otherwise. If I leave here shortly after seven, I'll have plenty of time to shower and beautify myself before Sebastian arrives. He said he'd pick me up from home at ten.

With the music resounding in the room, I slump in my chair and start typing away. Bring on the Saturday work mood.

I eat take-away pasta for lunch, an unhealthy portion of carbs being exactly the fuel I need to keep going for another few hours. And coffee, of course.

To my astonishment, I finish two hours before my alarm goes off. I jump to my feet, in dire need of stretching my muscles. I could go for a run; but since I went running with Sebastian, I found that doing it alone is no fun. Truth be told, I hate running with a passion. Or, well, any kind of sport. Why do I have to love food and hate sport? It'd be easier if I hated or loved both.

So instead of running, I dance.

I turn the music louder and start moving to the rhythm, closing my eyes and pretending I'm in a club. I'm actually glad I'm not in one. My dance moves royally suck, but there is no one here, so who cares?

At some point, I find myself singing too, giggling in between lyrics. If there's something more atrocious than my dancing, it's my singing. This is so much fun.

"Now, this I could come home to every night."

I yelp. "Jesus Christ."

"No, it's me."

Sebastian's standing in the doorway, holding a bottle of wine. I lose my balance for the second time today. My instincts kick into overdrive, and I grab my desk for support, stopping short of a second encounter with the floor.

I turn down the music.

"What are you doing here?" we ask at the same time.

"I came to do some work," I say at the same time he says, "I came back early."

We both smile.

"I bought a bottle of wine and decided to stop by the office to drop off some papers - so I'm not tempted to work from home. I want a clear schedule for the rest of the weekend."

"Really?" I put on my most flirty voice and even bat my eyelashes. Not sure it'll help much. I mean, the man did just see my ridiculous dance moves in all their glory. "What for?"

"You."

I swallow hard as he strides inside my office. He puts the bottle on my desk with such precision that one might think his life depended on it. He pins me against the wall, his lips crashing on mine, his arms slinging around my waist. I let him ravage my mouth, enjoying the loaded heat, the barely restrained passion. Then it's not restrained at all anymore, because Sebastian's hands find their way under my dress, grazing my inner thighs, and I begin to unbutton his shirt.

With great effort, I break off the kiss, pushing him a bit away. "Sebastian, stop. We can't do this here. It would be very inappropriate."

"I found you dancing that beautiful ass of yours to deafening music. That was appropriate?"

I giggle, hiding my face in the crook of his neck. He smells so impossibly good. "No, but sex and dancing aren't in the same league."

"I'm the CEO. I make the rules in my own company."

"Sebastian."

"Okay, let's pause."

We're both panting and quivering—about five seconds away from damning the pause, the rules, and everything else.

"If I have you here on your desk, I'll never be able to concentrate on work again knowing we did this. Let's take the party to my apartment. We can keep it as highly inappropriate as we want."

"I finally figured out who you are." I look up at him. "The inappropriate brother."

"Only with you." He tilts my chin up with his fingers. "I had a great plan to take you to dinner and do things the proper way."

"What happened to that plan?"

"I discarded it when I got hard from seeing you dancing."

"That can't possibly be true."

"Why don't you see for yourself?"

Without waiting for my answer, he puts my hand right on his erection. Fuck me. How can this man be so hard for me?

"Let's go," I say in a throaty voice.

***

Sebastian lives in a quiet and luxurious neighborhood on the other side of the city. The five-story building in front of which he parks looks expensive, but tasteful. The apartment itself is enormous on the ground level, and it has a beautiful garden in the back, complete with a swimming pool.

"This is a huge place to live all by yourself." I look around as Sebastian pours us wine in the kitchen. For some reason, I was expecting to find minimalist furniture in tones of black and gray. On the rare occasions I've visited the homes of the CEOs I worked for, they very much resembled hotel rooms. Cold and lacking in personality. Sebastian's apartment brims with life.

"I like my space. Make yourself comfortable."

I sit on the couch. The smooth leather molds to my skin, and I enjoy the cool feeling. I close my eyes, stretching my neck. Warm hands touch the back of my neck. I open my eyes, peering sideways. Sebastian stands behind the couch.

"You're tense," he whispers.

"I need a massage again."

"I know what you need." He presses his fingers

into my skin and I let out a moan. "Don't do that, or I'll lose what little self-control I have."

"Then don't touch me like this."

He drops his hands, leaving me with a sense of loss. I shift on the sofa, following him with my gaze as he fetches the glasses of wine, glancing at me with heavy-lidded eyes. Handing me a glass, he sits next to me.

What am I doing? This man will make me fall completely and lose myself. I can't afford that; but sweet heavens, I need it badly. I yearn to know what it feels like to have a man rock my world so devastatingly he'll become the center of my universe. If there's a man I'd allow to take over so completely, it's him.

"You're quiet," he says.

"Enjoying the wine."

He slides closer to me on the couch. "I missed you."

"I missed you too." He can't possibly know how much.

"I can't stay away from you, and I won't."

"I don't want you to stay away," I whisper. "My contract—"

"Fuck the contract."

"I was about to say the same thing."

He sets his glass on the coffee table, and I do the same with mine. He covers my mouth with his, but his kiss isn't as urgent as the one in the office. He takes his time, exploring my mouth, tasting my lips as if they're the most exquisite things in this world. He pulls me closer to him, and I climb into his lap. Sebastian drags his lips from my mouth down to my neck. I lean back, giving him better access, and my arm touches something behind me. A noise follows, a thump. Belatedly, I realize the sound was our wine glasses crashing to the floor.

"The wine—your carpet."

"Fuck the carpet," he says, and goes back to kissing my neck. "I'll buy a new one."

"Good plan."

I undo the buttons of his shirt hurriedly, enjoying the feel of his granite muscles beneath my fingers. He discards my dress, pulling my bottom lip between his teeth while busying his fingers with my bra. He unclasps it, freeing my breasts, as I get rid of his shirt altogether. We pause a few moments, drinking each other's bodies in.

"You are so beautiful, Ava."

He drags his thumbs across my nipples, flicking them tenderly, until they turn to hard nubs. He takes one in his mouth, and then the other.

"Sebastian. This feels so good."

"I'm far from done," he whispers against my skin. When he hoists me up, I hitch my legs around his waist, kissing him hungrily. I am wearing nothing but a thong, while he's still in his jeans. My throbbing core pushes against his waistband as he crosses the apartment. The friction deepens my need for him. He comes to a halt, shouldering open a door, switching the light on with his elbow. I barely have time to take in my surroundings before he lays me on the bed, and then there is nothing but him for me. We could be in the most luxurious bedroom or in a tent for all I care.

"I like that look in your eyes." He smiles, peering at me.

"What look?"

"The one that says I'm your whole world right now."

A wave of cold shoots through me, and I have to steel myself not to wince. How can he read me this well? His watchful gaze melts my fears. His eyes are hooded with desire, yes, but also so much more. I trust him.

"It's true," I admit. "Now, it's high time you lost your jeans."

In the blink of an eye, he's naked and proceeds to remove my last item of clothing. He positions his hands at my hips, tugging my thong down my legs. Finally, he tosses it somewhere in the room. I push myself up on my elbows, watching him watch me. His gaze travels along my bare skin. This man worships my body—every single part of it. After caressing me with his gaze, he proceeds to torment me with his lips. They leave a trail of fire on every spot he kisses on my body.

"I love your skin." He makes his way up my neck, pulling with his teeth at my earlobe. His large hands roam over my hips, one of them settling between my legs. He pushes his fingers against each of my folds, igniting my pulsing core.

"Sebastian."

"So wet already," he murmurs.

"I want you."

"Be patient. It's all in the foreplay." His voice is too calm, too composed. I must change this. Narrowing my eyes, I wrap my palm around his hard shaft, pumping up and down, relishing the sight of him losing control. A deep groan reverberates from his chest, and he tosses his head back. I drag my lip across his exposed neck.

"Patience doesn't sound so appealing, now, does it?" I tease.

The next second, Sebastian grabs both my hands, pinning them against the bed above my head. Breath whooshes out of me as he brings his face so close that there are only a few inches between us. The air crackles with tension.

Gulping, I lick my lips at the delicious promise in his voice. He keeps my hands together, his free hand roaming over my breasts. My puckered nipples almost hurt from being so turned on. He circles them with his thumb, avoiding my nubs. Fuck, he knows how to drive a woman crazy. He drops his hand between my legs, dipping a finger right into my core. I gasp, arching my back, pushing myself into his finger. He retreats quickly.

"Don't."

"Don't what?" I feel his smile against my ear. The bastard.

"Don't take your finger away."

He touches me again, this time caressing my clit. His fingers circle it until I pant underneath him. This man will turn me craaaaazy.

Licking my lips, I look up pleadingly at him from between my lashes. He kisses me hard, his mouth greedy over mine. That's it, he'll take me now.

Wrong. He pulls back and flips me on my tummy. I feel him lounging on top of me, his hard chest pressing against my back as he kisses my neck, intertwining his fingers with mine. I push my butt up into him.

"Fuck, Ava, do you want me to lose all my self-control?"

"That's what I want." I'm so horny I'm surprised I can utter words at all. Every inch of my body is alive with the need for him.

"Tell me exactly what you want," he whispers, making the hair at my nape stand on end.

"Damn it, Sebastian. I want you inside me right now."

"Ava." He lets out a deep groan, moving off me. I hear the blessed sound of a condom package being ripped open. He rolls it over his length, then picks up a pillow and pushes it under my belly, lifting my butt up. He positions himself at my entrance. I lick my lips, my thighs quivering. When he pushes inside, my whole body trembles.

"Oh." I breathe in and out, succumbing to his delicious torture. Because torture is the right word. Sebastian enters me with exquisite slowness. Inch by inch he fills me up, spreading my legs wider. This man is driving me insane. Finally, he stops pushing inside me, and I take it as a sign that he's all in.

"Can you take all of me in?"

I lick my lips. I thought I already was. "Yeah."

He thrusts inside me completely. I cry out, fisting the bedsheet.

"Ava," he grits. His hands cup my ass cheeks. He starts moving, and my whole world spins on its axis. Each movement leads to an explosion of sensations, starting in my core and lighting the nerve endings in my entire body up to my fingertips. With each stroke, he claims a more intimate part of me. His lips trail on my back, the gentleness forming a stark contrast to the crushing rhythm of his hips. Sebastian's forearms are at my sides. He's slowly coming undone. I can tell by the way that his nails dig into the mattress. This recognition ignites something deep inside me.

My sex twinges as I feel drops of sweat falling onto my back.

"I want you to come with me, Ava." He all but grunts out my name. I almost come because of that sound alone, but then Sebastian's propping himself on one forearm only, and he slips his free hand between the pillow and me, circling my clit.

I lose it. I pinch my eyes closed, stars erupting behind them. "I cwdunter. . ."

"That's not English, babe." His voice is trembling.

"Sebastian." I gasp as the orgasm takes hold of me. I succumb to it, every nerve singing with pleasure and need, the sensations intensifying when I hear Sebastian's cry of relief and feel him widening inside me.

He drops on top of me, careful not to crush me.

He laces his fingers with mine, squeezing lightly as he whispers, "You are an amazing woman, Ava."

Chapter Nineteen

Ava

When I wake up, ribbons of sunlight drop inside the room, and the birds' medley reaches me through the open window.

It takes me a few seconds to realize I'm not in my bed. To my right, Sebastian sleeps peacefully. The bliss from last night paints a smile on my face, but panic creeps in too. Should I leave? I have had a single one-night stand, and it was humiliating. He woke me up in the middle of the night, asking me why I was still there. I slipped into my clothes and ran out the next minute. But Sebastian isn't like that, and this wasn't a one-night stand.

Rolling on one side, I take in this fine specimen of a man. Even in his sleep, the one word to describe him is yummy. I once read that we feel when someone is watching us. It might be true, because within a few minutes of my blatant staring, Sebastian's eyelids flutter open.

"Good morning, gorgeous." His morning voice is so sexy. In one swift move, he pulls me to him.

I instantly relax in his arms. "Right back at you."

He drags his fingers down my cheek and my lips. "You look beautiful."

"Stop it." I avert my gaze, focusing on his chin. "No one looks beautiful in the morning."

"You do. Your eyes are a little puffy, and your lips swollen." His mouth curls into a satisfied smirk. "Why, your lips betray what a nasty girl you were last night."

"Mmmm." I pinch the skin on his chest. "My body shows how nasty you've been. I'm a little sore."

His expression turns serious. "A little? Then I didn't do my job right. You're about to get much more sore. That's a promise."

A shiver runs down my spine, goose bumps dancing on my skin.

"Are you cold?"

"No," I reply quickly. "Not at all. It's a good morning."

"Why, because the bed was comfortable?"

I grin, joining in on his game. "No, that's not it."

"Is it because of the pre-sleep activities?"

"Sebastian Bennett, are you fishing for compliments?"

"Depends. Are you about to hand some out?"

"Maybe."

He plants a smooch on my lips. God, he's adorable. "Well, then. Yes, I believe I am."

"I need to shower," I inform him.

"What a coincidence. So do I. Let's go together."

We disentangle ourselves from the sheets. I

stretch for a few seconds, while Sebastian goes straight to the bathroom adjacent to the room.

The bathroom consists of a Jacuzzi and a separate shower. They're both large enough for us to fit in.

"We can play around in the Jacuzzi later." Sebastian stands in the shower, and I join him. "Ava, meet shower. Shower, you're about to see many inappropriate things."

I giggle as warm water sprays my skin. "I can't believe it took me so long to figure out you're the inappropriate brother."

"I'll spend my days proving to you how much I deserve that title."

"Last night was very convincing. You have no idea how sore I am."

"Tell me."

"Sebastian," I whisper. "If you continue like that. . ." I swallow the rest of the sentence, distracted by the water running down his chest, his abs, and further down. Biting my lips, I add, "We're supposed to shower."

"I'll help you do that." A grin takes hold of his features. That's when I see the dimples.

Oh, my God, this man has dimples. I might fall in love with him. How come I never noticed them before?

"There's something different about your smile this morning."

"Mmm. Might have something to do with waking up next to a beautiful woman."

He pours some shower gel on his palms, lowering

himself to his knees. He starts rubbing the gel on my ankles, working his way up to my knees. His hands move further up my inner thighs.

"Such a beautiful body," he murmurs. As his hands travel to my hips and to my stomach, he leans forward. His tongue touches the sensitive skin between my legs. I part them to give him better access. This man can do amazing things with his tongue. Abruptly, he pulls back, standing up, his hands continuing to soap my breasts and shoulders, as if nothing happened. Such a tease.

"My turn," I say, after my entire body is covered with shower gel.

"Okay."

I pour gel on my palms and mimic his earlier routine, starting with his ankles and working my way up. There is something incredibly erotic about touching him like this. I trace every inch of skin on his legs with my fingers, enjoying the feel of his steel muscles. I take him in my mouth, watching him the entire time. He keeps his composure at first, but as I move my lips up and down, his breaths become more labored, his eyes more hooded. When he fists my hair, I know I've brought him exactly to the point I wanted, and pull back.

"You're being a bad, bad girl," he says as I stand up, soaping his chest, tracing the lines of his muscles, pressing my breasts against him.

We let the water wash away the soap.

After planting a quick kiss on my lips, he steps out of the shower. I linger inside, washing my hair. Every single part of my body aches for him. Damn, damn, damn, Ava Lindt. What are you doing? I have three months left here. The clock is ticking, and I already dread the day I'll have to kiss him good-bye. This won't be a purely physical relationship; it was never about that. Falling for this amazing man could be fatal, but what a delicious way to go.

After I finish with the shower, I blow dry my hair and throw on a robe. The smell of bacon greets me when I step out of the bathroom. Mystified, I hurry down to the kitchen.

I can't believe my eyes. Sebastian stands in front of the stove, wearing nothing but shorts. Cooking.

"What are you doing?"

"Breakfast. And then I'll happily do you again."

"You cook?" I ask unnecessarily. I can't shake off the surprise. Tiptoeing around him, I peer at what he's doing. Yep, my man is cooking. There are bacon and eggs in the pan, which he moves around very proficiently, as though he's on some cooking show, demonstrating how to do it correctly.

"Of course, I do. Everyone who was tall enough to stand over the stove had cooking duty at the ranch."

"You're amazing."

"We established that already."

I elbow him. "Cocky much?"

"Pun intended?" Sebastian smiles, those delicious dimples making an appearance again.

"Maybe." I plant a small kiss on the corner of his mouth.

"You are naughty."

"Can I help you with anything?"

"Is there anything you can do in the kitchen?"

"I'm an expert at heating stuff up in the microwave. I'm also very proficient at cutting and burning myself."

"Thought so."

"What do you mean?"

"You have a lot of talents, but you didn't strike me as the cooking type."

"What kind of talents?"

"Why, Ms. Lindt, are you fishing for compliments now?"

"After we established that you're amazing in every department, and I suck at cooking? You bet I want compliments."

He turns away from the oven, looking me straight in the eyes. "You are smart, funny, and can do amazing things with your mouth. Sit there and let me cook for you."

This is the first time a man has cooked for me. Damn it. There are too many first times with him, and he has a way of making them all unforgettable. Because really, who could forget the sight of him in boxers, cooking?

After we eat breakfast, I help clean up, and as I sip from my glass of orange juice, enjoying the view out his window, Sebastian sneaks behind me, taking me in his arms and nibbling at my earlobe. His fingers graze through my hair, tugging at it.

"I love your hair," he murmurs against my neck.

"Last night you loved my skin."

"I love every part of you."

"Mmmm. Charmer. Are you complimenting me to get in my panties?"

"You're not wearing any. But if you were, you bet I'd try. I'm not lying. You're perfect."

I snicker. I'm proud of my body, but I know it's not perfect. My love for food and disproportionate hate of sports are showing.

"Don't tell me you're self-conscious of your body."

"I'm not. . . mostly." In a whisper, I add, "My hips could be smaller."

"They are fantastic. I especially like how they grind against me when we make love." Sebastian lets go of me, and I turn around to protest, but before I even open my mouth, he holds up his hand.

"I want you to dance for me," he says.

"You mean like a striptease?"

"You're wearing a robe. That'd be an awfully short striptease. I meant dancing as in dancing. Like in the office."

Crossing my arms over my chest, I shoot him a look. "I'm not dancing in front of you."

"You did it yesterday."

"I didn't know you were watching."

"Come on, you don't have to be self-conscious in front of me. Your dancing is fun."

"I was having fun," I admit, putting my glass of orange juice on the table. "Okay, I'll do it, but you'll dance with me."

Sebastian fetches his smartphone. My hips take over as the music starts. Before I know it, Sebastian has yanked down my robe.

"Naked dancing," I say appreciatively. "Now we're talking."

"I love how smooth you feel." He touches my pubis lightly, electrifying me. Abruptly, he pulls his hand back.

When Sebastian starts dancing, I shriek, a fit of laughter overtaking me. "Oh, now I know why you like my dancing. You suck even more than I do. I can't believe there's something you're not good at."

He pulls me to him, encircling my waist, half-walking, half-dancing with me toward the couch. We must look ridiculous, but I love this. "I can do something else very well."

"Please do."

He lowers me onto the soft leather and climbs on top of me. "I could stay with you inside this apartment forever." He caresses my lips, then leans in and kisses me senseless.

Chapter Twenty

Ava

Forever lasts until Monday. I insist on Sebastian driving alone to work after he drops me off at my apartment.

When I arrive at the office, I have this dopey grin again. It grows wider during my presentation with Sebastian and Logan, even though we both act professionally. By the look on Logan's face, it's obvious he knows about us. I manage to convince both of them to go forward with my suppliers for the show, so I spend the rest of the morning on the phone, trying to convince said suppliers to take us on. Most of them put up a good fight because they're already solidly booked. By the time I'm done, I'm exhausted enough that my enamored-puppy-grin has faded somewhat. It returns in full force during the meeting with the marketing team in the afternoon, because Sebastian attends it. I might come across a bit maniacal. I love my job, but no one in their right mind can believe that talking about suppliers and deadlines makes me that enthusiastic.

On Tuesday, the tables turn. I'm talking total overhaul here.

The nastiest cold I've had in a long time keeps me from getting out of the bed. My eyes water and my forehead burns. I barely manage to send Sebastian a text, announcing that I'm too sick to work, before collapsing in a coma-like sleep.

When I come to my senses again, I don't feel much better. I've soaked my pillow and nightgown, and the inside of my mouth feels like gum.

I sneeze as I try to sit up, so I give up on the endeavor, lying back down. Then I hear a voice. With the greatest effort, I push myself up on my elbows, trying to peer through the open door into the main room. At first, I don't see anything; but then I notice Sebastian as he paces back and forth, his phone plastered to his ear. Noticing me, he mutters something into the phone, and then yanks it away.

"You're up," Sebastian says.

"Barely." I turn to one side and catch my reflection in the wardrobe mirror. I look as horrible as I feel. "What are you doing here, Sebastian? Go away," I mumble, pulling my pillow over my head. "I don't want you to see me like this."

"Don't be ridiculous. I'll stay here and take care of you." He sits at the edge of the bed, holding a cup in his hands. "Here, sit up and drink this tea. You look adorable with your red, puffy nose."

"You're a CEO." I pull my covers up to my chin, because I'm shivering all of a sudden. "Go do CEO stuff."

"Woman, let me take care of you." His tone doesn't leave any room for discussion. A fuzzy feeling of warmth overtakes me at his words. Sebastian helps me sit up and drink. His phone rings twice, but he ignores it. After I'm done with the tea, I cuddle against his chest, starting to feel drowsy again. I know the medicine I need, but I don't have any with me. Come on, Ava. You've done this before. Get your sick ass to the pharmacy before you fall asleep again. Clumsily, I attempt to get out of bed.

"What are you doing?" Sebastian asks.

"Going to the pharmacy."

He raises his eyebrows. "You're mad if you think I'll let you go anywhere in this state."

"Sebastian, the pharmacy is around the corner; I'll make it. I need that medicine or I won't feel better. I have a fever, so I might have the flu, not a common cold."

He stares at me as though I've grown a second head. Hell, I feel like I've grown a second head, and both heads are swimming right now. "How about you tell me what you need, and I'll get it for you? You know, since I'm here anyway."

"Oh," I say. "I hadn't thought of that. Are you sure?"

"Yes. How did it even occur to you to get out of bed?"

"I take care of myself all the time. I get sick at least once on every project. I should carry a bag of medicine with me."

"What do you need?"

I tell him the name of the medicine, and he's off. Either he knows how to teleport, or I fall asleep, but it seems like only a few seconds have passed when he returns.

"Here you go."

He holds me in his arms after I take the medicine, and it feels so warm and impossibly good that I don't ever want to let go. I fall asleep again.

I wake up to whispers—this time they belong to two different people. One voice belongs to Sebastian, the other one to a woman. There is the sound of a door closing and the whispering stops.

"Who was that?" I ask.

"My mother. She dropped off some chicken soup. Homemade."

"Oh, that is very kind of her."

"Pippa also stopped by. She brought you some sweets. Self-bought."

I snicker. "Can I have some soup?"

"Yeah, not a good idea."

"Why not?" I ask, genuinely puzzled.

"My mother is a woman of many talents, but a very unpredictable cook. Her pastries are delicious, her soups horrible."

"I'm sure that's not true," I counter. "I want to try it."

Sebastian smiles. "At your own risk." He opens the lid of the Tupperware container, putting the spoon inside. As I eye the soup, my throat constricts, rejecting the mere idea of food. I need liquids in my system, though. Soup is perfect. I shove a spoonful in my mouth and it takes all I have not to spew it back out. With the greatest effort, I swallow it.

"My God, this is horrible."

"Told you so. We never had the heart to tell her. But you'll like the sweets Pippa brought." He puts them in front of me, and I dig in, suddenly full of appetite.

"Now we're talking," I say. "Sebastian, I feel a little better. You can go back to the office, you know."

"I've canceled all my meetings for today."

I look at him, stunned. "You didn't have to do that."

"No, I didn't have to, but I wanted to. Now, stop being such a mule and accept that I'm going to stay with you today and tomorrow if you don't feel any better."

"Okay."

"You're accepting it?" he asks suspiciously.

"Do I have a choice?"

He grins. "Not really."

"But I have to warn you, I won't be much fun."

"You're always fun."

"I mean that kind of fun."

"Ava Lindt, I'm not here for sex."

Now it's my turn to be suspicious. "That's a sentence I haven't heard from any man."

"I'm not just any man."

"No," I sigh, "you're not. You're perfect." I begin to sneeze. After I calm down, Sebastian presses his hand on my forehead.

"Your fever isn't going down," he says worriedly.

"Well, that medicine should kick in at some

point."

"It might not be strong enough. I also bought some Tylenol."

"Ugh, I don't want more pills."

Sebastian laughs softly. "Are you five years old?"

"Yes, I am."

I frown the entire time he pulls out the package of Tylenol, releasing a pill into his palm.

"Now, don't be a bad girl, Ava."

I open my mouth obediently and swallow it. Then I pull my sheet up to my nose, shivering. "Oh, wow," I say. "Wow."

"Okay, you're starting to worry me. This is Tylenol, not some fine whiskey. Why are you so wowed by it?"

"It hasn't kicked in yet, and my fever is stronger than whiskey. My head is swimming worse than before. Hey, the good part of being sick is that I see two of you. Twice that sexiness. Too much for my eyes to take in."

Sebastian frowns. "You should sleep."

"Okay. Can you lie next to me?"

When he obliges me, I cuddle against him, burying my head in his skin.

"Can you thank your family for being so nice to me?"

"I will."

"I never had someone take care of me like that." Damn this fever. It loosens my tongue.

"How about your mother?"

"She wasn't around much. She worked three jobs,

and taking care of me while sick would've meant one meal less, so she had no choice. I miss her. I wanted to take care of her, like you do with your family, but she died before I got the chance. You're very lucky, you know. To have all of them."

"I know," he says. "They are great."

"So are you. No guy I've dated treated me like you do."

"That's because they were all idiots. You deserve to be taken care of and spoiled every day."

"Shhh, stop," I mumble. "You're going to make me fall in love with you."

I'm not sure if I imagine the next words, but I think I hear, "That wouldn't be so bad."

I fall into a deep sleep within minutes.

Chapter Twenty-One

Ava

The worst of my cold goes away after two days, but I work from home, afraid I'll make everyone at work sick. I only go to the office on Friday. I've barely settled onto my chair when Sebastian bursts into my office.

"What are you doing here?"

I swear this man wears a suit like no one else. Trouble is, now I know what hides beneath his designer clothing. I know exactly how defined his muscles are, because I caressed every single one of them, and I can't wait to do it again.

"Working."

"I thought we'd agreed you wouldn't come in this week."

"No." I barely contain my smile. "You said that. I never agreed."

Sebastian eyes me, stepping past the table and stopping in front of my chair. Leaning in over me, he tilts my chin up. And there goes my breath. "There was definitely a yes there somewhere."

"I was referring to something else." I lick my lips, reminiscing about the naughty things we'd done. In the tangle of limbs and kisses, he said I shouldn't come to the office the whole week. Then he asked me if I liked what he was doing to me. He was dragging his thumb across the slick spot between my legs, so of course the answer was a resounding yes. Maybe too resounding.

"Really? And what was that?" He's so close to me now that his intoxicating scent fills me, making me squirm.

"You know what."

"I want to hear you say it."

Before he can muddle my thoughts any further, I push him away. "Stop teasing me. We're at the office."

"We established that already." He rests on the edge of the desk, peering straight at me. "I want to take you to dinner tonight."

"Mmm, what's the occasion?"

"I don't need one. I can take my girlfriend to dinner if I want to."

"I'm your girlfriend?" I ask, stunned.

Sebastian's brow furrows. "What did you think you are? Wait, a better question is what am I to you?"

My head's spinning. There are so many things going through my mind right now. Sebastian saw a part of me I thought was long gone. When Tylenol clouded my thoughts, that little girl hungry for security and love surfaced. It was as if he was holding up a mirror, and in it, I could see myself bare. He was the mirror, and even after witnessing everything, he didn't run away. Because Sebastian Bennett is a real man.

I go for the one thing I know for sure. "You're the most wonderful man I've dated."

"Charmer." He caresses my cheeks, his fingers igniting my skin. "You're trying to distract me with compliments."

"Maybe."

"I'll pick you up at eight. We're going to the Sense." He looks at me as though I'm supposed to know the place.

"I haven't heard of it. How fancy should I dress up?"

"Fancy enough."

"Oh, I have a perfect dress. It shows a lot of cleavage," I tease. The effect is instantaneous. He presses his lips into a thin line, his eyes darkening a notch.

"I'm taking you there as my date, not so you can find a date."

Unable to maintain the charade any longer, I chuckle. "I was trying to bring out the caveman in you. You're adorable."

"Adorable and caveman don't go together."

"Yes, they do, and you're the result. Now go, because I want to get some work done."

That's when Logan walks in.

"What is this?" he inquires, his head snapping from Sebastian to me and back.

"Your brother is shamelessly flirting with me," I

fill him in. Sebastian stands and joins Logan in the doorway.

"Okay, let's set some ground rules." Logan squares his shoulders.

"I'm not having the talk from my brother," Sebastian says. I grin at his warning tone. Ah, nothing like the banter between these two to start my day at the office.

"I'll give it anyway," Logan replies.

"Of course you will." I barely stifle a laugh.

"Whose side are you on?" Sebastian asks.

"No sex at the office," Logan declares.

Straightening in my chair, I lay my elbows on the desk, steepling my fingers under my chin. "I agree."

"Well," Sebastian says. "I agree as well. You two"—he points at Logan and me—"have no business having sex anywhere. The two of us, however—" he adds, giving me a loaded look.

"You're impossible," Logan says as his assistant comes to inform him and Sebastian that they have a meeting starting in five minutes.

I watch them leave with a large grin on my face. These past few days have been out of this world. Sebastian came to my place every evening, taking care of me and spoiling me. I get all fuzzy remembering it. If I thought concentrating was hard before I gave in to him, it's nothing compared to how it's going to be from now on.

***

The day is surprisingly productive. Since I couldn't

do everything I had to from home, I had a humongous to-do list for today. I bulldoze through it, growing more satisfied with each task I check off. The collection launch will be one of the best achievements of my career.

At six o'clock sharp, my phone rings, displaying Pippa's name.

"I'm in the mood for a girls' night out," she says.

"No can do. I have a date with your brother tonight."

I hold my phone to my ear with my shoulder while gathering my stuff to leave.

"Oooh, where is he taking you?"

"Some fancy restaurant. I forgot the name."

"Can I help you prepare?"

"You really need an estrogen-filled evening, don't you?"

"Actually, I'm in dire need of some testosterone. But since I can't get that, I'll settle for a girls' evening in."

"Can you be at my apartment in an hour?"

"Sure."

***

I don't remember ever putting so much effort into preparing for a date. Stopping at the cosmetics shop next to my building, I pick up a body kit that promises to make my skin as smooth as a baby's. I'm skeptical, but what the heck. Once I'm in the shower and rub the peeling gel on, I become a believer. The thing removes two frickin' layers of skin. Afterward, I apply the body cream, and I'm surprised at how soft my skin really is. Next in line is nail polish. God, I feel so girly painting my nails, but I love it.

When Pippa arrives, she sports a large grin, eyeing me from head to toe. "I see you're taking this preparation process very seriously. Let's see what you've got."

Grinning in equal measure, I lead her inside the room. She reminds me a lot of my best friend, Nadine. "So, I can't decide between these two." I gesture to the dresses I've laid on the bed.

"These are both yummy," she comments. "From the way my brother looks at you, he'll go berserk."

"That's the goal," I confess. I was going to go for some safer choices, but I can't resist. Riling him up makes him hotter.

"I'm always for a little black dress," Pippa says.

"The black one it is." I pump my fist in the air triumphantly. It's a bandage dress I bought a few months back, and it's the least cleavage revealing of the lot. But combined with the way it hugs my curves, it'll have exactly the effect I want on Sebastian. He woke something deep inside me, a desire to ensure by any means that he needs me as desperately as I need him.

"Girl, you've got some great choices here. I'm envious."

"All bought on sale," I declare proudly, looking at my outfits. Growing up, I owned few pretty things. My mom made most of our clothes. In her youth, she came to New York to study fashion. Then my father happened, and then I happened, and she put her dreams aside, working every job imaginable: waitressing, cleaning, babysitting. She had an old sewing machine with which she made our clothes. They were simple and practical. Getting her a kick-ass machine was on the top of my to-buy list when I got my first job after graduating college.

She surprised me on my prom night with the most beautiful dress. She told me she'd saved the entire year to buy that fabric. It was the color of the sky when the sun is about to set. We laughed and danced as she helped me prepare, and since there was no one to take a picture of us, we took a selfie—before selfies were all the rage. We both looked radiant. I keep that picture in my living room back in New York.

My career as a sales shopper began after I started at Dirk's consultancy. I like pretty things, but growing up the way I did, I have a healthy disgust for overpriced items.

"You're like Alice. Both of you are lucky you have such a petite frame," Pippa comments, snapping me back to the moment. "I can rarely find what I want in sales. Okay, we have the dress. Shoes come next. Bring out your best heels."

Laughing, I whisk out a pair of black shoes with straps. Pippa pinches her nose. I put them back and then get out a red pair with sky-high heels.

"How about these?" I ask.

Pippa's eyes widen, and then she bows her head, peering at the shoes. "They're my size. I'm going to steal them."

"Nope."

"Borrow?"

"Maybe."

"I'm salivating here. You have to promise you'll lend me those."

"Oh, fine, I will. Can't believe we have the same shoe size, but you're a head taller than me."

I dress quickly and do a pirouette. Pippa nods in approval.

"Let me style your hair," she says. "I'm a pro."

"How come?"

"As the oldest sister, I was on hair duty for all the younger ones when they had any school dances, dates, proms. You can call them if you want references."

"I trust you. Go ahead."

Hair styling was never my forte. My hair is thick and there's too much of it. I usually brush it and wear it in a bun or ponytail. Pippa wasn't kidding. She's an expert. Using only my round brush and the hair dryer, she turns my wild mane into beach waves, all in less than half an hour.

I do the makeup myself. A little something on my eyes, but I put on red lipstick.

"Oh, shucks," Pippa says.

"You don't like it?"

"I do, but I'm afraid the two of you won't make it out of the room at all tonight."

"Oh, we will."

Chapter Twenty-Two

Ava

After Pippa leaves, I take a picture of myself then text it to Nadine. Instead of replying, she calls me.

"Yum, you look fabulous. Taking out the big guns tonight?"

"Yep. I figured go big or go home." I laugh into the phone as I slip my lipstick into my tiny purse.

"He's sold on you already."

"I don't know about that, but I can barely think straight around him."

"You're falling for him, aren't you?"

Straightening up, I stammer, "I—it's too early."

"Too early to fall or too early to admit it?"

"Both?"

"I've always loved your honesty."

That's when I hear a knock at the door.

"Listen, I've got to go. I'll call you later, okay?"

"You better. I want every dirty detail."

I snicker. "Like I ever give you those." Shaking my head, I end the call. Nadine always tries to fish every detail out of me. She was half-cheerful, half-jealous as I told her about everything that's happened over the past weeks.

The second I open the door, the air between us sizzles. Sebastian says nothing, his eyes raking over me. This man can make me shiver with his gaze alone.

His fingers tug at mine and he pushes me inside, hoisting me up against the wall as the door bangs closed. His hands are tight on my waist, his forehead pressed against mine. "You look fucking gorgeous."

With one strong hand, he pushes my tight dress up around my waist, reducing me to a puddle of need when his fingers graze my thigh. "Your skin is so smooth," he growls. I grin with satisfaction. Point for the skin-removal kit.

"And these lips. You know where I want them?"

"Yeah," I tease. "I want you to think about it all night while we're at the restaurant."

"Going to the restaurant seems like a very bad idea right now." His voice is low and throaty, arousing me further.

"Pippa predicted this."

"What?"

"She was here, helping me prepare, and said we might not make it to the restaurant."

"So that's how little Pippa thinks of me."

"Oh, there's nothing little about you." My voice is low and shaky. Sebastian's eyes widen at the sound of it. He presses himself against me, and I can feel how hard he is already.

"I told you I never back off from a challenge. Let's go to the restaurant. I won't touch you again until we leave."

"We'll see about that."

***

The restaurant isn't just fancy. It's Hollywood stars kind of fancy. I swear to God I notice one of my favorite movie directors at a table in a far corner talking to a very well-known star.

"What is this? The weekend getaway from LA?" I whisper as we advance inside the restaurant.

"You could say that."

"Are there paparazzi around here?" Granted, with stars parading around they'd take less interest in Sebastian, but still.

"No, the restaurant has a strict policy, even outside the perimeter. No cameras allowed. Don't worry, the world won't know I'm your dirty little secret." Though his tone is playful, there is an edge to it I don't like.

"I want to keep Dirk in the dark. I don't care if the world knows."

That puts a genuine smile on his face. Despite promising he won't touch me, Sebastian has kept his hand at the small of my back from the moment we stepped out of the car. I settle into his touch, wishing we could stay like this until the night is over, and even longer. We're seated at the edge of the terrace, where the breeze is strongest. I inhale deeply, letting the air fill me.

"I love the breeze."

"I know, that's why I requested a table here," Sebastian says. I lock my gaze on him. At once, my stomach does a somersault. We've done this before, yet it feels so different. I have to wrap my head around the fact that we're on a date.

After the waiter brings us the menu, I ask, "Are you going to play caveman again and order for me?"

His expression is best summed up by the word well.

"Don't bother," I say, peeking at the table next to me. I lower my voice. "I want what they're having. Steak with that brownish sauce. My mouth is already watering."

"You're adorable."

I pout, tugging with my teeth at my lower lip in an attempt to turn that adorable into irresistible. I want to be a sexy vixen tonight. Remembering I'm wearing bright red lipstick, I almost face palm myself. Instead, I lift my hand in front of my mouth, pretending to inspect that tall candle in front of us while I run my tongue over my teeth vigorously to make sure I don't have lipstick on them. Sebastian looks on the verge of laughter. Okay, sexy vixen was a bad idea. I'll try to be myself. When the waiter asks what I'd like to drink, I order a Sex on the Beach. At Sebastian's inquisitive look, I explain, "It's only appropriate. We're in a coast town, and later on, we'll have sex. And I'm rambling. Jeez, you make me nervous."

He offers me a smile, asking casually, "How was your day?"

"Much better after a certain someone left my office."

"Someone. . . hm. . . Do I know him?"

Joining his game, I say, "Oh, he's my current

client."

"Do you like him?" Sebastian teases.

"He's smart and hot. That combo should be illegal."

"Why is that?"

"Because it's irresistible."

We pause as the waiter comes with our drinks. Sebastian orders the food. Steak for both of us and an appetizer. I slurp from my cocktail, and the alcohol immediately calms some of my nerves.

"What else do you like about him?"

"His family." The words are out of my mouth before I can stop myself.

Sebastian's eyes widen, an unreadable expression taking hold of his features. "That's lovely to hear."

Feeling this deserves more of an explanation, I add quickly, "I've always hungered for a family, and yours is so. . ."

"Big? Loud? Noisy?"

"Perfect. And they're very warm. Don't worry, I won't intrude or anything. Pippa was the one who offered to—"

He holds up a hand to stop me. "My family already loves you. If you like their company, you can do whatever you like. You wouldn't intrude. In fact, I'd like nothing better than for you to get closer to them."

"Okay." I slurp from my cocktail, wondering—again—how different Sebastian is from the men I've dated. They postponed until the last possible moment introducing me to their family, as if they thought I'd be expecting a ring the next second. I rarely imagined that, but as I sip from my drink again, a crazy thought rumbles in my head. Ava Bennett would sound so elegant. Even my initials would look beautiful in my signature. A.B. Oh crap, I'm only on my first Sex on the Beach. I'll be picking names for our imaginary kids by the time I drink the second one. You're in this deep, Ava.

"What are you thinking about? You have a beautiful smile."

"A and B—" I stop midsentence, horrified.

"Are the start of the alphabet?" Sebastian raises his eyebrows.

"Never mind." The waiter saves me, putting a large plate with three different kinds of spreads—orange, white, and blue—in front of us. "This looks delicious." Immediately, I smear some of the blue stuff on the bread and take a bite.

"I love your appetite for food," Sebastian comments.

"Why, thank you."

"Actually, I love your appetite for everything."

"What do you mean?" I ask through mouthfuls.

"You put passion in all things. Your work, your food. Me."

I giggle. "Especially you."

Midway through dinner—and my second cocktail—I lose my pseudo-first-date jitters. At some point, Sebastian leaned over the table, laying his fingers over mine in a gentle touch. He's kept them there the whole time.

We've been eating and laughing loudly for what feels like hours, when someone stops at our table: a woman in her thirties with beautiful red hair and legs up to her armpits. I bet she can play vixen, no problem. Remarkably, I don't feel threatened. I'm sure the fact that Sebastian interlaces his fingers with mine while looking at her with disdain contributes to that.

"Sebastian, long time, no see." She gives me a curt nod.

"I didn't have the impression you wanted to see me at all the last time we talked. Ava, this is Lisa."

Lisa narrows her eyes. Clearly, she was expecting a different welcome. "I see you found another trophy." She points at me, scanning me up and down.

"I see you found another sponsor." Both Sebastian and Lisa turn to look at her date. He looks vaguely familiar, but I can't place him. "He doesn't have quite the caliber of the last one. Or do you have multiples now?" Lisa purses her lips as her companion joins us. He's a plump man in his late fifties.

"My, my, Sebastian Bennett." He holds his hand out, and Sebastian shakes it politely but coldly. He and I exchange pleasantries, and when he tells me his name, I realize why he looks familiar. He's a local media mogul.

"Lisa's told me a lot about you," he tells Sebastian. "Maybe we could get together, discuss some business opportunities."

"Maybe." It's clear from Sebastian's voice he has no intention of doing that.

"Did you tell him the good news?" the man asks Lisa. "We're getting married."

"Good for you." Sebastian smiles, but it doesn't reach his eyes.

"Let's go, Lisa. We're interrupting their date."

Sebastian shakes his head as he watches them leave. We return to our course, and after about ten minutes of silence, I ask tentatively, "Sebastian?"

"Hmm." He's lost in thought, watching his plate. A frown is on his face that wasn't there before the interruption.

"What was that?"

He takes a sip of wine, leaning back in his chair. "Lisa and I dated a few years back."

"I kind of gathered that. What happened?"

He watches me for a few seconds, as if considering his words. "There's no point skirting around this, so I'll be straightforward. I thought she loved me. She loved my money. After two years of dating, I found her fucking someone at the golf club. She told me to my face she was after my bank account."

"That's horrible. I'm sorry."

"Yeah, well." He makes a dismissive gesture with his hand, but I can tell this is still bothering him. "It was my own fault. I should've looked at the signs earlier. They were there to see."

"Like what?"

Sebastian shakes his head, giving me a smile laced

with bitterness. "She barely made time for me, and when she did, it was only so we could attend whatever social event was most popular. If I brought the issue up, she tossed in my face that I didn't make time for her either, that I gave priority to my family over her. She never wanted to attend any family gatherings, said they were boring."

"It sounds like you dodged a bullet."

"Bullets are all I had for years."

"Surely not all women were after your money."

"Some weren't, directly. But they were more interested in what they could get from me, like a leg up in society or in their careers. I was naive about this at first. Growing up in my family, I thought my parents were the norm. Finding someone, falling in love, staying in love and having a family. It seemed simple enough. The reality turned out different. I was trying to wrap my mind around the idea that I'll end up like that schmuck Lisa's marrying. Knowing she wants to tie the knot with my bank account, but preferring that to being alone."

"Sebastian," I admonish. "I told you before money isn't all that people see in you."

"Money complicates everything. It changes what people see in you."

"Not all people."

"What do you see in me?" He wiggles his eyebrows. Flirty Sebastian's back. Good.

"Look who's fishing for compliments now."

"Humor me. Hot and smart don't count. You already said that." His eyes glint with mischief, but I detect a hinge of insecurity in his playful tone. The thought that even a man like him—especially him—has doubts, breaks my heart.

"You are funny, caring, and loyal to your family." Before I can stop myself, I add, "You are the only man I've felt safe with." I suck in my breath. "Emotionally, I mean."

"I know what you meant," he says softly. Taking my hand in his, he plants a small kiss right in the center of my palm, sending electrifying sparks dancing across my skin.

Why am I so open with him? With other men, I guarded my feelings because I was scared that saying them out loud would send them running for the hills. With Sebastian, I have no such fears. Maybe because I know I'll lose him anyway.

"For what it's worth, you're unlike any other woman I've met. You make me feel. . . everything."

The waiter interrupts us. "Can I get you another round of drinks?"

"We're good." Sebastian doesn't take his eyes off me, and the waiter gets the drift, leaving at once.

"I wanted another cocktail."

"Bad idea. You're tipsy already; you'd get drunk. I'd rather you be sober to feel all the delicious things I'll do to you."

"So much talking," I complain, brushing my ankle across his. "Show me."

"Patience."

"Then tell me." I smile wickedly, seeing Sebastian lick his lips as I drop my shoe and lift my leg higher up on his thigh, under the table.

"I'll take each nipple in my mouth and suck until you writhe beneath me." At once, heat pools between my legs. Sebastian drops his voice to a whisper. "I'll do the same to your clit, until. . ."

"Yes?"

"You want to know more?"

"Uh-huh."

"I will make love to you hard and wild, Ava. And you'll be begging for more."

"More." My voice is breathy, but I'm not ashamed at all. Sebastian opens me up in every way. Emotionally, sexually. I have no restraints with him, and it feels damn good. I push my leg even higher up his inner thigh. "Tell me more."

"No. Now it's time to show you."

Chapter Twenty-Three

Ava

The next half hour passes in a haze. In the cab, Sebastian keeps me close to him, one arm around my shoulders, while I lean against him. Keeping our fingers interlaced, he plants kisses on my neck, running his lips up and down. The move is gentle, but it arouses me to no end. No matter what he does, Sebastian can undo me. Once we're inside the apartment, we barely make it to his room with our clothes on. By the way he kisses me, I know he left the gentle touches back in the cab.

"I will be rough tonight," he growls against my skin. "I can't be otherwise."

"I want you to be rough. Don't hold back, Sebastian."

He captures my mouth with urgency, cupping my face in his hands. His lips are delicious, and I enjoy licking the honey remnants of our desert off them. He presses his body against mine. He's already hard for me.

"You drive me crazy," he mutters.

"Back at you."

His hands are everywhere, fisting my hair, grazing the skin on my thighs. He pushes my dress up and attempts to hoist me up on the vanity.

"Not so fast." I push him away, amused at his confused expression. When I drop to my knees, he lets out a sharp exhale. With sure hands, I pop the button and unzip his pants, pushing them down past his ass.

I palm his erection over his boxers, taking immense pleasure in seeing him come undone. Keeping my eyes on him, I push down his boxers too, freeing his shaft. In one quick move, I run my tongue along it.

"Ava!"

Sebastian grips the furniture behind him, leaning his head back. Wrapping my palm around his erection, I pump up and down.

"You're so good, Ava."

Slickness pools between my thighs at his words.

"That's enough."

I retreat, frowning. "But we both like it."

"I want to make love to you." He hoists me up. "If you continue with your wonderful mouth, we won't get to that at all."

I giggle as Sebastian finishes what he started earlier, namely removing my dress and underwear. When I'm completely naked, he takes a moment for his eyes to rove over my body before pushing me onto the bed and lunging over me. Sebastian sucks my bottom lip while kneading my breast with one strong hand. My already hard nipples become too sensitive for his touch, and at the same time hunger for more of his ministrations.

"You're greedy tonight," I whisper.

"I'll always be greedy for you."

My breath catches as Sebastian reaches to the nightstand, retrieving a condom. Then he kneels back, ripping the package open and sliding the condom on. He hitches one of my legs on his shoulder, and then the other. He rubs himself against my entrance, teasing me. I've never been so slick in my life. I want him so much I feel I'm going to break out of my skin.

Sebastian drives into me with one hard move, whipping my breath away. My back arches, my pelvis lifting to meet him. With this angle, he fills me up even deeper than before. A slow tremble spreads through me from the spot where our bodies are joined. It's subtle yet so devastating I don't know what to do with myself. I will come undone from this one tiny quiver. It spreads through me like a hurricane.

"Sebastian, oh God." Taking deep breaths, I focus on the impossibly intense sensation of having him inside me. As he rocks in and out of me, arousal races through me, his strokes bringing me relief, and at the same time, inciting the burning need for more. He fills me so completely, stretching me more with every movement.

He's as rough as he promised, and I love it. There is no restraint in him as he slams in and out of me, giving and taking pleasure in equal measure. I lose myself in the swirls of sensations, sliding in and out of reality, his grunts of pleasure being the only thing grounding me.

"Fuck, you feel so good, Ava," Sebastian mutters, groaning with pleasure. His expert fingers flick my clit, making me come undone. My pulse ratchets up as pleasure dances along my nerve endings, erupting into stings. Sebastian plunges deep inside me with ferocious moves, his desperation igniting an orgasm deep inside me. I writhe, bucking my hips, fire ripping through me. He scoops my ass up, driving into me with even more desperation. Pleasure sears me, singeing my center. I don't know if it's icy or flaming darts shooting through me, but the pressure building in my core explodes with a vengeance as I push myself into him. It extends into tendrils of relief gripping my entire body. I close my eyes as Sebastian rasps out my name, release engulfing us both.

Chapter Twenty-Four

Sebastian

I wake up before her the next morning and move to the living room so I don't disturb her. As is my habit, I open my laptop, checking the latest e-mails and reports. My mind starts making a list of people I want to call and e-mail, and then I realize I'm being an ass. Ava's here; I won't waste my time working. It can all wait until Monday.

A few minutes later, I hear her approach with quick steps. When I turn around, I let out a grunt. She's completely naked.

"Jesus, woman. Do you want to make me crazy this early on?"

"I always want to do that." She smiles coyly as I pull her into my lap. I find myself searching for ways to keep her happy. I want to anticipate her every need and fulfill it, because seeing her happy makes me happy.

"Why don't you get dressed? We can go get breakfast. I know a restaurant about twenty minutes from here. You'll love it. Afterward we could go to the club. We can do whatever you like there. Swim, play tennis, golf."

She licks her lips, moving her hot little body against me, but she doesn't look impressed with my offer.

"If you want to do something else, I'm open to alternatives."

I try to anticipate what she'll say, running a number of scenarios through my head. Shopping might come up. I used to give my credit card to other women, but I'll actually enjoy watching her try on clothes.

"Let's stay in," she whispers the words playfully, resting her palms on my chest. "I like having you all to myself, and you spoil me so much when it's just the two of us."

"What do you mean? I spoil you all the time."

"Yeah, but more when we're alone. I don't want anything today. No club and no fancy restaurant. I just want you."

"We'll stay in." I kiss her senseless, pulling her tighter to me, taking her mouth like a man possessed. If this woman knew how strongly I feel for her, she'd lock me up. In the month I've known her, I've let her in more than anyone in years except my family.

Letting my guard down is a dangerous thing. I should take a step back and clear my head, consider everything I have to lose. It'd be the sensible thing to do. But I can't be sensible around her.

She's too good to be real, and it's killing me. I lay her on the couch, doing to her the things I was too desperate to do last night. I first cup her breasts, pulling her nipples between my lips until they're rock hard. Then I stop and lift up, looking her straight in the eyes as I lower my hand between her legs. The expression in her eyes makes me want to hug her and not let go. I can't get enough of her. And she just wants me. Not the things I can buy her, but me.

I drop my mouth to the skin between her breasts, trailing down in a straight path, past her navel, right to her clit.

"Sebastian. . ." She arches against my mouth when I slide a finger inside her. The way she clenches around it is beautiful. She's so ready, and so close. I keep my eyes on her chest, watching it heave up and down with increasing speed. A lovely blush spreads on her skin as I continue to pleasure her with my tongue and finger. My balls tighten when her fingers claw at the surface of the couch, as if she wants to fist the fabric to ground herself.

"That's it, Ava. I want to see you come."

Closing her eyes, she lets out a beautiful cry as she spasms around my finger. I unhitch my lips from her tender spot, kissing down her inner thighs then up her torso until I'm over her completely.

Grinning, she says, "Now that's how every day should start. Who needs coffee if you can have an orgasm?"

"Not sure how I feel about my skills being compared to coffee, but—"

"Coffee is important to me." She nods very seriously, which only makes me guffaw.

"I suppose that makes it all right."

She laughs softly, pushing herself against my chest, looking up at me. "I don't know about you, but I'm not hungry. I ate a lot last night. Let's swim."

"Let's."

"Uh, I just realized I don't have a bikini."

"There is one in my closet somewhere."

"You have a woman's bikini in your closet?"

My hand is over her breast and I swear I feel her heart stop for a second.

"It's Pippa's. She bought it a few months back so she can swim when she's here, but she hasn't used it yet."

Her body goes lax underneath me. "Sorry. I'm silly."

"No, you're not." I trace her lips with my fingers. "But do you really think I'd tell you to wear the bikini of a woman I've slept with?"

She shrugs. "A man once tried to convince me that the thong I found in his pocket belonged to me. It had glitter on it. I hate glitter."

"He was a jerk." A vein pulses in my neck at the thought that anyone dared to hurt and humiliate her; that they didn't appreciate how wonderful she is. I do, and I will make sure to let her know every damned day.

"Yeah, he was. I figured most men are."

"I'm not most men."

"I see that." She smiles, this time coyly, and I lower myself to kiss her. Ava pushes her body into me, but she's not looking for a sexual response, just reassurance. This is one of the rare moments—like when I overdosed her with Tylenol—when she lets the vulnerable part of her show. At least her body does. I know she won't admit that aloud. Yet. I'll earn her trust. I don't want her to feel like she has to hide anything from me.

After we pull apart, we go upstairs. She puts the bikini on, I jump into swimming shorts, and then we go outside.

"I can't believe you have your own swimming pool. Why do you ever leave your home?"

"Work?"

"Oh yeah, that."

Facing the pool, she raises her arms, closing her eyes. "I love the wind," she announces unnecessarily, because I can read it on her sweet face. She enjoys it like it's an expensive wine or caviar.

It's refreshing to be around someone who finds happiness in such small things. Other women would've snorted at the idea of a weekend in. Who wants to stay in when there is a hot, expensive restaurant opening? Or so many shops she could hit? I remember those days as if they happened in another life. Fake, meaningless. No matter how much I gave a woman, it wasn't enough. Her birthday? A new car was in order or diamonds as expensive as a car. I didn't mind, not at all. I'm glad to share and make a woman happy, but I'd never dreamed women only wanted from me the luxury my money could buy.

Ava wants me, and in a few short months, I'll

have to let her go.

I enter the water first, and she follows.

"Gaaaaaah," Ava exclaims. "The water is freezing. Fuck."

I don't get the rest of the sentence because her teeth are chattering. I hurry to her, wrapping my arms around her as she presses her breasts against me.

"The water is a bit chilly. It's not freezing." I try not to laugh at her, really, I do; but I end up laughing anyway.

"Yeah, a thousand degrees chillier than I expected. Why didn't you tell me?" She looks at me accusingly, but all it does is make me want to kiss her. I rub her back and arms.

"You'll be warmer in a sec."

"Yeah, right." Despite her protest, she lays her head on my shoulder as I continue to rub her. After a few minutes, she says, "That's better."

"If you swim, it'll be even better."

We end up swimming for hours, intermingled with lying in the sun and fooling around like we're teenagers. That's what I love most about Ava. She makes me forget who I am.

"I'm hungry," I announce at lunch.

"Me too. Let's shower."

***

Ava showers first, and then I do. She's sitting on the bed punching a pillow when I come out of the shower.

"Why are you beating the crap out of that pillow?"

"I'm not; I'm picking my hair off it. Sorry, I didn't realize I left hair everywhere, including your pillow."

"Well, you should be sorry for hijacking my pillow in the first place." I hug her from behind, wrapping my arms around her waist and pressing my crotch in her delicious ass.

"Like you minded." She turns to face me with a devilish grin. "You slept on my boobs."

"Men are resourceful in times of need. You didn't just take my pillow. You hijacked the entire bed."

Her mouth forms an O. "I did not."

"I should've taken a picture. You practically kicked me out of the bed. You did that in your apartment, too."

"I won't believe that unless you show me proof." She pinches her nose, frowning. "I'm getting really hungry. You don't want to argue with me when I'm hungry. Will you cook again?"

Tilting my head, I laugh against the soft skin of her shoulder.

"So, the princess wants to be spoiled. What do you want to eat?"

"I get to pick?"

"Yeah."

"I don't care what I eat, really. As long as you cook naked."

"Feisty, I like it."

With her hand in mine, I make my way to the living room.

"I'll grill us something," I say.

"Cool. I want to help. Give me stuff to do."

"Nah, stay there and look pretty. It'll be safer for both of us."

She squints, breaking into a grin. "So you think I'm pretty?"

Wiggling my eyebrows, I say, "Very. Especially when you're naked, like now."

The grill is on the terrace, so we move there as I prepare the meat. We also throw on robes, because the breeze isn't too forgiving. As I watch her savoring every bite, I can't help grinning. I become intoxicated with her enthusiasm and good mood.

"This is the best food ever." Sighing dramatically, she adds, "You are perfect. Can I keep you?"

"Which part of me, my cooking skills or my mad in-bed skills?"

She looks up at me from between her lashes, offering me a seductive smile. "I'll have to wait to see what other skills you have before I decide."

After we finish eating, I ask, "Do you want to go to your place to get some clothes?"

I register a strange surprise in her eyes. She turns her back, pretending to clean the table, and I can't gauge her reaction anymore.

"You want me to stay here the whole weekend?" she asks.

"Of course I do. I'm not nearly done with spoiling you."

"Okay."

Hooking my arms around her waist, I rest my

head in the crook of her neck, inhaling her sweet woman scent.

"Move in here," I find myself saying. She freezes in my arms, and if I'm honest, I'm doing some freezing myself. Well, now it's out there, and it feels damn right. "I want to know you—all of you. I can't get enough of you."

She fidgets in my arms, her ass pressing against me.

"Sebastian. . ."

I breathe out in relief, because there's no protest in her voice, just confusion. Well, since I'm already on a slippery slope, to hell with it. Here goes nothing. Wrapping my arms tighter around her, I whisper against her neck, trailing up to her ear. "I like waking up next to you, and having you here. I like your hair on my pillow, and even getting kicked out of the bed. If I had it my way, I'd spend every minute with you from now until you have to leave."

"Me too." The confession comes like a mouthful of fresh air. Damn it, why does this feel so good and so right?

Finally, she turns to face me. The mix of emotions in her eyes mirrors my exact feelings. This is uncharted territory for both of us.

"But I'll keep my apartment."

"Sure. Your boss has to believe you live there."

***

We return from her apartment late in the afternoon. The woman owns a lot of clothes, and I grew up with three sisters. At sunset, I grab my woman, a bottle of wine, and two glasses, and we sit outside, watching the sky.

"This is hands down the best view of the sunset ever. It should be in one of those guides for tourists. Great house, great view," Ava comments.

"Hmmm, could this be the best because you're in my arms?"

"Oh yeah, that too. Better not put it in the tourist guide though. Wouldn't want visitors expecting this. I don't like to share." She shudders lightly in my arms, and I hug her more.

"You won't have to share me, Ava. Don't worry about that."

"I do worry. That I'm not enough."

"What are you talking about?"

"I wasn't enough for my exes. If I was, they wouldn't have done what they did." She pastes a smile on her face, like it's a joke, but I can see right through her.

"Ava." I cup her head in my hands. "Any man who doesn't spoil you every day doesn't deserve you."

"That applies to every man except you." She giggles.

I grin, towering over her, and drag my knuckles lightly over her cheeks before kissing her. This sweet woman, with a body made for sin and a smile to match. She's barely moved in, and I already dread the day she'll leave.

Chapter Twenty-Five

Ava

The next three weeks go by in a blink of an eye, or so it seems. There's plenty to do at the office—which I am used to. What I am not used to is coming home and not being alone. Since the Bennetts found out I moved in with Sebastian, they find an excuse to drop by every other evening.

Like the eternal pessimist I am, I keep waiting for the fairy tale to end. If something is too good to be true, it probably is—that's what Mom always said. The trouble? Sebastian's more amazing with each passing day, and his skills in bed are unmatched. Seriously. This man can do things with his mouth that should be illegal. Okay, so maybe fairy tale wasn't the right name for this.

Unless it's the adult version, that is.

"Sebastian, stop, or I'll be late," I say, without much conviction in my voice. He smiles against my swollen flesh and lifts his mouth. He keeps his finger on my clit, applying pressure.

"You're the one who said you want to be woken up like this every morning," he whispers in my ear as I dig my fingers in his back, my breath frantic. Tension builds inside me. My hands roam over the hard lines on his naked torso, his manly scent overwhelming me.

"I don't, thiwatonow," I babble, spectacularly aware of all my nerve endings. The rhythmic movement of his finger ignites me.

"I love it when you forget English."

That's when I come. Hard and fast. I plant my heels in the mattress, bucking against his strong hand. He captures my orgasm in a kiss, holding me close to him until my breathing and heart rate slow down.

"Good morning," Sebastian says.

When I'm certain I can string coherent words together, I say, "Good morning to you too, handsome." Supporting himself on his forearms and knees, he towers over me. "I really need to shower and go meet your sister." It's Saturday morning, and Pippa and I scheduled a girls' day out for today.

"You're taking advantage of me, you know that?" he asks, tracing my lower lip with his thumb.

"And I'm enjoying every minute of it."

I shower quickly, putting on a light green dress. When I arrive in the living room, Sebastian's talking on the phone. He has his business face on. I catch the word senator, and grin. Yes! This is Sebastian Bennett, ladies and gentlemen. Wakes me up with an orgasm, and then talks senators into doing whatever he wants. More proof that his mouth is magic.

Tiptoeing around the place, I make myself a sandwich and eat it, then strap my sandals on. Sebastian catches up with me as I'm about to leave the apartment.

"You're taking over my family." Hooking his arms around my waist, he pulls me to him for a kiss. He lightly brushes my lips, but he's only wearing boxers, and being this close to his bare chest is a dangerous endeavor. I might end up not leaving, after all.

"Does it bother you?"

"Well, I'm a greedy bastard and want you all to myself."

"You know what I mean."

"No, Ava, why would it bother me? You're not my dirty little secret. Even though you can be dirty in bed."

"I thought you liked it," I say shyly.

He pushes me against the door, spreading my legs with his knees. In a quick move, he pins my hands above my head. "I love it when you're feisty. You look at me like there isn't anyone else in the world you'd rather be with."

"Well, there isn't," I say truthfully.

"I'd better let you go, beautiful."

"You call me beautiful a lot."

"It's true."

"Mmmm. . ." He plants a soft kiss on me and lets my hands go, caressing my shoulders. Sebastian doesn't just say those things, he makes me feel them by the way he looks at and touches me. He worships my skin and my lips.

When we break apart, he says, "Have fun."

"Jealous you're not joining us?"

Sebastian steps back, finally leaving me free to move from the door. "It's a girls' day out. Enjoy it. Besides, I have a hunch Pippa's going to take you to her favorite interior design shop. I love my sister, but spending more than five minutes there makes me want to punch someone."

I grin. "She did mention she wants to go there. Do you want me to buy anything?"

"If there's anything you think fits here, go ahead."

I lick my lips, swallowing twice. "You want me to bring my own decorations in your apartment?"

"Yeah." There is a strange glint in his eyes as he leans against the wall, folding his arms across his chest. "I want you to feel at home here."

"But I'll only stay here for another six weeks and then my placement will be over." Suddenly, no air reaches my lungs. I open my mouth to breathe and there is no oxygen.

Sebastian's jaw ticks, the glint in his eyes more pronounced. "Let's pretend it won't." Oh, God, I trust this man with everything I have: my body, my heart, and my mind. I'm afraid I'll leave all of that here after I'm gone.

Deciding to be naughty and lighten up the mood, I add, "Pippa said we're going to a strip club in the afternoon."

He stiffens. "What?"

I bite my tongue to keep a straight face. "Yeah, apparently there's one with a new show, where the audience is also encouraged to get. . . involved."

In a millisecond, Sebastian unhitches himself from the wall, striding to me. "I won't allow you to—"

I burst out laughing, unable to keep up the charade. I'd make a terrible spy.

"You're pulling my leg, aren't you?"

"Guilty. I love it when you go all alpha on me. I mean, Pippa keeps talking about going to a strip club, but she's not serious."

Sebastian's smile melts into a frown. My stomach churns.

"What is it? You look worried."

Taking a deep breath, he says, "I should spend more time with Pippa. She closed herself off from me after her divorce, and I'm not sure how she's really doing."

"You're out to save the world, aren't you?"

"Nah, I'm too selfish. I care about my family. And you."

My heart bounces. "I'll make sure Pippa has fun today. I'll take her mind off things."

"Thank you. That means a lot to me. She's not even talking much to Alice or Summer. Maybe she'll open up to you." Sebastian looks at me as if I indeed told him I'm saving the world today. I feel like Wonder Woman.

"You don't have to do everything on your own, you know. I like to help."

"I see that. But if helping will include strippers, I'll have a word with my dearest sister."

***

A day filled with estrogen and girly activities turns out to be exactly what Pippa and I need. We're going textbook on this. Manis and pedis are first on our list, followed by hours of shopping. We stop by the interior design shop, and while Pippa buys half their stock, I only buy a small fruit bowl. It'll look great in Sebastian's apartment, and it'll be a nice, unobtrusive reminder of our time together in six weeks.

The thought depresses me, and as I pay for the item, I find my lower lip quivering and my eyes stinging. Soon, a burning ache settles in my chest. I'm missing him already. God, how will I survive my Sebastian-less future? Thankfully, Pippa drags me to a cupcake shop next. Nothing like an overdose of sugar to stuff dark thoughts right where they belong, in the recesses of my mind.

Turns out, I don't need any spy skills to make Pippa talk about the divorce. Over coffee and cupcakes, she opens up to me.

"Sebastian has to stop worrying about me. I'm not okay, of course I'm not, but I have my big girl pants on." Looking sadly at her empty plate, she adds, "If I keep stuffing myself with cupcakes, I will literally become a big girl."

"He's your older brother. He'll always worry."

"Yeah, I know. It's always been like this. There were two camps when we grew up, the older ones and the younger ones. I remember Logan, Sebastian, and I making a pact when I was about eleven years old that we'd always look after the younger ones. Of course, Sebastian, being the oldest of the lot, took it upon himself to take care of everyone."

Adoration for her older brother is etched on her every feature. Her smile is contagious, and I find myself imagining the scene and a younger Sebastian being as bossy as now. I feel like hugging her.

She lounges back in her chair, crossing her legs and arms and keeping her eyes on the wooden table. "And now I feel like I failed them. I mean, how did I choose so wrong? Was I blind?"

Ah, so that's why she isn't talking to her family about it. The urge to hug her grows stronger.

"Pippa, I've seen enough of your family to know that they'll love you no matter what. None of them thinks you've failed. If anything, they're relieved you got rid of—"

Her gaze snaps up to me, her shoulders going rigid. "Don't say his name."

"—him. They want you to be happy, honestly. And your sisters aren't kids anymore. It's not like you have to be a role model or something. Don't push them away. You've always had each other's backs, didn't you?"

"Yeah, when that meant covering for mischief, or going through a high school breakup. But every single person in my family—that includes about half of the adopted Bennetts—more or less told me he wasn't right for me. I didn't listen, and it turns out they were right. I'm ashamed on top of hurt."

"You're the one shutting them out, and no one's chanting I told you so."

She sighs. "I know. I'm mishandling all of this. I need more time to pull myself together. I tried yoga, meditation, and whatnot to stop feeling like crap about myself. I'm one failed meditation away from trying voodoo."

Pippa says this with a steady voice, but my stomach clenches nonetheless.

I choose my words carefully. "It's okay to wallow for a while, Pippa."

"The problem is I feel the ground slipping from underneath my feet. I'm not wallowing. I'm drowning." For the first time, her voice wavers, and her eyes are glassy as she looks up at me. "I grew up with parents who loved each other to death and brothers who worshipped me. I felt safe. When I started dating, I felt like a sheep among wolves. I thought Terence was different. Turns out he was just better at pretending."

I try to imagine how she must be feeling. Maybe because I grew up without a father, or I'm a natural pessimist, but I went into most of my relationships half expecting them to end badly. Even so, I was brokenhearted when they were over. I can't imagine how a divorce feels to Pippa, who grew up watching her parents' perfect marriage and probably took happily-ever-after as a given.

"It'll get better eventually," I say. "But it'll suck badly for a long while before it does."

To my surprise, Pippa smiles. "That actually makes me feel better."

"Really?" I ask skeptically.

"Yeah. It sounds realistic, gives me something to look forward to." Eyeing my half-eaten cupcake, she adds, "Are you finishing that?"

"No."

With a grin, she draws my plate to her.

It's early afternoon and we're on our way to the beach when I notice a familiar face in the line to an ice-cream stand.

"Anna," I exclaim, stopping dead in my tracks. Anna is my least favorite coworker. Though she's older than I am, she came to the industry later on and has a lower position, which frustrates her. She's nosy and gossipy, and takes immense pleasure in seeing people going through difficult times. "What are you doing here?"

"Took a few days off, and my husband's family lives here." She swings her bushy red hair behind her shoulder. "I'm flying to New York on Monday. Aren't you going to introduce me to your friend?"

"Ah, sure, this is Pippa Bennett, Sebastian's sister. Sebastian's the CEO." I speak very fast, almost babbling.

"You're on a first-name basis with him," Anna remarks, an unpleasant smile appearing on her face.

Pippa takes a step forward. "Everyone in the company is on a first-name basis."

"Everyone also goes shopping with the CEO's sister?" She eyes the bags in our hands. "That's a cozy. . . enterprise."

Welcome to the advertising industry, where everyone is out to get you. Maybe it's like this in every industry, I don't know, but if she takes her gossipy mouth to Dirk, I could be in trouble. He could become suspicious.

"Have you heard about Laney?" Anna asks, referring to one of our colleagues.

"No, haven't had much time to check in with the other girls."

"Dirk fired her."

"What? Why?"

"Well, you know it was her third project with the real estate mogul in LA. Dirk found out she was actually sleeping with him."

Next to me, Pippa stops in the act of searching for something in her bag. When Anna moves forward in the line, it takes me a few good seconds to order my numb feet to follow her. Anna's not done. I can tell that by the hungry look in her eyes.

"It was a scandal at the office, since it hadn't happened in forever. Young girls today, they are so tempted by the forbidden fruit. Lucky I'm married. No temptation for me."

"Yeah, lucky you," I murmur, hunching my shoulders as if a ton of bricks fell on them. "Is Laney okay?"

Anna shrugs. "Haven't talked to her."

Typical.

"Well, it was nice meeting you, Anna." Pippa's words come out clipped. "But we must get going. We have a full schedule for today."

Anna purses her lips. She doesn't say anything more than, "It was nice meeting you too, Pippa. Bye, Ava."

"She's such a bitch," Pippa hisses when Anna's out of earshot.

"Yep."

"You're worried." It's a statement, not a question.

"Wouldn't you be?"

"Listen, your boss won't find out. And if he does, Sebastian will sort it out. We have shark lawyers, but it wouldn't even come to that. Sebastian can be very persuasive."

I straighten. "I don't need Sebastian to save me. He's got enough on his plate already, watching over your family."

Pippa gives me a long look. "Oh, I could tell you weren't looking for a knight in shining armor since I met you." At my raised eyebrows, she adds, "I'm the people reader in the family, haven't you heard that?"

I shrug noncommittally, even though I do remember Sebastian telling me that. It scares me.

"Anyway, as I was saying, you didn't strike me as the type who needs a knight, but an equal—someone who doesn't save you, but who you can count on."

I gulp. Holy crap, she does read people well.

"He's my brother, and I'm biased, obviously, but Sebastian fits that role perfectly."

I burst out laughing. I can't help it. "Pippa, I recognize a sales pitch when I hear one. I've moved in with your brother already. You don't have to sell him to me."

"Yeah, I do. You said Sebastian has enough on his plate with the family." Pippa gives me a long look, and then her features light up in a smile. "You are part of the family now."

Chapter Twenty-Six

Ava

The meeting with Anna didn't have any consequences, but I know I'm playing with fire. For the next few weeks, I am careful. Dirk calls more often to check in, but that's normal because we're approaching the final phase of the project. Whenever I talk to him, I make sure to speak of Sebastian in the most impersonal way possible, and I asked Sebastian and Logan to follow suit in case Dirk contacts them.

As the show approaches, the hard work pays off big time. We score a myriad of high-class and exclusive editorials, and there are more requests than ever from overseas giant luxury retailers to partner up for distribution. Martha and I are very pleased. Sadly, I don't think she'll remain at Bennett Enterprises too long after the show. She keeps talking about wanting to move to Seattle. The two of us come up with more publicity ideas to keep building on the momentum.

I take it upon myself to sway Logan, the most rigid CFO I've met, to pour more budget into the campaign. Who would've thought that Logan, with his angelic eyes and I'm the nice brother line, would be so impossibly stubborn? I spend an entire

Saturday at the office going over the new budget proposal with him and Sebastian. Thankfully, Sebastian sides with me—sleeping with the CEO totally has its perks—but it still takes hours to convince Logan.

"You know what's unacceptable?" Logan asks, tossing the report on the desk and leaning back in his chair.

"That you've changed your mind about the budget? Again?" I give him a murderous look. I swear to God, I will forge his signature and call it a day if he goes back on his decision one more time. "Sebastian, you're a very democratic CEO. Tell him it's a done deal."

Logan narrows his eyes, while Sebastian bursts out laughing and says from behind me, "We do things differently here. It's unhealthy for a company if one person has too much decision-making power. Logan isn't changing his mind again." Stepping to my side, he gives Logan a pointed look. "Are you?"

Logan flinches. Almost imperceptibly, but he does, which brings me immense pleasure. "No, I was about to say that it's unacceptable that it's five o'clock on a Saturday, and we're the only three morons in the office."

"You want to call in more people?" Sebastian asks skeptically.

"I want to get out." Logan leaps to his feet, pacing the room. "I need to stretch my legs."

Sebastian grins. "Well, Alice did ask us—"

"And we stupidly said no. Can't believe I turned

her down so I could have you two crawling up my ass the entire day." As is always the case when they tease each other, Logan sports a flashy smile.

"But we can still play a bit if we leave right now."

"What are you guys talking about?"

"She's officially part of the family, isn't she?" Logan asks Sebastian, his thumb pointing at me.

Sebastian nods, which fills me with all kinds of warm and fuzzy feelings.

"You're coming to a soccer game," Logan announces.

"Oh. I thought it was off-season now, but what do I know? Who's playing?"

Both brothers burst out laughing.

"We're playing," Logan offers.

"Define 'we.'"

"Our family," Sebastian explains.

I snort, convinced they're humoring me. "No, you're not."

"You'll see." Logan rubs his hands together in excitement. "Let's go."

"But now that you've approved the budget, I want to make some calls and set up—"

"It's Saturday." Logan emphasizes the last word as if I somehow missed the point. "You'll find that most people don't look forward to hearing from you today. Sebastian, convince your woman to move her sweet ass off that chair and join us."

"Oh, I can convince her in no time. One question, is sex at the office suddenly acceptable?" Sebastian inquires. I catch his gaze and we both refrain from laughing.

Logan's face falls. "No."

"I'll go, I'll go. Lucky we're all wearing outdoor clothes." I don't know if they planned it this way, but they both showed up in jeans and t-shirts. My dress is appropriate for a beach, but it's not like I will play anyway.

***

"Whose idea was the soccer thing?" I ask as we get into Sebastian's car. There's a beautiful sunset today, the color of juniper, with some orange thrown in for good measure.

"Alice's," Sebastian and Logan say in unison.

"I didn't know she liked soccer so much," I say.

"Sebastian and I used to play all the time when we were kids. Eventually she learned it too," Logan says.

"That's not how I remember it, Logan," Sebastian says, looking at Logan in the rearview mirror.

"Well, no," Logan admits. "Alice was a few years older than the little ones, but still closer in age to them than to Pippa, Sebastian, and me, so she wasn't part of the older group. We told her that if she wanted in with us, she had to learn to play ball. She actually did it. She practiced in secret and surprised us all."

"Surprised is an understatement." Sebastian turns the wheel with a nostalgic frown. "She kicks ass. She's even better than Logan."

"No, she's not," Logan says indignantly.

"Did she or did she not kick your ass when you played against her last year?"

"That was one time," Logan says.

"And there was the—"

"Okay, okay, she's great at it," Logan admits, clearly wanting to avoid more proof of Alice's superior skills. "You'll see, Ava."

"Actually, I'll have no idea. I've never played or watched a game. Except in high school, when I had a crush on a jock. At his games, I was more preoccupied with eyeing him than paying attention to what was happening on the field."

"A jock?" Sebastian gives me an incredulous look, but Logan perks up.

"Don't look so surprised. He was hot, but he didn't know I existed. In senior year, he asked me to tutor him in chemistry. He managed to crush all my hopes in one sentence." I shake my head at the memory. "His IQ was insultingly low. He was as dumb as jocks come."

I was expecting this to garner me appreciative nods, but both brothers are suspiciously silent. And the silence stretches. . .

Uh-oh.

"I was a jock," Logan says seriously.

Cringing, I glance at Sebastian for a sign that Logan is pulling my leg, but nope. "Seeing as how you are a CFO, my dumb comment doesn't apply to you." I smile brightly as I say this, but Logan raises both eyebrows. I spend the rest of the drive trying to get back in his good graces. When we arrive at the Bennett house and get out of the car, I completely put my foot in my mouth.

"Wait a minute, if you were a jock, how come Alice's better than you?"

In response, Logan narrows his eyes and walks away, just as Pippa comes to greet us. She looks after Logan with raised eyebrows, then shrugs and walks to us.

"I'm not sure Logan will forgive me anytime soon," I tell Sebastian.

"That's okay. He needs to have his ego taken down somewhat," he replies.

"I agree," Pippa says. "Haven't met the woman yet who can do it."

"I should introduce him to Nadine. She has a degree in it." Also in falling in love with jerks. Except, Logan is not a jerk. On second thought, I should really tell Nadine to come down here.

"Oh, you should totally introduce her to him." Pippa's eyes widen.

"What's this, Pippa?" Sebastian inquires, putting one arm around his sister's waist and the other around mine. "I thought I was your current matchmaking project."

"Oh, you two are a done deal." She gestures between the two of us. I lower my eyes to my feet. Yeah, for one more month, we're a done deal. Then we'll have to deal with the aftermath, which will be too much heartbreak. That's a done deal too. Sebastian's voice is uneven as he tells me I'll have to play at least one round with them before I dismiss soccer for good. His grip on my waist tightens as he leads me to the immense garden turned soccer pitch—otherwise also known as the place where Ava Lindt will make a complete ass of herself. There are even two nets.

I try to get out of it, using my dress and sandals as an excuse. Pippa makes the case that she's played in a dress before, and Alice gives me the extra pair of sneakers she brought just in case.

"I won't be good at it," I mutter for Sebastian's ears only. "I've never played ball without hitting myself or other people. . .you have no idea how much I suck."

Sebastian lifts my jaw, planting a quick kiss on my lips. He moves his mouth to my ear. "You just used ball and suck in one sentence. Do you have any idea what that does to me?"

"Pervert," I hiss as Alice tells us all to take our positions.

Soccer is a family event for the Bennetts. Save for the twins who are overseas, everyone is here. Thankfully, only one couple and their adorable baby, Adrian, from the cohort of adopted Bennetts are here, so all in all, only a dozen people will experience my humiliation firsthand.

Badly. That's how much I can suck. In the span of fifteen minutes, I manage to get hit with a ball three times, the last time in the head. I've also managed to injure three players. I've muttered more apologies in these fifteen minutes than I have in the past year. My right side hurts like a bitch from falling on it, and so does my knee.

"Okay, this is clearly not working," Sebastian says.

"Really? I thought I was doing an exceptional job," I snap.

"I have an idea. Why don't you babysit Adrian, and Jenna can come play?"

I look over to where he's pointing and nod. Jenna is beyond happy when I tell her she can play in my stead, and I'll take care of her son. She practically flies to the field, and plays well.

She, like everyone else, has embraced this sport. I turn my attention to the little bundle in my arms. Apparently, he and I are the only ones around unable to competently kick a ball.

"Well, hello, little baby."

Baby Adrian turns out to be the cutest baby in the world. He doesn't cry once, and smiles at me the entire time. I hug him to my chest. So this is all the fuss about babies. They smell like sugar and heaven, and they radiate happiness. He plays with my hair for a while, and then falls asleep. I redirect my attention to the field, and discover Alice is a bona fide tomboy. The few times I've seen her, she was wearing feminine dresses—and wearing them well, but it's obvious she's as comfortable in sneakers, shorts, and a tank top. Even with my limited understanding of the game, I can tell she and Logan are the best on the field. I cannot properly assess Sebastian's performance, because I'm too preoccupied inspecting how beautifully his muscles contort with effort, but I'm sure he's great. Not that I'm biased or anything.

After what seems like an eternity, the game is

over.

Sebastian walks straight to me, smiling as he gazes down at Adrian. "The two of you seem to be getting along well."

"There's not much I have to do. He's laughed at me the entire time. Look. Oh, he's adorable."

"You're going to be a great mom one day."

His words stir something inside me. I don't know if it's because I'm holding a baby in my lap, but my desire to have a family hits me hard. I've always wanted a large family, but over the past couple of years and unfortunate experiences, I put those dreams on hold. Truth is I didn't see myself starting a family with my past boyfriends. I guess deep down I knew none of them was the one.

Yet as I look at Sebastian explaining the rules of soccer to Adrian as if he expects the toddler will play the next round with them, my heart constricts. This feels too real, beautiful, and perfect. How will I go back to empty afternoons and weekends?

"Can't imagine how your mom managed with all of you," I comment as Mrs. Bennett announces the grill is ready.

"I'll go shower real quick," he informs me. I hug baby Adrian tighter and stare after Sebastian as he enters the house, lost in thought.

"Ava."

I snap my head up, startled to discover Alice standing right in front of me. "Sorry, I wasn't listening."

"What were you thinking about? You looked sad."

Okay, so apparently Alice is the no-bullshit sibling. Something in her attitude demands honesty.

"That I'll have to leave in a few weeks. I don't feel ready to leave all this behind."

"Then don't." Alice shrugs, as if the matter's settled.

"I wish it were that simple."

"Oh puh-lease. Where's the fun in simple?"

I smile, remembering she practiced soccer in secret just to be allowed to be part of the older group. Alice is determined and competitive.

Unexpectedly, she takes baby Adrian from my arms, returns him to his mother, and tells me, "I challenge you to kick balls until you score a goal."

"Alice, we'll be here until the end of time."

"I am patient." She says this so nonchalantly I can't help but laugh. I join her on the field. She defends the post, while I kick the hell out of the ball. Obviously, I manage to kick my own feet twice, falling to my knees. But after a lot of tries, I finally score a goal.

"I scored. I can't believe this." I jump up and down despite my aching knees.

"How does that feel?" Alice asks.

"Like I'm the baddest badass and invincible."

"Good. Was getting here simple?"

I narrow my eyes. "No."

"Point made." She saunters to the grill area without another look back.

Yep. My assessment was spot on. She is the no-bullshit sister. I like her. I join the grill party, only to discover there's no food left. Groaning, I slump in a chair. With the adrenaline leaving me, I'm more aware of the pain in my knees.

"Here, I saved some steak for you before everything was gone," Sebastian says, handing me a plate and kissing my forehead. "Alice did the impossible. She deserves a medal."

"You watched the entire time?" I eat with quick bites.

"Yes. Thought of coming to rescue you, then decided to just watch."

"Very funny. My knees hurt." Pulling up my dress, I wince. Both knees are bloody. I raise my legs, inspecting the damage. "Holy crap."

To my astonishment, Sebastian laughs. "City girl. You never went hiking or stuff, did you?"

"I did too," I reply indignantly. "But I walk on my feet, not my knees."

"Let's get you cleaned up." Sebastian is still sporting a mischievous smile when Mrs. Bennett joins us.

"Oh, dear, you need to tend to those immediately." She points at my knees, looking as worried as I feel.

"That's where we're going," Sebastian informs her.

"Oh, no. You stay here, and I'll take care of her. You gave me nightmares when you were little, always insisting on cleaning your own scratches, doing a half-assed job and getting infected."

I feel my eyes widen, unsure what surprises me

more: that she used the word half-assed or that Sebastian actually cowers a tad. Ah, nothing like a mother's wrath.

"By all means, Mother, take care of Ava. She'll appreciate it more than I did. Ava, be a good girl and let me know if Mom tries to give you antibiotics for a simple scratch."

Mrs. Bennett tsks, and Sebastian takes off with a smile.

"I was a mother hen when they were little," Mrs. Bennett confesses, "but I worried about them all the time. There were so many of them, and at least three of them were up to no good half the time, and the others were covering for them. It was madness." Her smile tells me she wouldn't have had it any other way.

"Isn't that what mothers do? Worry?" I remember my mom always worried about putting food on the table, about my education, about not spending enough time with me. Mostly, she worried about my future. She wanted me to have a better life than she had. I look up at the sky, believing, as I always have, that my mother can hear me, and I smile. Oh, Mother, if you could see me now. I am happy. Very happy indeed.

Mrs. Bennett puts a protective arm around me and leads me inside the house.

***

Sebastian

"What happened to Ava?" Dad asks.

"She scraped her knees. Mom's nursing her."

He pats my shoulder, eyes gleaming with satisfaction. "I'm happy for you, son."

Ah, the dreaded talk with Dad. I knew it was coming. Strangely, now that it's upon me, I even find myself looking forward to it. We both sit on a bench further away from the group.

"Ava's a great girl."

"She is, but don't get your hopes up. When her assignment ends, she'll leave."

Dad nods, as if considering my words. "I told you this before, son, but it bears repeating: nothing is more important than having someone strong to share your life with."

"Dad—"

"Whenever there are ups and downs, we'll be here for you. However, we'll never replace the woman you love. You know how hard those years were before you built your business."

"I do."

"I wouldn't have gotten through them without your mother. Now, I'll go get a beer. Think about what I told you."

***

Ava

The smell of cinnamon and raisins inside the house welcomes me, rich and warm.

"Sit here, dear." She points to the couch in the living room. I sit and wait patiently until she returns with rubbing alcohol and cotton pads. Raising my hands, I intend to relieve her of the items and nurse my knees by myself.

"I'll do it. You can let someone else take care of you once in a while, dear."

"I'm not used to it." It feels wonderful though. I remember when I was sick and Sebastian took care of me, and when Pippa did my hair. "Your son takes good care of me."

"He'd better. That's how I raised him."

I offer her a smile.

"So, let me see your knees. Humor an old lady."

I laugh. "You're not old, Mrs. Bennett." I point to my knees, and she immediately pours alcohol on a pad.

Holy hell, that stings.

"Motherf—" I clamp a hand over my mouth, squeezing my lips together as she tends to my wounds. The burning sensation lasts even after she's done, though it lessens in intensity.

"I want to thank you."

"For what?" I ask, confused.

Mrs. Bennett smiles and sits on the couch next to me. "For making my son so happy. I haven't seen him like this in years. I don't know if others notice the difference, but I do. He's opened up to you and welcomed you into his life in a way I feared he'd never do."

I remain silent, unsure what to say, my emotions rolling to form a lump in my throat.

"I was so happy when I found out he asked you to move in with him. He saw how special you are. If you aren't next to him, he searches for you. I've watched him. He's not even aware. He simply needs you." She pulls me into a hug that I return wholeheartedly. She smells of warmth and love, and it's wonderful and motherly. Oh no. My eyes sting. God damn it, I have to control the sprinklers. Taking a deep breath, I calm myself, and my eyes are surprisingly dry after she lets me go.

"What's taking you two so long?" Sebastian's voice booms from the hallway.

"Like I said, he can't stay away from you." Mrs. Bennett winks at me, pushing herself up from the couch and leaving the room. She and Sebastian exchange a few words in the hallway, and then the front door shuts.

Sebastian enters the living room.

"How is my girl? Ready to go back out?"

Sinking deeper in the couch, I confess, "I want to stay here a little longer. It smells like heaven."

Sebastian furrows his brow, as if he's considering something. "Let's go to the kitchen and steal some pie."

"It can't be ready."

"I know Mom. The pie's been ready for at least an hour." His eyes light up with a look of mischief. Suddenly, he appears younger by at least ten years. Taking my hand, Sebastian helps me stand, leading me to the kitchen. He's right, the pie is ready. I cut two slices, putting them on the plates Sebastian hands me. I'm about to dive right into it, but he stops me.

"Wait, it's better with whipped cream."

Armed with whipped cream and the plates,

Sebastian shoulders open a door that leads directly into the garden on the other side of the house. There's no one here, and the moon is the only source of light. We settle on the small, wooden bench next to the door. I add whipped cream, and we dig in.

"This is delicious," I mumble through mouthfuls. Sebastian grunts in agreement. Neither of us speaks until we've finished eating and put the plates on the floor.

Chapter Twenty-Seven

Ava

"You have cream on the tip of your nose," Sebastian says with a smile. I wipe myself clean, a little embarrassed. He covers my mouth in an unexpected kiss. Our tongues meet in a clash, and everything blurs for me except him. Everything about him comes into focus. His taste, for one. Cinnamon mingled with the flavor of him. His scent excites me: mint shower gel and the underlying smell of him—oh, I know that one so well. In a haze, I feel him pulling me into his lap, careful not to touch my knees. Our lips don't part at all, as I fist his hair with both hands. He rests his fingers on my waist. Remembering what Mrs. Bennett said about his feelings for me, I shudder. I feel the same way about him, and it's damn frightening.

As if sensing my predicament, he pulls back, resting his forehead against mine. "Is everything okay?"

I cannot withhold the truth from Sebastian. Also, the darkness around us gives me courage.

"I'm scared," I confess.

His fingers tighten on my waist, but his voice remains gentle. "Of what?"

"My feelings for you. I've. . . It's the first time I. . ." My voice fades as I search for the right words. "I've never had feelings this strong for anyone else."

"This makes two of us." Sebastian raises one hand to cup my cheek, and I liquefy at his touch, my heart growing twice in size.

"I'm scared," I repeat.

After a beat, he says, "So am I."

"No, you're not." Chuckling, I pinch one of his nipples. "Nothing scares you."

"This does. You complete me, Ava, and I don't know how I'll carry on without you."

Wham. The force of his words knocks the wind out of me, as if I've been hit with that damn soccer ball squarely in the chest again. The best thing that's ever happened to me is temporary and it's killing me. By the look of him, it's killing both of us. My heart shrinks until it feels the size of a small diamond, yet it's heavy. It carries the weight of all the lonely days and sleepless nights awaiting us.

"So what do we do?" I whisper.

"Run with it and enjoy it while it lasts. Or—" I put a finger on his lips to silence him.

His gaze ripples through me. I lower my eyes to his chin, heat creeping into my cheeks. He demands I give up my inhibitions and he tears down the walls I carefully built. Sebastian makes baring my soul remarkably easy by revealing himself in front of me. This man knows not only to demand but also to give.

He kisses me again, this time like a man possessed. His mouth demands everything of me, and I savor him right back. Desperation tinges our passion, pushing us further and further on the spiral of need. Sebastian Bennett is not a man who gives himself easily, but when he does, he's all in. So am I. Lowering my hand between us, I moan into his mouth. He's hard for me already. The recognition sends arrows of heat between my thighs.

"Fuck. How can you turn me on like this, Ava?"

Sebastian buries his head in my neck, his lips nibbling at my sensitive skin. I sling my hand behind my back between us, caressing the rows of hard muscles.

"Get up. I want to take you from behind," he unexpectedly says into my ear. My knees weaken at his strong, no-excuses-allowed tone.

"Yes," I say in a small voice, too aroused to bring up any objections. We both rise from the bench, Sebastian guiding me away from it.

"Lean forward and put your hands on the wall."

"Okay." I do as he says, equal parts curious and nervous.

"Spread your legs." He pushes my dress up around my waist.

As soon as I do what he instructs, I peek over my shoulder and see him kneel. He moves aside my thong and dips his tongue between my folds. My knees buckle as he licks me on the inside, desire ensnaring me. I need something to hold onto. The wall doesn't provide much support, and I dearly need it. I wish we'd stayed closer to the bench. My thighs are quivering already. Sebastian drags his tongue from my clit all the way back, tipping my ass out, cupping my cheeks with his hands. When he slides two fingers inside, he rouses all of my nerve endings, sexual need overpowering me. It's raw, primal, and delicious. He removes his fingers from inside me, but keeps his hand at the apex of my thighs, spreading me wider.

He swears loudly, and I whirl around in alarm.

"What's wrong?" I ask.

"I don't have a condom with me."

I lick my lips, my heart thudding in my chest. "We can do it without one. I'm on birth control pills." I avert my gaze, cringing at the last words. I didn't keep this from him on purpose, but the topic never came up. Sebastian tips my head up so I have no choice but to look at him.

"I know you are. I saw you take them." There is no accusation in his voice.

"Are you mad at me?"

"Of course not. I don't want you to feel pressured into saying yes right now. If you're not sure, we can wait until we get home." A smile plays on his lips, but his eyes remain serious. "I might also die of sexual frustration; but I'm a grown man, I can handle it. Or we can do. . . other things."

My only answer is, "I want you inside me. Now."

"It goes without saying that I'm clean. But do you trust me?"

"Yes."

"I want you to say it, Ava."

"I trust you."

His eyes warm, and he places the sweetest of kisses on my lips. The fact that he patiently waited for me to trust him and didn't confront me with his knowledge tugs at my heartstrings.

He flips me around again. I hear him unzip his pants, fiddling with his clothes, and then he poises himself at my entrance. I press my palms into the wall for support.

Sebastian tortures me, dragging the tip up and down my sensitive flesh. When I can't stand the pressure anymore, I push my ass into him. He loses control, driving into me at once.

"Avaaaaaaaaaaaaaaaa. Fuck."

I swallow hard, blind from the impossibly intense sensation. Everything is magnified. His sharp exhalations against my nape burn me. My nipples pulse urgently. My palms aren't enough, I rest my forearms on the wall, desperately trying to ground myself, fearing my legs will give in. Sebastian fists my hair as I push my hips against him, the pulsing between my legs begging for release.

"I won't last long, babe. You feel so good." His strokes get faster, harder. "You are mine," he says, gripping my hair tighter, tipping my face to him. With a guttural groan, he empties himself inside me, driving me over the edge. My orgasm rips a loud cry from my mouth. "Mine."

Chapter Twenty-Eight

Sebastian

"This was a brilliant idea," Pippa says two weeks later, on the deck of Logan's newest yacht. We're inaugurating it Bennett style. That means most of my siblings are here, as well as a few close friends.

"I can't believe Mom and Dad are sitting this one out," Logan says. He, Pippa, and I are the only ones on the deck, lying in armchairs in the sun. The rest, including Ava, are swimming around the boat.

"Their way of telling you they don't approve," Pippa says.

"Way to rub it in, sister," Logan says, annoyed. "After all these years, they're still not used to it."

I smile. My parents are simple people. Yachts, fast cars, and expensive outings are unnecessary luxuries for them. Vain. Even convincing them to accept that house was a lot of trouble. I admire the values they taught us, but find nothing wrong with indulging in the sweeter side of life. When one becomes more fortunate, it's no sin to enjoy it. My personal mantra is to also help those less fortunate, which is why

Bennett Enterprises donates a hefty percentage of our profits to various causes.

Rubbing more oil on her arms, my sister says, "This outing is just what the doctor ordered. Otherwise, I would've spent this weekend at the office too."

"You should take it easier," I tell her.

Logan perks up. "How come you never tell me that?"

"Because I'm his favorite sister, so I get special treatment."

"What she said," I reply. I don't have a favorite sibling, but Pippa needs all the attention she can get right now. I know why she spends so much time at the office lately. It's not only because the collection launch is approaching. She's made a few trips to her lawyer in the past two weeks to settle the divorce. I offered to accompany her, but she refused, often returning to the office with red eyes and working until late at night. She does the same thing I do when she feels her personal life slipping through her fingers. She puts all her time and energy in the one thing that's solid—Bennett Enterprises.

"Anyway," Pippa comments, "you two are workaholics all the time. I'm like that only when a launch approaches. By the way, I can't believe what a fabulous job Ava's doing with the campaign."

"Yeah, she's very talented," I agree, but don't elaborate, a knot forming in my throat. Instinctively, I peer across the yacht railing and into the water to where I saw Ava last. She's still swimming with Alice and Summer. The closer we get to the date of her departure, the harder talking about her becomes.

"You have it bad for her, brother," Logan says.

"It's that obvious, huh?"

"I work with you, remember? I see the way you look at her. It's. . ."

"What?" I frown at him, shifting in the chair.

"Everyone's happy about the two of you."

"I'm not just happy," Pippa interjects. "I'm thrilled. So are Mom and Dad."

"Tell them to keep the thrill low. She's only here for another three weeks." The thought suffocates me. Where did the time go? I make a grab for my glass, only to find it dry.

"Have you thought about asking her to stay?" Logan asks. He and Pippa exchange a glance that tells me they've talked about this.

I clasp the glass tighter. "She has a job and a life, and I respect that. I can hardly tell her to leave everything behind for me."

"She travels a lot," Pippa says. "Relocating wouldn't be too hard for her."

"I can't ask her to give up her job. When the project is over, she'll move to the next one." My voice is hollow. Why the fuck is this thought so depressing?

"Dude, you already sound like a love-sick puppy. No way am I going to listen to your drunk ramblings about your lost love after she's gone." Logan hefts the glass in my direction as if he's toasting me.

I stare him down. "When did I ever get drunk and

talk about women?"

"Oh, that's right," he admits. "Never."

"Damn right."

He takes a sip from his non-alcoholic cocktail, looking at Pippa with wide eyes.

"Oh, Logan, stop the puppy dog eyes. Though you'll always be known as the family puppy," Pippa informs us with a lovely grin. "Sebastian's the family's lion, nursing his wounds alone and all that shit."

Logan leaps to his feet. "How does Sebastian get to be the lion and I the puppy? Why can't I be a tiger, or at least some scary dog breed?"

Ah, a good old Bennett brawl.

Pippa puts a hand on her hip, squinting at Logan as if she's considering something. "Yeah, you're right. Not a puppy. I'll look up the appropriate breed later. Must be one that barks a lot but doesn't bite."

"Don't forget it must have an oversized ego," I supply.

Pippa nods. "I'll keep that in mind."

"I'm very glad the two of you are having fun at my expense." Logan's tone clearly indicates he's not glad at all. Pippa and I grin. "But we were talking about Sebastian, and how the family lion will be stupid enough to let the woman he loves walk away."

My smile drops.

"Sebastian, don't be an idiot," Pippa begins, now turning to me, placing both hands on her hips. "If you love her—"

"I didn't say that."

"You don't have to," she insists, tilting her head.

"Oh, you can just see it?" I ask sarcastically.

"I can," Pippa says triumphantly. She glances at Logan, who backs her up with a strong nod. Oh, here they go again.

"Yes, yes, Pippa, we all know you've been blessed with Mom's exceptional people-reading skills." I give them a dismissive hand gesture, but they won't let me off so easily today.

"Except when it comes to the people I date or marry, apparently," she adds. I pull a face, fully aware of what she's doing, bringing up her broken marriage so I don't brush her off. I'd get mad at her for being so manipulative if I didn't love her so much. Which she knows very well.

"How is it that every time we do something together out of the office, you two corner me about my personal life?" I inquire, tapping my fingers on the glass.

"You want us to do it at the office too?" Pippa asks with mock surprise. "Why didn't you say so? Logan, are you up for it? Hey, we could even call in Alice for a Bennett sibling meeting now and again in the CEO's office. Or in the meeting room."

Groaning, I drag my palm down my face. "Please don't."

"Let's get through this step by step," Pippa says. She sits down on the floor, crossing her legs as if she's about to do some yoga or shit. Damn it. I know that expression on her face. Lifted eyebrows, lips curled into a half smile. It reminds me of our days as kids, planning our way into or out of a mess. "The point is you can't let her go."

"You jumped a few steps in the process," Logan tells her.

"What will you do after she leaves?" Pippa continues, and now a shred of seriousness tinges her playful tone. "Get back to your old life? Find a Terence, like I did? You've had enough sharks have a go at you over the years, wearing silicone and Botox to mask their teeth. You're the billionaire CEO of one of the biggest companies in San Francisco, and we're in a sexy industry. Everyone knows you, and you're one of the most eligible bachelors around."

Logan and I groan in unison. He gets up. "Okay, it's time for some adult drinks. Whiskey for everyone?"

I nod. After a few seconds, so does Pippa.

"Make mine a double," I instruct.

"Go, tiger," Pippa tells him. We all laugh, but without much humor. The discussion has taken a turn for the serious. Logan shoves the drinks in our hands, and we spend a few minutes in silence, nursing the whiskey.

"I don't want to talk about Ava right now," I say eventually. Logan leans back in his seat, averting his gaze, but Pippa persists.

"I don't care. You found a great woman, and as far as I can see, you really let her in."

"Yeah, but when I did that, I knew it was only for a while."

There's a loaded pause—a very loaded pause in

which I gulp down the entire contents of the glass.

"Sebastian Bennett," Pippa says through gritted teeth. "Are you telling me that you only went all in because you thought it was a temporary thing?"

"What? Yea—No. Maybe? I don't know. Fuck no. I can't think straight."

"You can't blame it on the double whiskey," Logan warns. "You've just had it. No one gets drunk so fast."

"Burning sun and alcohol isn't a good combo," Pippa says. "Recap time. Yes or no, Sebastian?"

"No, it wasn't because it's temporary. It was because. . . I couldn't help it. I didn't even realize I was doing it until I was in it up to my head. Over my head, actually."

"Good boy." Pippa pats my arm. "If you'd told me you're one of those assholes that get the urge to run at the thought of forever, I would've beaten the crap out of you."

"I'm not like that, you know it. I want to carry on the Bennett name and have my own soccer team of kids; but with only siliconed and botoxed sharks in sight, I gave up on that dream years ago."

When I saw her at the soccer game holding baby Adrian, I could practically see our future together. In fact, I see no future without her. This woman has wedged her way into my heart. She's glorious. And mine.

Only when Logan sputters his drink and Pippa hugs me, telling me I'm an adorable lion do I realize I've actually said at least part of all that out loud.

Logan goes to pour himself a fresh glass of whiskey, shaking his head.

Well, it's all out there already. She might've called me a pink panther for all the manliness adorable lion has to it, but I'll find a way to pay her back. Not now though. Now I need her help. "What do I do, Pippa? I feel like I'm drowning and she's not even gone yet."

"Fight for your HEA, brother."

"I thought you no longer believed in those."

She puts her hands in mine, leaning closer. "It didn't turn out well for me, though God knows I tried. He wasn't worth it. But Ava is, you know that."

"I do. Damn right, I do. I. . . I know it won't work. She won't stay."

Pippa juts her chin forward, speaking slowly, as if I'm a child. "Then convince her."

Logan returns empty-handed. "I changed my mind. No more alcohol. Let's swim to clear our heads."

"You two go," I say. "I want some time to think."

"See," Pippa tells Logan. "Lion behavior, like I said." She whisks Logan away before he even opens his mouth, throwing me an encouraging look over her shoulder.

***

Pippa was right. Alcohol and sun is a bad combo. When I stand up, I wobble on my feet, which hasn't happened in years, so I slump back in my chair. Sometime later, Ava appears on the deck, carrying a heap of something in her arms.

"There you are," she says. "Logan told me you're drunk, but I thought he was messing with me."

She walks to me with the shy smile I've come to love. Hell, I've come to love everything about her, and that's the problem. How can I let her go now?

"I like your bikini." I slur the words so badly, it's a miracle she understands any of them. She straddles my lap, facing me. Her tits are in my face and her crotch right over mine. I'll take that any time.

"I brought shells."

"What?"

She holds up a white shell, looking at it with a bright smile and squinted eyes. "This is so pretty. I swear it changes its color every time I look at it."

"Looks white to me."

"It is white, but it has these colorful hues. They're different colors, depending where you're looking from." She holds it in the sunlight, tilting her head from one side to the other. Ah, yes, one other thing I can add to the list of things I love about her: the way she can find beauty in the simplest things, and shows me how to do that too. If I weren't drunk off my ass, maybe I'd see what she means.

"Where did you find it?"

"I went snorkeling with Daniel and Blake. We went into a cave and I found this there."

"Did they take good care of you?"

She nods, dropping the shell between us and resting her palms on my chest. "They're great. And so much fun."

"Watch it, I might get jealous." I run my hands up

her thighs to her hips.

She laughs, tilting her head back, exposing her throat to me. "Of your brothers?"

"Of any man." I cup her left breast with one hand. "This is mine." I slide the other hand into her bathing suit, finding her wet pussy. "This is mine too."

She huffs out a breath, her chest heaving up and down.

"You are mine, Ava, and I won't let you go."

Her eyes widen, and she murmurs, "You really are drunk."

"Yeah, but you're still mine."

I kiss her hard, possessing her mouth, my hand cupping her wetness. Entangled with her like this, I make myself a drunken promise: I will not let her go.

Chapter Twenty-Nine

Ava

Two weeks to D-day, and everyone's running around crazily already. I'm definitely leading the crazy pack.

"Okay, everyone. Let's start this," I instruct.

This is the first rehearsal for the show, and I'm impressed that all the models showed up. The prep team did a wonderful job, and now the girls are ready to hit the runway. They're wearing mock jewelry, of course. The real items will only be here on the day of the show.

I sit next to the runway, but don't look much at the models; Pippa's in charge of that. I inspect the rest of the decor and the way the technical equipment blends in. I've had nightmare issues with shows before, with designers deciding the day before that they want to change the entire color scheme. Luckily, Pippa looks very pleased.

Finally, content with the decor, I turn my attention to the models. I'm impressed with the high-caliber models they hired for this. The star of the show is Simone Candella, an Italian beauty who took up residence in the United States six years ago. Watching her stroll on the runway, I understand the world's fascination with her. She's the personification of beauty. Her waist-long black hair and tan skin give her an exotic air, making her striking blue eyes nothing short of mesmerizing. A visible dash of arrogance accompanies her every move, but that's to be expected.

Midway through the rehearsal, I notice a shift in the models' behavior. They smile more, occasionally winking at something behind me. Baffled, I turn around and find Sebastian there. I let out an audible groan. Both Pippa and Sebastian laugh.

"What are you doing here, brother?" Pippa whispers over her shoulder. "You haven't been at a rehearsal in years."

"Thought I'd take a break, delight my eyes with some beauty." He looks at me pointedly, and heat rushes to my cheeks. I know he's teasing me, but I feel a tiny pang of jealousy.

As the rehearsal progresses, the models become bolder, giving him hot looks. Out of the corner of my eye, I peer at Sebastian, who wanders around the room. To my astonishment, he's not looking at the runway, instead inspecting the lighting equipment.

Finally, he sits next to me and says, "This is going to be our most expensive show."

"The buzz around it got you enough partners to offset the cost."

"I know. You're a genius."

Pride swells inside me at his words. Shortly afterward, we take a break. The models wear robes, milling around, drinking nothing but water, even though the catering company also brought model-approved food like salads and low-calorie everything.

Sebastian speaks in a hushed voice to Pippa, still ignoring all the hot looks he gets. He speaks to the technician who's behind all the magic that will happen during the show, especially the opening stunt. Since Sebastian and I aren't displaying our relationship (very) publicly, we try to keep our distance to what would pass as professional interest.

Pippa walks to me and says in a low voice, "Looking at these girls makes me feel bad about all those cupcakes I eat."

"You look great," I reassure her.

"I like my body, though I have my unfavorable spots, but it's hard to look at them and not get self-conscious."

Silently, I agree.

"I mean, look at Simone. She's practically perfect," Pippa says. "Well, she's a total bitch, but other than that. . . Anyway, I wanted to ask you something else. I need to change something."

Oh, crap. I knew it. Here it comes.

"The dress Lily wears the second time she comes out isn't right."

I wait for the blow—something like—oh, and I want the entire color scheme changed, but Pippa seems to be done with the requests.

"I know a designer put the models' looks

together," she continues, "but I trust you. You have excellent taste in clothing. Would you mind looking backstage? Maybe you'll find something more suitable?"

"Yeah, of course. I'll bring you a few other choices you can look at and decide."

"Perfect." With a chuckle, she adds, "Look at my brother. He came just to see you. He hates coming to these things. Models are drawn to him like moths to a flame."

"They are, aren't they?" I ask with a dry mouth.

"I give him five minutes before he bolts, or goes to another room," she adds in a low, conspiratorial tone.

***

The prep room smells like overheated hair spray. It's empty right now, since all the stylists are at the buffet. The clothes are stuffed in an adjacent room, which also houses a couch. There are hangers upon hangers with clothes, and I head to the back of the room, where I spot two hangers chock-full of cocktail dresses. Browsing through them, I find four that'd be appropriate.

Suddenly, I hear voices from the front of the room. I hadn't even realized someone was there. I don't know what makes me do it, but I instinctively bend my knees and duck, hiding behind the hanger.

"Sebastian Bennett, what a surprise to see the CEO himself here. You've never joined the rehearsals before," a woman says. Her voice is throaty and low. Simone. A sinking feeling forms in my stomach, my heart suddenly weighing a hundred pounds. I saw the way she ogled Sebastian; and she's so beautiful.

"It was about time I paid a visit," he says.

I look around for a way to escape. Damn it, there is no way out except through the door I came through, and they'd see me immediately. With trembling hands, I part two dresses, looking between them. I have a direct view of the back of Sebastian's head. He sits on the couch while Simone stands in front of him. She's wearing nothing but a robe, and her stance is provocative, revealing too much of her generous cleavage and perfectly toned legs.

"Like anything you see?" she asks. Tears spring to the corners of my eyes. This can't be happening to me. I can't witness my man cheating on me. Again. I simply can't take it. . . not from Sebastian. My heart grows so heavy, I feel like I'm choking. I bite my forearm, afraid a sob might come out, giving me away. How much bad luck can I have? Isn't it dreadful enough that I walked in on my ex, John, doing it with that ho? Do I now have to watch the man to whom I've given myself completely do this here? My eyes water. Damn it, I don't want to cry. This can't be happening. I must look away and cover my ears. Yeah, that's what I should do. But like the masochist I am, I keep looking. This is like watching a car wreck, only now I see my life getting wrecked.

"I'm not here for any of this." Sebastian's voice is brisk, but it does nothing to calm me. Sweat dots my palms. I tug at my lower lip with my teeth.

"Oh, really? I bet I can change your mind."

"Listen—what is your name?"

"Simone."

"Listen, Simone, I don't get involved with people I work with."

"Why not make an exception? Don't you like what you see? I won't tell if you don't. It'll be our secret."

"You are a beautiful woman, but I'm really not interested."

"Ah, you're playing hard to get. That's no problem. I can make you hard in an instant."

"Simone, please return to your work."

"Let me suck you off," she says in a very seductive voice, letting her bathrobe fall to the floor. She's completely naked. "You can come all over me if you want to."

Sebastian rises to his feet, Simone's robe in his hand.

"Put this on. Now," he commands.

I don't dare to breathe. Simone puts on her robe.

"I can give you my number and we can meet after work," she says.

"I will tell you this one last time. I am not interested in you. If you don't stop this right now, I will have your contract with our company dissolved."

Simone steps back as if Sebastian's cracked a whip in front of her.

"Get over yourself, Bennett. I can sue you for sexual harassment."

Sebastian laughs. "Please, try. I can afford the best lawyers. They will destroy you in court. I'll make sure no one hires you again. Ever. You know I have the power to do that."

Simone whirls on her heels and leaves the room.

I blink, stunned. He actually told her no? My mind must be playing tricks on me. She's the most beautiful model I've ever seen, and she practically offered herself to him on a silver platter. Relief washes over me, and I begin—of all things—to sob.

Sebastian turns around, startled, and heads straight to the back of the room. To me. I pull myself to my full height.

His eyes widen. "Ava, what. . . Were you here the entire time?"

"I didn't mean to. I came here to search for some clothes," I babble, speaking so quickly I'm afraid he won't understand a word. "I didn't hear you come in, and I didn't have a way to get out. I wasn't spying, or. . ." I take a deep breath, fighting tears. "It's not my fault."

"What isn't? Babe, you're not making sense. Talk to me. I want to understand."

I can't open my mouth, because if I do, I'll break down. It was always my fault. With Trey, it was my fault that I traveled so much. He had no choice but to cheat. With John, it was my fault that I wanted to surprise him on our anniversary. I mean, who goes to their boyfriend's apartment without calling first? They always blamed me.

Sebastian puts his arms around me, snapping me back to reality.

"Shhh, Ava, relax. Why are you trembling?"

"You told Simone no?" The words come out as a question.

"Of course I did."

"You didn't even hesitate." I still can't believe it.

"I had no reason to. I have you."

I breathe in and out rapidly, searching for words to tell him how much this means to me. He's single-handedly restored my faith in humanity. I hadn't had any idea I had lost it so completely, until I thought I was losing him too.

"You're a great man, Sebastian," is all I can whisper, though it doesn't even begin to cover what I feel for him. Someone calls my name outside, and I pick out the dresses I chose earlier, carrying them on my forearm. I want to stride toward the door, but Sebastian remains in front of me, blocking my way.

"Ava. Wait."

"The crew outside needs me."

"They can wait a few more minutes. Why do you want to avoid me? Did I do something wrong?"

"No, absolutely nothing."

He tilts my head up, looking at me with desperation. Oh, damn. How do I explain this to him without coming across as a clingy, insecure little girl? This isn't me. I'm a strong woman. I didn't have a privileged upbringing, and I had to fight for everything. I don't regret it, and I am proud of how far I've come. But after being cheated on twice, my confidence in this department vanished into thin air. I can do a lot of things. Put a campaign together from the ground up? Check. Make my clients gain a significant advantage over the competition in just a few short months? Check. Make a man love me enough to keep it in his pants around other women? Im-freaking-possible. Or so I thought, until Sebastian.

"That's the thing. You're too perfect. If I stay in here with you one minute longer, I might say something silly."

"Like what?" he asks, exasperation on his beautiful features.

"Like, I love you." I catch my breath.

His frown melts into the sweetest smile. "Let's be silly together. I love you, too, Ava."

"You do?" My knees weaken. As if realizing that, Sebastian wraps his arms around me, pulling me close to him. I rest my hands on his chest.

"Yes, and I'd never cheat on you. That's not the kind of man I am. It's a privilege loving you."

"Oh."

He kisses me with tenderness, his hands cupping my cheeks and drawing me up to him. His arms give me warmth and a sense of safety. God, this feels so wonderful, so absolutely wonderful, that I don't want to worry about anything. My eyes brim with tears. I've never felt so cherished or loved.

Our kiss grows more urgent, and Sebastian pushes me further, until we reach a wall. Unhitching his lips from mine, he kisses my neck, dropping his hands to my thighs, his fingers lifting my dress until they touch my bare skin. I shiver, heat pooling between my legs.

"I want to make love to you, Ava," he murmurs

against my skin.

"Not here. The people outside. . ."

"Let's go. Right now."

Sexual tension crackles between us. It's so thick and loaded that one single spark would be enough to make us both forget where we are. He locks his gaze on mine, and the mix of emotions in his eyes almost convinces me to give in to his request. The need to be alone with him hits me hard.

Swallowing hard, I say, "I still have to check on a lot of things. Give me two hours, and then we can leave."

Leaning in to me, he says in a tight voice. "Two hours."

Chapter Thirty

Sebastian

I watch her from afar for the next two hours. Ava's her confident self again. She orders everyone around and keeps checking every little detail that could lead to confusion on the presentation day. As I expected, she treats Simone as if nothing happened.

Ava is a strong, independent woman. The thought that the lowlifes who cheated on her made her doubt herself even one bit, makes me want to find those idiots and smash their faces. She's amazing, and any man who doesn't see that is a fool. Their loss, my gain.

I almost came undone seeing her like that inside. My beautiful Ava was so fragile, so scared that I might hurt her. I flex my palms, rage coursing through me. No one will hurt her again. I'll see to that. I want Ava just the way she is. She wiggled her way into my every thought, filling a void I thought would remain unfilled. I won't ever desire another woman.

After precisely two hours, I walk up behind her. She's dismissed almost everyone, and she's now looking for something in her bag, with a lovely frown on her face.

"Your two hours are up," I tell her over her shoulder. She flinches, but then turns around, a grin spreading on her face.

"I know."

"Where do you want to go?"

"Home, but I'm starving. Let's pick up some food on the way."

"That's my girl. Nothing can stave off your appetite."

"Nope, not really."

We buy tacos on our way home and devour them in the car. She's silent the whole way, as if struggling with something. She wants to tell me something, but I won't pressure her. When she's ready, she'll talk. Once inside the apartment, that moment seems to arrive. Ava looks up at me, her face flushed.

Leaning against the kitchen island, she says, "Sebastian, I want to apologize for the way I reacted back there."

"What exactly do you think you must apologize for?"

"Crying. Trembling. Basically, losing my shit. You didn't have to see me like that."

"You were vulnerable." I push a strand of hair behind her ear, kissing her forehead. "When you moved in here, I told you I wanted to know every part of you. I meant that. I'm not here just for the fun or sexy times. I'm here to love you. Every part of you."

Her tiny body squirms, and she offers me a shy smile.

"I want to make one thing clear. The fact that those assholes cheated on you is not your fault. Trust me. You're wonderful."

"You, Mr. Charmer, must give me the name of the charm school you attended. Men worldwide need to follow suit."

"Oh, it's Mom's school of I'll-kick-your-butt-if-you-mistreat-a-lady. It was very effective."

"Well, I'll let her know she did a wonderful job."

"She did. Now," I drop my head to her ear and whisper, "I believe we have unfinished business."

Instantly, goose bumps form on her arms, which is one hell of a turn-on.

"Is that so?" Her voice is playful and, at the same time, uneven. "I don't remember."

"You don't?" I feather my lips on her neck and shoulder, enjoying hearing her breathing pattern become more labored.

"No, was it dessert?"

"You can call it that if you want to."

I hoist her up in my arms and she tilts her head back, laughing. I'll never get enough of her laughter. After getting us to the bedroom, I lay her on the bed and lean against the windowsill.

"Strip," I tell her.

Ava wets her lips and unzips her dress in one swift move. She picks up the hem of the blue fabric, pulling the dress over her head. I suck in my breath when she remains in nothing but her bra and thong.

"Take off your bra."

As her breasts spill free, my erection threatens to explode in my pants. I lean down to her, kissing her lips, cupping one breast greedily, letting my hand slide further down.

"You soaked your thong." I groan, stroking her slit with my finger over the damp fabric. Shuddering, she closes her eyes. I discard my clothes fast, and take her thong off too. She moves to the center of the bed, watching me. She's so fucking sexy.

I join her in the bed, wrapping my hand around my erection, pumping up and down, squeezing it the way I like it.

Ava's eyes widen in surprise.

"Touch me," I tell her. Obediently, she closes the distance between us, coming so near that her delicious breasts touch my chest. She looks me straight in the eyes as she takes over stroking me. "God, you're good, baby. So good."

I want to drive her crazy tonight. I want to drive her crazy every night. Tasting her mouth, I claim her lips, dragging my knuckles down the sides of her body, enjoying the goose bumps forming on her skin. I squeeze her sweet ass with both hands. She's gorgeous, perfect, and knows what to do with that hand of hers.

In one second, I change everything. I kiss her hard, pushing her back on the bed, parting her legs with my knee. I move my mouth downward, paying attention to first one of her breasts, and then the other. The way she arches her back drives me crazy.

"You're fucking perfect," I mutter against her skin as I continue my descent, settling between her legs. I run my tongue over her inner thigh, inching toward her sex with exquisite slowness. By the way she digs her nails in the mattress, I know I have her exactly how I want. I place my mouth on her clit, sucking it gently.

"Sebastian."

She pushes her heels firmly in the bed, her breathing becoming more labored. That's it. Lust shoots through me. I plunge one finger inside her, and another one, caressing her inner flesh. I crook my finger. She fists my hair, moaning. I continue to kiss her until I feel her tighten around my fingers, right before crying out from the orgasm. Watching her come apart completely burns my control. I grind my erection against her still sensitive flesh before driving into her, stretching her tight passage. Her breasts press against my chest.

"You feel amazing," I tell her.

"You make me feel things I didn't even know existed." She pants underneath me, her skin glistening with sweat.

"I'm very pleased to hear that."

She giggles in my ear, and I swear it's the damned sweetest sound. I make her moan. Hard. I plunge into her faster, deeper, spreading her legs wider apart. I watch her unravel, fighting to keep my control, to last longer. Breathing through my mouth, I time my strokes, rocking in and out of her as she succumbs to her orgasm.

I spiral over the edge, coming hard, burying my head in her neck, screaming out her name at the same time she calls mine. Afterward, she cuddles against me, and I cradle her in my arms, kissing her forehead. This woman makes me want to have her and protect her. It's the first time I want to give a woman everything.

As her breath falls into that peaceful pattern that indicates she's asleep, I'm more certain than ever that I'll never want another woman. She's it for me. The one. I'll be damned if I'll let her slip away.

***

I can't sleep. Not wanting to wake Ava, I'm leaving the bedroom when an idea strikes me. I open my laptop and start researching. One hour later, my master plan is done. I debate waiting until morning to tell her, and then decide not to.

Ava sleeps on one side, hugging a pillow. Her luscious hair is spread everywhere.

Sitting at the edge of the bed, I hover over her for a few seconds before whispering, "Ava." No reaction. "Ava."

"Mmm." She hugs the pillow tighter, squishing her breasts against it. I'm tempted to push her on her back and suckle one of her nipples, but restrain myself. I'm on an important mission.

"I have an indecent proposal."

"Can't wait to hear it," she says sleepily. "In the morning."

"Nope, now."

Lazily, she blinks her eyes open. "Is something wrong?"

"Nothing wrong, but if I tell you this when you're up and buzzing, you'll come up with a hundred reasons to say no."

"No to what?" She closes her eyes again.

"Don't fall asleep."

"Then talk."

"You said Dirk didn't assign you to a new project right after you finish here."

"Not yet, but I bet he'll come up with something."

"Tell him you want two weeks off. Let's go somewhere, just the two of us."

She opens her eyes again, and this time there's no sleepiness in them. A smile playing on her lips, she pushes herself up on an elbow.

"Mr. I-didn't-take-a-day-off-in-five-years wants to take two entire weeks off?"

"You make me do things I didn't even contemplate before. You make me want those things." I lean in to her, kissing her cheek.

"I'll go with you, Sebastian."

On that vacation, I will ask her to stay here in San Francisco with me.

Chapter Thirty-One

Ava

Next morning at the office, I make a to-do list of all the things I need to get done before the show. It's enormous. Looking at it, I decide that sleep is overrated. I'll run on coffee, adrenaline, and the knowledge that afterward I'll spend two weeks with Sebastian, without work or anything else getting between us. Dirk wasn't happy when I told him I want two weeks off, but he can suck it. I haven't taken a single day off in the last year, and I'm not eager to repeat that experience. I work hard. I deserve a damn break. One last trip before this dream ends. I'm surprised at the ache blooming in my chest. I always knew this wouldn't last, but I never expected to fall in love with Sebastian. It'll make going back to the way things were so much harder. Imagining my life without Sebastian depresses me. Back to empty hotel rooms and dinners alone in the office, long after my colleagues are gone. Empty beds. I shake my head, trying to clear my thoughts. A job is something fixed;

something I can count on. A man can always leave. My job won't keep me warm at night though. Sebastian does.

"Bah. Get your act together, Lindt," I admonish myself. For the remainder of the morning, I work through my monstrous to-do list.

I will always remember the moment all hell broke loose. Lola and Sandra, two girls from the marketing department, burst inside my office, looking like they're about to confess a mortal sin.

"What's wrong?" I ask them.

"Martha quit."

"What do you mean, she quit?" I leap to my feet, nearly knocking over my computer. No, no, no. This can't be. "There is one week left until the presentation."

"Uh-huh," Lola says.

"She . . . Jesus." I bite my tongue, drawing in deep breaths.

"So, we wanted to know who will take over her duties," Sandra says.

I suspected Martha would leave soon, but I never thought she'd quit now.

A vein pulses in my right temple. "Right. You two go back in your office and continue with your tasks. I will let you know how to proceed."

After they leave, I take a deep breath and stroll into Sebastian's office. He and Logan stop talking when they see me.

"Your marketing manager quit," I announce.

"We've been informed," Logan says. "She

received a job in Seattle she couldn't refuse, and they required her to start right away."

"You need to hire someone now."

"There's not enough time until the show," Sebastian explains. I swear loudly, because I knew this was exactly what they were going to say.

"I know, but I needed to vent somewhere and I couldn't do it in front of the team."

Both men burst out laughing.

"This is not funny," I say.

"We know it's not." Logan's expression turns somber.

"Can you do it without the marketing manager?" Sebastian asks. "Logan and I can try to jump in, but between the meetings we've already scheduled, there won't be much time."

"Well, it'll mean pulling a hundred hours this week. Nothing I haven't done before, but I hate it when it happens. I'll get back to work."

Sebastian looks at me intently.

I pull myself up straighter. "Just so you know, all these long hours mean you'll get laid a lot less."

"We'll see about that," Sebastian replies, a rueful smile on his face.

"Does anyone care that I'm in the room?" Logan throws his hands up in the air.

"No," Sebastian and I reply in unison.

"Okay, glad we settled that," Logan concludes.

"I'll leave you two now and get back to work."

***

One week later, I've used up every ounce of energy. I'm convinced my body will give in any minute now. Thank God, it's the day of the show. I can do plenty of collapsing after it's over.

I'm in a chic boutique in downtown San Francisco, trying on dresses for tonight. With everything going on, it completely slipped my mind that I don't have anything to wear for the occasion. The vendor brings me two gorgeous dresses, but my enthusiasm fails when I see the price tag. They're both over three thousand dollars.

"Unless you have something on sale, don't bring me any designer items."

To his credit, the vendor doesn't look disappointed in the slightest. He hurries off, returning with three dresses that are within my price range.

"I'll try this one on first." I point to a dark blue dress. It's floor length, and made of light chiffon. I put it on quickly, asking him for help to zip up.

I step in front of the mirror and he nods appreciatively. "You look fantastic."

I smile. The dress hugs my figure surprisingly well, making my boobs stand out and my waist appear smaller. I wish it weren't so long though.

"I'm going to need killer heels with this one," I say. "Luckily, I have just what I need."

The door opens and a new customer comes in. I notice her in the mirror as she looks through the store. Simone.

"You look familiar," she remarks.

"I'm the marketing consultant at Bennett Enterprises."

"Oh, that's right. I saw you at the rehearsal. Will you be at the show tonight?"

"Yes, of course."

She eyes my dress dismissively, telling the vendor, "Bring me a dress from the Red Valentino collection you have in the front."

My eyebrows shoot up as the vendor eyes her with disdain and hesitates, as if he doesn't want to serve Simone. Finally, he moves to bring her the requested items.

"It's for the after-party tonight," Simone explains. Not that I asked her. "I have a man to seduce."

Looking away from her, I return my attention to the mirror, pretending to inspect my neckline.

"Do you know if Sebastian Bennett is dating someone?"

I swallow hard. "He is."

"Well, it doesn't matter much. Whoever she is, she can't compete with me. Men leave their wives for me. They always fall for this." She gestures at herself. I turn to her in disbelief. So this is what a homewrecker looks like. Does she know how much hurt she causes? All for what?

I look at Simone, pitying her. Strangely, I don't feel the need to compete with her. "You have a very low self-esteem."

"Excuse me?"

"Going around, offering your body," I clarify as

the vendor arrives with a Red Valentino dress.

"At least, I have something to offer," Simone says viciously. "Unlike you."

"We don't allow this kind of behavior in our shop," the vendor tells her.

"She insulted me first," Simone says.

"I don't see how telling the truth is an insult."

"Do you know who I am?" she asks him dismissively.

"Yes, I do. The owner of this shop is one of those women whose marriage you take so much pride in having ruined. I thought you looked familiar. Now, get out."

Simone stares down at him, but he doesn't back off. After a few seconds, she leaves.

"Don't listen to her," he tells me. "You look beautiful."

I look at myself in the mirror again, pleased with my choice of dress. Still, I feel uneasy.

***

When I enter the venue for the show a few hours later, I'm dazzled, even though I've been at the rehearsal and I know play-by-play how this will go. The opening act is a show of diffused lights. Simone is lowered slowly from the ceiling to the stage, looking every inch the beauty she is. The rest of the models come out next. The collection is exquisite, though one can barely see the jewelry on the models. That's what the large screens on either side of the stage are for.

I sit at the table with the marketing department, right next to the runway. Sebastian sits with Logan, Alice, Blake, and Daniel at a table on the other side of the runway. I'm proud that he's finally attended his own show and sits in the front row as opposed to hiding in the back room. He catches my eye on several occasions during the show. I blush every time. We've planned to stay for about an hour after the show, so he can answer questions from attendees. Then we're going to celebrate—just the two of us, while everyone else attends the after-party. Tomorrow, I'll clear my office while he attends a daylong meeting, and then our vacation will start.

The show ends with Pippa walking down the runway with all the models, bowing as the crowd applauds. As the girls return backstage, she jumps off the runway, coming straight to me. I stand up and give her a hug.

"You were wonderful."

"Let's get out of here," she says in my ear.

"You don't want to stay at the after-party?" I ask in surprise.

"Not really. I had a fight with my ex-husband over the phone before the show. I'm in the mood for a girls' night out. I say we grab Alice too and go out. You can't say no."

"I'm all in, but Sebastian—"

Pippa holds her hand up, rolling her eyes. "My brother will have you for himself for two whole weeks. He can do without you tonight."

"Okay. Where are we going?"

She grins. "I don't know, but a good friend of mine, Caroline, is somewhere around here. She always has great ideas."

"Okay, let me tell Sebastian I'm leaving."

"Meet you in front of the entrance in fifteen minutes?"

Wow. She must want to leave this place badly. "Okay."

Getting to Sebastian is not as easy as I thought. Though the press was invited to leave right after the show ended, there are plenty of people fighting for his time and attention. When I finally do reach him, a tall guy in an expensive suit extends his hand to shake Sebastian's.

"Bennett, this is extraordinary. You always had great marketing, but this surpasses everything."

"The merit belongs to our consultant and our team." Sebastian points at me, and the man takes a step back, nodding appreciatively. "She was the fresh mind we needed in our company and worked well with our team."

"Are you free to take up new projects? You could do wonders in my company." The man gives me a sleazy look that tells me he'd also want me to do him. Not happening, buddy.

"I'm afraid you'll have to discuss that with my boss," I answer politely. "I already have projects lined up, but we have a large team of consultants."

The man opens his mouth, but Sebastian cuts him off. "Sorry, we must leave you. I have to make the

rounds, and everyone will want to meet the brain"—
he points at me— "behind this show."

Sebastian looks uneasy as we leave. "Our private
celebration will be impossible tonight. There are too
many people I have to talk to, and that'll last well
into the after-party."

"You don't need me here though, do you?"

"Why?"

"Pippa wants to get out of here for a girls' night
out."

Sebastian frowns, looking through the crowd. "Is
she okay?"

"Yeah. She wants to let some steam off. She's
worked hard these past weeks."

"So have you. Go with them. Blow off some
steam."

"Are you sure?"

"Yeah."

I nod, but instead of leaving, I start tugging with
my teeth at my lower lip.

"Ava, is something wrong?" Sebastian asks me.

"I met Simone today when I was shopping. She
has this great plan to seduce you."

He laughs, cupping my cheek. "She'll fail hard. Go
and have some fun with my sister. The two of us will
have fun at home. Don't doubt me. "

"I trust you. Completely."

Chapter Thirty-Two

Ava

Holy crap.

I dearly hope Sebastian trusts me, because Pippa's friend brings us to a strip club. I keep hoping it might be a regular pub with a very shady name, but when we step inside, there are scantily dressed men everywhere. To my left, to my right. Dressed in overalls, thongs, or in nothing at all. Wait, no, that guy I took for naked actually does have a thong. But it's nude. And another guy wears a thong with a penis painted on it!

"Why would he wear a thong with a penis on it?" I ask Pippa, bewildered.

"Look at that one," Caroline points out. "His thong is transparent."

"Dear God, I need some alcohol," Alice announces. "There's too much testosterone around."

We attract stares, because we're all wearing long, elegant dresses, but I have to admit, it's kind of fun. We make our way to the bar and find some empty seats.

"Bartender, bring on the tequila," Caroline says. "We'd like a shot each."

He places glasses in front of us almost immediately. Arming ourselves with lime slices and salt, we clink our glasses, and down the tequila. I grimace, feeling it burn my throat.

The bartender looks at us carefully. "Are you girls on a bachelorette party? I can ask the boys to give you a special round of. . .dancing."

"Well, no one's getting married," Caroline says.

"That we know of." Pippa gives me a doubtful look. Oh, Pippa. I wish this were my bachelorette party. Nadine's been dreaming about organizing it ever since I told her about Sebastian turning Simone down. She's convinced he's the perfect man. So am I.

"You can totally ask your guys to give us something special," Caroline concludes.

"Actually, I don't feel comfortable with that idea," Pippa says. Next to her, Alice nods. "Let's watch from afar."

"This is no fun." Caroline pouts. "I have another idea. Let's play truth or dare."

"Are we in high school?" Alice asks. I study Pippa for a beat. Behind her apparent exuberance, there's sadness in her eyes.

"Don't be a prude," Caroline says.

"Fine," Alice says. "Who's the best lay you've ever had?" she asks Caroline.

Caroline rolls her eyes. "Let's have another round of tequila before we start."

"Aha," I remark. "Who's a prude now?"

We down another round, and Caroline rests her palms under her chin, a dreamy expression on her face. "My best guy was in senior year at college. Sad, I know, but it's true. That man gave me the most amazing orgasms."

"Oh, my God," Pippa says. "I just realized you're talking about my brother."

"Which brother?" I ask at the same time Alice says, "You're still hung up on him?"

"She means Daniel," Pippa informs me.

"Oh." I smile, wishing I could dig a hole in the ground and disappear in it. It's ridiculous how relieved I feel.

"I'm not hung up on him." Caroline says not so loudly that several people turn to look at us, snickering. Okay, no more tequila for her. "But he did give me fond memories. If only he hadn't broken my heart. The bastard."

Alice puts an arm gently around Caroline's shoulders. "If it's any consolation, he does ask about you from time to time."

Caroline frowns, as if considering her words. "Nope, it's no consolation."

"Right." Pippa claps her hands hard. "Forget about truth or dare. No more talking about past guys. This can't turn into a sob night. We're here to have some fun."

"You two were the ones who shot down the offer of private lap dances." Caroline glares at Pippa and Alice.

"Well, I don't feel comfortable with a stranger

grinding his ass against me," Alice says.

"But we have no problem looking at them, do we?" Pippa wiggles her eyebrows. "I spotted a ten."

"We're giving grades?" I ask.

"If not here, where?" Pippa replies.

"Amen to that," Caroline says.

"Okay, show me, which one is supposed to be a ten?" I ask.

Pippa points to the left of the stage. There's a man there, all right. And his butt is. . . double. Right, if I see double ass, I should really ease up on the tequila. Narrowing my eyes, I concentrate until I only see one ass. "Nah, that's a nine, max. Sebastian is a ten though."

"Oh. My. God," Pippa exclaims. Alice shakes her head, laughing. "I need friends who haven't had sex with my brothers. This is weird. I don't want to know about my brother's ass." As Caroline opens her mouth, Pippa lifts a finger at her. "Or my other brother's skills in bed."

"Let's get back to giving grades," Alice says. She places her forearms on the counter, leaning on them, narrowing her eyes at something across the room. She reminds me of a cat preparing to jump on unsuspecting prey. "I saw one I'd definitely let give me a lap dance."

"Ohhh, you're starting to have a fun side, Alice. Let's get you some more tequila." Caroline raises her arm, gesturing to the bartender to bring another round, but I shake my head at him.

"Let's have a break," I tell Caroline. "We already

had two rounds."

Caroline snickers. "Aww, you're adorable. Why have we never met until now?"

"Because you missed my parents' anniversary." Pippa gives her the evil eye.

"You know I don't like to be around if Daniel's there." Caroline sighs.

"You're not an adopted Bennett?" I ask in surprise. "I thought you'd qualify, since you're Pippa's friend."

"Nope. You lose the right when you bang one of the brothers," Caroline says in a dead-serious tone.

"Oh," I reply sadly. "I'll have that tequila now."

Two hours and countless shots later, I am slurring my words and miss Sebastian terribly. I excuse myself from the table and walk outside, in dear need of fresh air. Thank God for speed dial, because I couldn't find Sebastian in my phone book if my life depended on it.

"Hello, handsome."

"You're drunk," Sebastian says.

Well, he catches on fast. "No," I reply vehemently, giggling. "Maybe. A little."

"Where are you? I can take you home."

I lean on the wall next to the entrance.

"You don't want to know where we are." I giggle again, imagining the frown he must have right now.

"Now I want to know more."

"Well, remember my joke about the strip club last time?"

Sebastian lets out a sound between a growl and a snicker. "My sister brought you to a strip club?"

"No, her friend Caroline did."

"Oh, that explains it. So how drunk is everyone?"

"I'd say we're seeing double butts, and that's butt overload because there are enough butts as it is."

Sebastian laughs into the phone. "I only got the word butt. Let's leave it at that, I don't want more details."

"Where are you?"

"Home. I left the after-party about half an hour ago."

"Were there no naked butts around there?" My voice is playful, but despite the drunken state, my heart grows heavy.

"Should I come pick you up?"

"Yeah. The girls need a lift too." I realize he hasn't answered my question. I give him our address and go back inside to tell the girls they have to prepare to leave.

***

"This is fancy. We're having a private driver," Caroline giggles while Sebastian helps the four of us in the car. Or tries to, because we're not making this easy on him. He holds his sisters by the waists, and they are each kissing one of his cheeks, muttering something about best brother in the world.

"More like babysitter," Sebastian says.

"I want shotgun," I announce, elbowing him.

He indulges me and helps the three girls climb in

the back.

"This was fun," Caroline says as Sebastian hits the gas pedal. "Ava, we should go out again."

Pippa answers before I even get to open my mouth. "She can't. She's going on a short holiday with my dear brother, and then returns to New York, or wherever her job sends her next. "

"Oh, but aren't you doing her, Sebastian?" In the rearview mirror, I see her frowning, looking from Sebastian to me.

"Really smooth, Caroline," Alice remarks.

"I'm drunk. I can get away with this." She shoos Alice away good-naturedly. "Don't break her heart, like your brother did with mine."

"Thanks for the advice." Sebastian's tone is clipped, but he places his hand over mine, and I melt in my seat.

We drop the girls one by one: Caroline, Pippa, and Alice.

Chapter Thirty-Three

Sebastian

"Up we go." I lift her in my arms, and she immediately rests her head on my chest.

"I can walk. You don't have to carry me. But this is nice."

Laughing, I kiss the top of her head.

Once inside the bedroom, I lower her to her feet and unzip her dress, pushing it down. Her glorious body greets me. She's wearing nothing but a thong. I can't help myself and knead one of her breasts, kissing the nipple of the other one.

"Perv, you want to get me naked," she murmurs, grinding against me. I pull back.

"Usually yes, but tonight I'll just tuck you in."

"Why?"

"Because you're drunk, and I've been taught not to take advantage of drunk women."

"Not even if I want you to take advantage of me?"

"No."

I tuck her into bed, drawing the sheet right up to her neck, then lean next to her.

"I missed you," she tells me.

"Even if you were surrounded by sexy butts?"

"You have the sexiest butt." She says the words with a vehement nod. I want to kiss her senseless. "How was your night?"

"I answered a lot of questions, caught up with my brothers." I hesitate, wondering if I should tell her everything that happened tonight. I decide in favor of honesty. She deserves it. "Simone won't work for us for future shows anymore."

She gulps, her beautiful eyes widening. "What happened?"

"She had someone send me backstage under a ridiculous pretext. She was waiting for me naked back there."

"Oh." She makes herself small in the bed, pulling the cover up to her lips.

"It was very pathetic."

A shadow of fear crosses her eyes. "Did anything happen?"

"No, silly. I wanted to tell you so if you found out from someone else you didn't think I'm keeping it from you."

A smile spreads across her face. "I like you."

"You'd better like me; otherwise, I'll think you were taking advantage of me, sleeping with me all these months."

"And I like your family," she mumbles. "Why can't I have them too? Your sisters are great. I always wanted to have sisters and brothers." She's growing sleepier by the second. "A big family, like yours. Lots of kids."

"Define lots," I tease her.

"Mmm, four."

"That's not a lot."

She hugs the pillow under her head, mumbling, "Why do I have to leave? It's unfair," before falling asleep.

"You won't leave," I whisper to her, even though I know she can't hear me. "I'll make you stay."

I stay up, watching her for a long time. I'll give this woman everything she wants as long as she remains by my side. She makes me want all those things I dismissed because I lost confidence I'd find a woman to share everything with.

At some point during my stalkerish watching, a buzzing sound comes from the living room. What the hell? Who calls at this time? I check the nightstand. My phone is here, so Ava's is buzzing.

I ignore it, resuming watching her. Whoever is calling will take the hint that it's late. Except they don't, and if the phone continues to buzz, it'll wake her up. Grudgingly, I get up and go into the living room. I turn the phone on silent mode, but the caller doesn't give up. There's no caller ID either, so I can't send a message telling them to fuck off.

I decide to answer. "Who is this?" I bark into the phone.

"Who is this?" An unpleasant and vaguely familiar guy's voice sounds from the other end of the phone. My insides boil.

"Listen, douche bag. It's 2:00 a.m. and this is my

girlfriend you're calling. I get to ask the questions."

"You just answered mine, Sebastian Bennett."

The phone switches off. What the hell? I stare at it, expecting him to call again, but after five minutes, I give up and go to bed. This better not be some idiotic reporter trying to get the scoop on my private life, because I'll sue the fuck out of him and his entire family tree.

Chapter Thirty-Four

Ava

I arrive at the office at noon the next day. Despite having downed one too many tequila shots last night, I only have a slight headache. Sebastian woke up early. He's not at the office when I arrive, because he and Logan are at the bank, caught up in a daylong meeting.

Nostalgia grips me the second I arrive at my desk. I can't believe my last day is finally here. Taking a deep breath, I start packing my belongings, trying to focus on my upcoming trip with Sebastian, and push out the thought that I won't see him again after the trip ends.

Last night, we had a moment—at least, I think we did. I let my guard down. I know that for sure. I can't believe I told him I want four kids. And there was that moment just before I fell asleep, he might have told me to stay. I might have imagined it, and I don't have the courage to ask him. Maybe on our trip. . .

Smiling, I fetch a small box to put the gifts I've gotten from him in. I kept one chocolate, and let one rose dry. I place them carefully in the box, ignoring the feeling of finality sweeping over me as I close the lid.

I sit at my desk and check my e-mail, looking for any unanswered request from Sebastian's team. My eyes freeze on the subject of the newest email.

Termination of contract
With trembling hands, I click it open.

Dear Ms. Lindt,

We regret to inform you that your employment at our agency was terminated, effective today. The fourth clause of your contract was violated. As you were informed, this is grounds for immediate and irrevocable cease of work. You also lose your right to the contract termination compensation and to the bonus for your work with the client in this case.

We wish you best of luck.

I stare at the screen, reading the text again and again, until my eyes water.

No!

Sweat dots my palms, a strange coldness gripping me. I am on the brink of panic, unable to fight it much longer. Barely keeping it together, I call Dirk. He picks up immediately.

"You are firing me?" I'm surprised at how calm I

sound. "What is going on?"

"You know perfectly well what is going on," he sneers. "You are fucking Sebastian Bennett."

I draw in a sharp breath, clutching the phone forcefully. "That is not true. I don't know where you get your facts—"

"From Bennett himself. I spoke to him."

"You spoke to him," I repeat. My hand trembles on the phone, so I grip it tighter. Sebastian wouldn't do this to me. He knew I'd be fired if Dirk found out.

"Yes, last night. He answered your phone and I recognized his voice. He proudly announced you are his girlfriend. He had no idea who I was, but that's beside the point."

Despite everything, I let out a breath of relief. He didn't do it on purpose.

"I've been on alert ever since Anna told me you're cozy with the Bennetts," he continues.

I swallowed hard. Should've know that bitch would go right to him.

"She was in San Francisco again a week ago," Dirk adds. "She saw you and Bennett kissing. I waited for their show to be over to fire you to avoid a scandal. We are a serious marketing consultancy, Ava."

"I know that."

"Not an escort service. That clause is in place for a reason. We have a reputation to keep up." Dirk's voice is as dickish as it gets.

"I can explain." My mouth goes dry, and I press my knees together to stop myself from shaking.

"I'm not interested."

"This isn't what it looks like."

"Did you sleep with Bennett?"

"Yes, but—"

"Do we have a clause that specifically forbids it?"

"Yes, however—"

"Then things are exactly the way they look. You know very well the trouble that scandal caused us all those years ago."

"There won't be a scandal this time."

"It doesn't matter. It's best to cut the evil right from the root."

"What the. . . Damn it, Dirk. You can't leave me without my job, and refuse to pay my bonus and termination deposit."

"Yes, I can. It's written in your contract."

"I won't be able to afford . . . I'll lose everything." Something hard settles in my chest, making it hard to breathe. Keeping my phone between my ear and shoulder, I swipe my sweaty palms on my skirt.

"That's not my problem."

"I busted my ass off for you all these years," I say through gritted teeth.

"And then you opened your legs for Bennett and threw all that hard work away. I thought you were smarter than that."

"You dick," I yell into the phone. "You have no right to talk to me like that. The board might have named you CEO, but the reputation of the company was built on my back and on that of other consultants. Your incompetent ass wouldn't have gotten you where you are."

"Right. I was about to draft your recommendation letter, but I see one won't be necessary anymore."

I nearly swallow my tongue. "What? No, Dirk, look, I'm sorry I said that. I'm just—"

"Don't bother putting your time with us on a resume."

"I spent six years in your company," I shriek.

"If you put us on your resume and someone calls, I'll give them enough reasons not to hire you. You've been warned."

"I am your best employee—"

"Were. Best of luck," he says, before I hear dead air. The asshole hung up on me.

I stare into space, my mind blank, my entire body overcome by quivers. Reality seeps in slowly. Finding a new job will take me months. Without the bonus, there is no way I'll be able to pay my rent, even if I move to a cheaper neighborhood. I'll have to dig into my savings. Tears roll down my cheeks. The savings were meant to go toward a deposit for my own home. Good-bye, dream of owning my own place.

Good-bye, all dreams. Everything will go to hell. Everything will crumble around me. One little mistake, that's all it took to undo my hard work. How is this fair?

Dirk's words resound in my mind. That's not my problem. Of course not. Why should he care? Shit, why did I have to lose my temper like that?

Wiping away my tears, I steel myself, looking for a solution. First things first, I need to convince Dirk to change his mind on that recommendation letter. Without that, finding my next job will be a nightmare. A six-year gap on my resume will raise eyebrows. I have to put my job at the agency down, and I must convince Dirk to support me when future employers call him. I'll make him see reason. I've done great things for his company, even if I made a mistake.

The second thing I need to convince Dirk of is to give me that bonus. That'll give me a safety net until I find a new job.

I dial him again, but he doesn't pick up. Fuck you, Dirk the Dick. I need to fly to New York right now and do some damage control. The hours it'll take me to get to New York will be enough to allow Dirk to cool off, but if I let too much time pass, it'll become even harder to turn things in my favor. I'm about to go to Sebastian's office, then remember he won't be here for the day. I call him, but it goes straight to voice mail. Right, he probably shut off his phone during the meeting. Hanging up, I ponder what to do. I can call again, but my voice is too undependable to leave a voice message. I write him a quick e-mail.

I have to return to New York. Cancel the vacation. Sorry. Call me when you can.

I book myself the next flight to New York and head straight to my apartment. I pack all of my things as quickly as I can, then drop the key to the building administrator. I take a cab and stop at Sebastian's place to gather the few things I have here. That's when I realize I have to return his key. I stare at it in my palm, and then set it on the coffee table with a heavy heart.

On the way to the airport, I try calling Sebastian a few more times, but it goes straight to voice mail again. I really don't want to take off like this, with just the e-mail I sent him earlier, but squeezing all that's happened into a voice message will bring me to tears.

I also call Dirk a few dozen times, but he doesn't answer. I do my best not to flip out, but I burst into tears several times during the flight.

My most important goal is to convince him to give me a recommendation. If I achieve that, I can sort out the rest. It'll be a mess, but I'll manage. I always do.

I can't lose everything. Not after working so hard, for so long.

Chapter Thirty-Five

Sebastian

My last meeting ends at eleven o'clock at night, and I head straight to Ava's apartment. We agreed before the show that she'd pack up all the things she has at the hotel this afternoon and I'll help her move them to my place. Thank fuck we're leaving for the Bahamas tomorrow. She and I for two weeks. That's exactly what I need. I knock at her door, calling her name a few times, but she doesn't answer. I make a grab for my phone, and then realize I left it in the car. I go back downstairs. Maybe she decided to move the things by herself. It's late, after all, and our plane leaves very early tomorrow.

The building administrator throws me a fuck-me glance when she sees me. Jesus.

"Did Ms. Lindt check out already?" I ask her.

She frowns. "Yes, shortly after lunch. She requested a cab to the airport."

"What do you mean 'to the airport'? There must be a mistake."

"No mistake, I did the check-out myself. She said she needed a cab to the airport, but had to make a stop on the way."

I slam my fist on the hard wood, swearing.

"You look like you need a drink," she says. "My shift just ended, and I know a cozy bar downtown."

"That won't be necessary." I barely keep my voice straight. She drops her eyes to the floor, and I add a quick, "Good-night."

I stomp out of the building.

I want to call Ava the minute I'm in the car, and then remember my phone battery has been flat the entire day. Fuck. I hit the steering wheel hard, and nearly crash into a car on my way home.

"Ava," I call once inside the apartment. No answer. "Ava, are you here?"

With horror, I realize she's taken all of her things. There's no trace of any belongings of hers. It's like she's never been here. The punch to the gut comes when I see the key I gave her lying on the coffee table.

She wouldn't do this. Except. . . she did. There must be an explanation for this. Gathering all the calm I can muster, I plug the charger into my phone. The few minutes until the phone comes to life are excruciating.

She called me a few times, but left no messages. I dial her number, but it goes straight to her voice mail. I realize I haven't checked my e-mails. Sure enough, I find one from Ava.

I have to return to New York. Cancel the vacation. Sorry. Call me when you can.

I stare at the e-mail, dumbstruck. Call me when you can? Then she switches off her phone? Right. I grit my teeth. Right.

***

"Weren't you supposed to be in the Bahamas?" Logan asks two days later. He enters my office, dropping in the chair opposite my desk, staring at me. He was away from the office yesterday.

"I was, but Ava got cold feet and fucked off to New York."

"What? Why?"

"Ask her. She wrote me an e-mail, saying she had to return, I should call her, and now she's not answering her phone. It goes straight to voice mail."

"Have you e-mailed her?"

"I have my pride, Logan." I hit the table with a fist, drawing in a breath. "I'm not going to beg a woman who didn't even have the decency to tell me to my face that she wants out."

I almost e-mailed her. I must have drafted out at least fifteen e-mails, and then deleted them. Imagining her reply kept me from sending them. The mere idea of seeing her rejection written was enough to prompt me to press Delete. Yes, I've officially become a coward and am passing it off as pride.

"Ava's not that kind of person. Hell, she didn't

chicken out when the marketing manager up and left one week before the show. That woman's got some balls. Maybe she had an emergency."

"I thought about that, but she's not even picking up her phone. I don't know about you, but I can take a hint when it's thrown at me."

"You love her, don't you?"

"Does it matter?" I counter. "Yes, I do."

"Okay, let's talk about something else. I hate to break this to you, but we need to hire a marketing manager like. . . yesterday."

"I know, but I'm not in the mood right now."

"I've been looking into promoting someone from within the department, but they all lack the necessary leadership skills. On the other hand, if we bring someone from the outside again, we'll repeat history."

"I'll find a solution. Eventually. What else is on the agenda?"

Logan talks about the meeting he attended yesterday. I don't listen to one word. My concentration is atrocious. It doesn't help that I haven't slept at all since Ava left. I came to the office yesterday morning and remained here, sleeping on the couch. I keep asking myself why she did it, driving myself mad looking for an answer. Other women took my money when they left. Ava took my sanity, along with everything else that was worth it in my life.

Well, it is what it is. Everything will go back to the way it was. I hate how horribly depressing that thought is. Back to empty days and meaningless nights. I already put my assistant in charge of renting out my place. I won't return there alone.

Logan's monologue lasts about an hour before Pippa interrupts us.

"What are you doing here?" She stands in the doorway to my office, looking at me as if I grew a second head.

"I'm the CEO, this is my office," I answer sarcastically. "Why wouldn't I be here?"

"You're supposed to be somewhere else." Strutting into the room, she puts her hands on her hips, surveying me with wolf-like eyes. "You look terrible."

"Why, you're all sunshine and rainbows today. Thank you for the compliment."

"I wanted to point out that you look dreadful when I came in," Logan adds. "But I kept my mouth shut."

"That's because you're smart."

I have a two-day beard, and I haven't changed my shirt, which looks like crap after I've slept in it. I probably smell too. So what?

"You didn't answer my question," Pippa insists. "Why are you here?"

"Bahamas got canceled. Don't ask me for—"

Pippa throws her hands in the air. "Not Bahamas, you idiot. You're supposed to be in New York."

"Why would I be in New York?"

I look at Logan for a clue. I must be missing

something. Logan looks as lost as I feel.

"Because Ava's there."

I squint. "How do you know that?"

"She got fired from her job. She's there trying to put out all the other fires that broke out as a result."

"What do you mean 'she got fired'?" I ask.

"When?" Logan jumps to his feet.

"Didn't you know?" Pippa asks.

"No. How do you know?"

"A colleague of hers informed me. Apparently their boss found out Ava was dating you."

"Shit," I say.

"Yeah, shit. He kicked her out, no bonus, no termination clause. From what I was told, he didn't want to give her a recommendation either. Ava went to their office two days ago to talk to him, and he threw her out."

"The jerk. How did he find out?"

"You told him," Pippa says, clearly annoyed.

"I didn't. . ." I stop, remembering that late-night phone call. That's why his voice sounded familiar. I assumed only a journalist would call in the middle of the night. It didn't even cross my mind it could be a boss who has no respect for his employees. "This is my fault. Why didn't she tell me this?"

"My guess is she must be busy trying to solve her situation," Logan says.

"But I can help," I say, louder than I intended. Pippa flinches. "We all can."

"I assumed you were in New York already. Look, Ava's been fighting her way through life on her own for years," Pippa says. "She's not used to asking for help. You just have to give it to her."

"What if she doesn't want my help at all? She doesn't pick up her phone. I must have called her a hundred times."

Logan eyes me.

"What?" I bark at him, annoyed by his smile. "I wasn't about to admit that to you."

"You have your pride. I get it," he says, smiling even wider. "That's why you won't e-mail her."

"Don't get on my bad side today, Logan."

"Right now, you are both getting on my bad side," Pippa says. "Sebastian, get your sorry ass on a plane and fly to New York. Why are you hesitating?"

I hiss out a breath. All that talk about how it angers me she didn't have the courage to tell me to my face she wants out. I couldn't stand hearing it from her. Reading it was bad enough. What if the reason she isn't taking my calls is because she's not interested anymore?

"That woman loves you, you know that. And you love her," Pippa says. "Don't be stupid, Sebastian. You have to put yourself out there completely. You both deserve to be happy."

This sobers me up. "Logan, take over all my meetings for today. I'm flying out to New York."

"Hold it," Pippa says, stepping in front of me as I'm about to exit.

"What? You were all set on kicking me out of my own office."

"I would've done it too, but you can't fly out like

this. You need to change. You stink."

I groan. "I suspected as much." Without taking my eyes off Pippa, I say, "Logan, change of plans. Drop any immediate meeting and go to my apartment. Bring me clothes to change."

"Because I've been downgraded from CFO to your personal butler?"

"Because you're my brother, and I need to take care of something else while you bring me the clothes."

I hear Logan stand up fast. "Okay, I had enough dick lines today. I'm on it."

I give Logan the keys for my apartment, and then he leaves the office.

"You still must shower," Pippa points out.

"There are showers down in Creation. I'll use those. Meanwhile, is your prototyping guy here? I have a task for him."

"Yeah, he is." Pippa narrows her eyes. "I know that look. You're planning something."

"You're damn right I am."

Her eyes widen, and she drums her fingers on her cheeks, like she used to when we were kids and preparing mischief. Well, this will top all of them. "Tell me."

"Nope. Payback for telling me that I stink. Twice. Even if it's true." I enjoy immensely seeing her grow more restless by the second. My sister's never been one to accept there can be secrets between siblings. At any rate, I will have to tell her. I won't pull it off on my own, but I can tease her a bit more.

"Come on, give me a hint at least."

"What did you say earlier? It was a nice phrase. Oh yeah, I will put myself out there completely. And you will help."

Chapter Thirty-Six

Ava

You know you're a lost cause when even ice cream tastes like shit. It's my favorite ice cream too: Ben and Jerry's with almond and caramel. I eat it with a large spoon, sitting on the couch inside my apartment, watching some mindless reality show. There are packed boxes all around me.

My meeting with Dirk the Dick two days ago was a disaster. I didn't manage to convince him to give in to even one single request: no bonus and no reference. After my disastrous encounter with him, I announced to my landlord I have to leave this apartment; thankfully he understood my situation.

I found a rat hole outside the city where I can live until I'm back on my feet without burning through my savings. Let's hope I won't get shot until that happens. I went to visit the place yesterday and it creeped me out. Then I came home and packed my stuff the entire night. I collapsed on the couch this morning, and now I can't get up again. All my muscles are as sore as hell. The movers will be here in a few hours, which gives me plenty of time to wallow and obsessively check my e-mails. Dirk made me return my phone yesterday, since it was the company's. I do have my laptop, and I didn't get an e-mail from Sebastian. I bought a new phone, but he doesn't have my new number, and I'm too much of a coward to call him.

When the reality show gets too mindless, I switch off the TV and focus my attention on my laptop, namely on the list with jobs I want to apply to. I have a game plan. It's not perfect, but I'll make it work. Dirk refuses to acknowledge my efforts—but the clients I've worked with won't. They've all been thrilled with me.

I will call all of my clients, including Sebastian, and sweet talk them into letting me list them as references.

I let out a sigh at the thought of Sebastian. Dirk told me terrible things in his office. The old me would've been horrified at my actions, drowning in guilt over throwing my career away over a man— Dirk's words. As I sat across from him, watching him, I couldn't bring myself to feel one ounce of guilt about my relationship with Sebastian.

I felt more alive and happy with him than I've been in my entire life. My only regret is that it ended. Tears spring to my eyes, and I wipe them away quickly. I suppose that by leaving the way I did, I gave him an easy way out; and he took it, ripping my heart to shreds. I know I should call him using my new number, or write another email explaining everything, but I can't bring myself to do it just yet. Biting the inside of my cheek, I resolve not to think about that right now. I still have things to do and organize, and I know thinking about Sebastian will be my undoing.

***

I'm about to open the second carton of ice cream when the bell rings. Frowning, I drag my feet to the door. Are the movers here early? I open the door without looking through the peephole. I really must break that habit; it might get me killed, or at the very least mugged, in the hellhole I'm moving to.

"Sebastian."

"You look terrible," he says.

For a few seconds, neither of us says anything, and then I burst out laughing. "I really need you to shower me with compliments today."

I eye him, drinking him in as usual. Is it possible that it's been just two days since I last saw him? It feels like an entire year has passed.

"Did you take any other shower?" He smiles lazily.

I gulp, eyeing the floor. I didn't shower after I packed everything.

"Why are you here?" I ask him.

"Can I come in?"

"Sure."

He walks in, sizing up the boxes. "I'm sorry for exposing us to your boss. I wasn't—"

"You didn't know it was him." I lean against a stack of boxes. "Someone from work had seen us together in San Francisco earlier too. He was looking for a way to throw me out anyway. I chatted with some of the girls there, and apparently, I was getting too senior in the company—he wanted to hire someone younger and cheaper."

"He's an idiot. You're brilliant."

"Ah, now we're talking." Grinning, I wink at him. "Keep the compliments coming. I wasn't joking when I said I really need them." God, having him here makes everything brighter, better. He fills the space with his smile and twinkling eyes. Realization hits me hard, wiping my breath away. Right here in this moment, I realize I've never wanted anything more than this: him. It's not just that I want it. I need him.

"What's with all the boxes?"

"I'm moving to a cheaper neighborhood until I find a job." My words come out robotic, as if someone else utters them.

"Impressive. You managed to arrange all this in two days," he says. Peeling his eyes away from the boxes, he fixes them on me, unleashing the full power of his gaze. My knees weaken.

"Why haven't you answered my calls?"

"Dirk took my phone. It was the company's."

His face falls. "I didn't think of that."

"I'm sorry," I say. "I got a new one, but didn't have the courage to call or write."

"Come here, you silly girl." He pulls me into a hug, and I lose myself in his arms. God, this is so much better than Ben and Jerry's and making lists and plans. For the first time in days, I feel safe, and oddly—empowered. "You have nothing to feel sorry for. You should've told me."

"I was so busy with everything. Packing, finding a rat hole to move into. You didn't e-mail me, so I thought you wanted to end everything. I'm so tired."

"Shh." He picks me up in his arms, and then sits on the couch, keeping me in his lap. His arms are tight around me. "I'm here for you, Ava. You run into trouble, you let me know."

"I'm used to doing things on my own. I went on autopilot, into problem-solving mode."

"Well, I know you don't need someone to save you. That's partly why I love you so much. You're fierce and strong." He caresses my cheek, filling me with warmth. "I'll never let you go." Tilting my chin up, he feathers his lips on mine, and then claims my mouth with a deep kiss, full of longing and tenderness. This man. . . God, he's so perfect. I want to kiss the living daylights out of him for the rest of the day. Sadly, we must also breathe. Gasping for air, we pull apart. "I was going to ask you to stay with me in San Francisco during the trip."

"You were?" I ask in amazement.

"Yeah. I love you."

I fist his shirt. "I love you, too. So much. "

"I was still rounding up arguments to convince you to leave your job, but Dirk the Dick made it that much easier."

I grin against his lips. "Dirk the Dick? You're a fast learner."

"Always. I have a proposition for you." He cups my face, making me look at him.

"Sounds dangerous."

"It'll be irresistible. We've established already I'm the irresistible brother."

"Of course you are. Let's hear that proposition." I'm curious.

"As you know, the marketing manager ditched us." His tone is serious and businesslike, which cracks me up right now. "Luckily, we had that very efficient and talented consultant working for us, or the launch would've gone to the dogs. Now she's gone, and the manager position is still free."

"Sebastian Bennett, are you asking me to work for you?" I pull myself straighter in his lap. Amazing. A few minutes ago, I had the distinct impression I was carrying a rock weighing a ton on my shoulders. Now? I could fly.

"Yes, I am. The team likes you, and you're very good at what you do. Are you interested?"

"I don't know." Scrunching my nose, I massage my temples, pretending I'm thinking hard. "I have some requirements that must be fulfilled first."

"Like what?"

"Like having my office far away from the CEO so I can actually get work done."

"Absolutely not."

"That was the easiest request." I pinch his chest playfully.

"Why do I get the feeling I'll say no to all of them?" He lowers his hands to my hips and then my thighs.

"You'll jeopardize my work ethic."

"Not at all. I'll reward your efforts." The hint of a smile plays on his lips. It's my favorite one: sexy, with a dash of mischief.

"You're quite good with rewards."

"Am I?" He runs his thumb over my lower lip. "Say yes." To my astonishment, there is a shadow of doubt in his eyes, like there's a real chance I'll say no. As if.

"Yes. Of course. I'll—"

He drowns the rest of the words with a kiss that is as sweet as it is passionate. Tangling his fingers in my hair, he pulls me to him with thinly disguised desperation. We both laugh after we break apart.

"Out of respect to my future employer, I must tell you I am not as brilliant as you think. I thought through one hundred scenarios, but working for you wasn't one of them."

"Thank God you agreed. If you didn't come back with me to California, my family might have killed me."

"What are you talking about?"

"Pippa all but kicked me today. Logan joined Pippa in kicking me. Mom called to berate me. You're not alone, you know. My family cares about you. Once you become a Bennett, you're always a Bennett."

"An adopted Bennett?" I ask hopefully.

"A real Bennett."

He puts me down on the couch. Then he drops

on one knee, pulling a jewelry box out of his pocket. When he opens the lid, my heart leaps in my chest.

"My ruby," I whisper.

"Pippa turned the necklace into a ring today. Ava Lindt, will you do me the honor of being my wife?"

"Yes."

He slides the ring on my finger, and I can barely take my eyes off it. "It's beautiful, Sebastian."

We both rise to our feet, and he hooks an arm around my waist. Cupping my cheek in one hand, he laughs wholeheartedly, and I join him. "You complete me, Ava. Right from the beginning, something in you was beckoning to me. I can't imagine going on without you."

Too emotional for words, I rise on my tiptoes and plant a kiss right on the tip of his nose.

"I can't believe you proposed to me when I haven't showered, surrounded by a pile of boxes."

"Oh, we'll have to do a do-over in front of my family, don't worry."

"What?" My chest tightens as I imagine doing this in front of all the Bennetts, but then I visualize Pippa's dreamy expression and Logan telling us we still can't have sex at the office, and I relax. The thought of seeing all of them again fills me with joy.

"They'd never forgive me if they don't get to see the proposal. It's almost as bad as a runaway wedding for them."

Looking at the ring on my finger, I have to fight the tears threatening to spill on my cheeks.

"I'm a lucky man, Ava. There are a few things I'd

like to say."

"Mmm, don't you want to wait until the vows?" I'm dying to hear him out, but there'll be no stopping the tears if he's his usual sweet, charming self.

"Nah, there'll be too many people. I want to make you a few promises while we're here, just the two of us."

Cupping my cheeks in his hands, he pulls me to him, pressing his forehead to mine. "I promise I'll cherish every moment with you—"

"I'm sure you'll love having your pillow hijacked every night—"

"I will," he assures me. "I'll spoil you and take care of you, and our family." With a smile, he adds, "That'll include our many, many kids."

Pulling back a notch, I ask suspiciously. "How many?"

He answers with a grin. "We'll talk about that later." Caressing my face with the back of his hand, his eyes linger on mine, full of warmth. "You'll never feel alone again, Ava. I promise."

A lump settles in my throat, emotions overcoming me.

"You're going to make me fall in love with you more every day, aren't you?"

"I'm certainly going to try. You deserve to be loved, and you have so much love to give. I'm happiest when you look at me like I'm your whole world, so I'll make sure to work hard to earn that look."

A knock at the door startles us both.

"Oh, it must be the movers." Before I can utter another word, Sebastian marches to the door. Pulling it open, he tells the guys their service is no longer necessary and returns to me after they leave.

"I need to call the landlord of the other place to let him know I won't be moving in. He'll probably still keep my deposit. Then I'll—"

"Shh. I forbid you to go on your autopilot, problem-solving mode." His commanding voice spurts tendrils of heat through my body. Sebastian takes my breath away. He pushes a strand of hair out of my eyes, tilting my head up.

"Bossy fiancé," I say.

"We'll deal with everything later. Right now, I want to make love to my beautiful fiancée."

He leans in to kiss me. I smile against his lips, lacing my fingers behind his neck. He's right, we'll figure everything out later. Together.

Epilogue

Ava

"We will not call any child of ours Seamus." I stomp my foot, but all that does is make Sebastian grin and everyone else laugh out loud. We're at his parents' house, as are all his siblings. Pouting, I sit in Sebastian's lap. "Let's not talk about kid names anymore. I'm not even pregnant."

Right after our engagement party a few months ago, Sebastian informed me that he's planning to have as many kids as it takes to have a soccer team. I wasn't sure how many players there were on a team, so I googled it. Eleven. I still hope he was kidding, but I don't think so. He's already talking about names. Alex, Seamus, and William are what he came up with so far. I'd have the Bennett family vote on names, but some of them look far too thrilled about Seamus, so I'm not too sure they're to be trusted.

"I'm with Ava on this one," Logan says. "Seamus is a no-go."

I narrow my eyes at him. Logan's trying hard to get in my good graces. We've butted heads at the office all week over some budget plans—again. The marketing department accepted me almost at once. They'd already warmed up to me, so they didn't consider me an outsider anymore. A funny thing happened in New York after I left. The agency's board fired Dirk. Sebastian claims he had nothing to do with it, but he averts his gaze when I ask him about it. Simone carried out her threat. She sued Sebastian for harassment. The result was stellar. Sebastian won, and Simone's reputation was tarnished. One by one, she lost all her major contracts. Pippa bet Simone would be posing for Playboy instead of Vogue within six months. I gave her a year. Pippa won the bet after only three months.

"Why don't we talk about the wedding?" their mother asks in a gentle tone.

"There are still a bazillion months left," Blake says. "Besides, picking out names is more fun."

Sebastian holds his hands up in defense. "I keep myself out of wedding preparations. Last time I offered my opinion, it was shot down before I finished speaking."

I grin, still not believing my luck in finding this man and his hilarious family. There was a time when I thought the only way to be strong was not to count on anyone but myself; but I've never felt stronger than now, surrounded by a bunch of Bennetts who can't keep their noses out of anything—including shady names for future babies. I love them all to pieces.

"That's because you have atrocious taste, brother," Pippa says. With that, she whisks me away from the group, undoubtedly to talk more about our matchmaking plan. Last month, Nadine told me she's looking to relocate. I've been trying to sell her on San Francisco ever since.

"Did Nadine say anything new?"

"I've almost convinced her." Pulling out my phone, I show her the last e-mail I sent to Nadine.

From: Ava
To: Nadine
I still stand by what I wrote. I have my hands full trying to organize my wedding, and I could use your help. Also, there are three other sexy, single Bennett men running around San Francisco. They all have good references (actually the party brothers are still working on those references). Logan Bennett is driving me **CRAZY** *at the office. That man needs to have his ego taken down a notch. You're up for the challenge. Fly down here for a few weeks and see if you like the city. If you don't like it, you can move somewhere else.*

I look up from my phone and find Pippa grinning.

"You really think Logan and Nadine will make a good match?"

Her grin turns into a mischievous smile. "You just wait for her to fly here. We'll make it happen."

***

THE END

***

Dear Reader,

If you want to read Logan and Nadine's story,

Your Captivating Love, you can pre-order it here: http://laylahagen.com/books/the-bennett-family-series/your-captivating-love/

It will be delivered to your e-reader on April 19th.

Description:

Logan Bennett knows his priorities. He is loyal to his family and his company. He has no time for love, and no desire for it. Not after a disastrous engagement that left him broken-hearted. When Nadine enters his life, she turns everything upside down. She's sexy, funny, and utterly captivating. She's also more stubborn than anyone he's met. . .including himself.

Nadine Hawthorne is finally pursuing her dream: opening her own clothing shop. After working so hard to get here, she needs to concentrate on her new business, and can't afford distractions. Not even if they come in the form of Logan Bennett. He's handsome, charming, and doesn't take no for an answer. After bitter disappointments, Nadine doesn't believe in love. But being around Logan is addicting. It doesn't help that Logan's family is scheming to bring them together at every turn.

Their attraction is sizzling, and their connection— undeniable. Slowly, Logan wins her over. What starts out as a fling soon spirals into much more than they are prepared for.

When a mistake threatens to tear them apart, will they have the strength to hold on to each other?

***

Dear Reader,
If you want to receive news about my upcoming books and sales, you can sign up for my newsletter HERE: http://laylahagen.com/mailing-list-sign-up/

Author Contact
Website: http://laylahagen.com/
Email: author@laylahagen.com
Facebook: http://facebook.com/LaylaHagenBooks/
Twitter: @laylahagen

***

Other Books by Layla Hagen

The Lost Series

Novella Lost
Lost is a FREE is a prequel novella to Lost in Us and can be read before or after.

Whatever might help him forget his past and numb the pain, James has tried it all: booze, car races, fights, and then some. Especially women. College offers plenty of opportunities for everything. . . Especially when you have a trust fund to spend.

Serena spirals deeper and deeper into a hurricane of pain. But no matter how far she falls, there's no redemption from the overwhelming guilt. Two souls consumed by their pasts fight to learn how to survive. But all hope seems to be lost. Until they meet each other.

Available as a FREE Ebook download. You can find the links to all retailers here: http://laylahagen.com/books/lost-series/lost/

***

Lost in Us: The story of James and Serena

There are three reasons tequila is my new favorite drink.

• One: my ex-boyfriend hates it.

• Two: downing a shot looks way sexier than sipping my usual Sprite.

• Three: it might give me the courage to do something my ex-boyfriend would hate even more than tequila— getting myself a rebound

The night I swap my usual Sprite with tequila, I meet James Cohen. The encounter is breathtaking. Electrifying. And best not repeated.

James is a rich entrepreneur. He likes risks and adrenaline and is used to living the high life. He's everything I'm not.

But opposites attract. Some say opposites destroy each other. Some say opposites are perfect for each other.

I don't know what will James and I do to each other, but I can't stay away from him. Even though I should.

AVAILABLE ON ALL RETAILERS. You can find the links HERE: http://laylahagen.com/books/lost-series/lost-in-us/

***

Found in Us: The story of Jessica and Parker

Jessica Haydn wants to leave her past behind. Hurt by one too many heartbreaks, she vows not to fall in love again. Especially not with a man like Parker, whose electrifying pull and smile bruised her ego once before. But his sexy British accent makes her crave his touch, and his blue eyes strip Jessica of all her defenses.

Parker Blakesley has no place for love in his life. He learned the hard way not to trust. He built his business empire by avoiding distractions, and using sheer determination and control. But something about Jessica makes him question everything. Not only has she a body made for sin, but her laughter fills a void inside of him.

The desire igniting between them spirals into an unstoppable passion, and so much more. Soon, neither can fight their growing emotional connection. But can two scarred souls learn to trust again? And when a mistake threatens to tear them apart, will their love be strong enough?

AVAILABLE ON ALL RETAILERS. You can find the links HERE: http://laylahagen.com/books/lost-series/found-in-us/

***

Caught in Us: The story of Dani and Damon

Damon Cooper has all the markings of a bad boy:
• A tattoo
• A bike
• An attitude to go with point one and two

In the beginning I hated him, but now I'm falling in love with him.

My parents forbid us to be together, but Damon's not one to obey rules.

And since I met him, neither am I.

AVAILABLE ON ALL RETAILERS. You can find the links HERE: http://laylahagen.com/books/lost-series/caught-in-us/

***

Standalone USA TODAY BESTSELLER
Withering Hope

Aimee's wedding is supposed to turn out perfect. Her dress, her fiancé and the location—the idyllic holiday ranch in Brazil—are perfect.

But all Aimee's plans come crashing down when the private jet that's taking her from the U.S. to the ranch—where her fiancé awaits her—defects mid-flight and the pilot is forced to perform an emergency landing in the heart of the Amazon rainforest.

With no way to reach civilization, being rescued is Aimee and Tristan's—the pilot—only hope. A slim one that slowly withers away, desperation taking its place. Because death wanders in the jungle under many forms: starvation, diseases. Beasts.

As Aimee and Tristan fight to find ways to survive, they grow closer. Together they discover that facing old, inner agonies carved by painful pasts takes just as much courage, if not even more, than facing the rainforest.

Despite her devotion to her fiancé, Aimee can't hide her feelings for Tristan—the man for whom she's slowly becoming everything. You can hide many things in the rainforest. But not lies. Or love.

Withering Hope is the story of a man who desperately needs forgiveness and the woman who brings him hope. It is a story in which hope births wings and blooms into a love that is as beautiful and intense as it is forbidden.

AVAILABLE ON ALL RETAILERS. You can find the links HERE: http://laylahagen.com/books/withering-hope/

Cover: http://designs.romanticbookaffairs.com/
**

Acknowledgements

There are so many people who helped me fulfil the dream of publishing, that I am utterly terrified I will forget to thank someone. If I do, please forgive me. Here it goes.

First, I'd like to thank my beta readers, Jessica, Dee, Andrea, Carrie, Jill, Kolleen and Rebecca. You made this story so much better!!

I want to thank every blogger and reader who took a chance with me as a new author and helped me spread the word. You have my most heartfelt gratitude. To my street team. . .you rock !!!

Last but not least, I would like to thank my family. I would never be here if not for their love and support. Mom, you taught me that books are important, and for that I will always be grateful. Dad, thank you for always being convinced that I should reach for the stars.

To my sister, whose numerous ahem. . .legendary replies will serve as an inspiration for many books to come, I say thank you for your support and I love you, kid.

To my husband, who always, no matter what, believed in me and supported me through all this whether by happily taking on every chore I overlooked or accepting being ignored for hours at a time, and most importantly encouraged me whenever I needed it: I love you and I could not have done this without you.

Table Of Contents